Secrets

Enid Blyton

Secrets

The Secret Island
The Secret Mountain

Armada
An Imprint of HarperCollinsPublishers

The Secret Island and *The Secret Mountain*
were first published in Great Britain in 1938 and 1941
respectively by Basil Blackwell Ltd.

First published in Armada in 1964 and 1965

First published together in this edition
in 1993 by Armada
Armada is an imprint of
HarperCollins Children's Books,
part of HarperCollins Publishers Ltd
77-85 Fulham Palace Road
Hammersmith, London W6 8JB

1 3 5 7 9 10 8 6 4 2

Copyright reserved Enid Blyton 1938 and 1941

The Enid Blyton signature is the trademark
of Darrell Waters Ltd.

Printed and bound in Great Britain by
HarperCollins Book Manufacturing, Glasgow

The Beginning Of The Adventures

Mike, Peggy and Nora were sitting in the fields, talking together. They were very unhappy. Nora was crying, and would not stop. As they sat there, they heard a low call. "Coo-ee!"

"There's Jack," said Mike. "Dry your eyes, Nora. Jack will cheer you up!"

A boy came running by the hedge and sat down by them. He had a face as brown as a berry and bright blue eyes that shone with mischief.

"Hallo!" he said. "What's up, Nora? Crying again?"

"Yes," said Nora, wiping her eyes. "Aunt Harriet slapped me six times this morning because I didn't wash the curtains well enough. Look!"

She showed him her arm, red with slaps.

"It's a shame!" said Jack.

"If only our father and mother were here they wouldn't let us live like this," said Mike. "But somehow I don't believe they'll ever come back now."

"How long is it since they've been gone?" asked Jack.

"It's over two years now," said Mike. "Dad built a fine new aeroplane, you know, and he set off to fly to Australia. Mother went with him, because she loves flying, too. They got nearly there—and then nothing more was heard of them!"

"And I know Aunt Harriet and Uncle Henry think they will never come back again," said Nora, beginning to cry once more, "or they would never treat us as they do."

"Don't cry any more, Nora," said Peggy. "Your eyes

5

will get so red and horrid. I'll do the washing instead of you next time."

Jack put his arm round Nora. He liked her best of them all. She was the smallest, although she was Mike's twin. She had a little face, and a head of black curls. Mike was exactly like her, but bigger. Peggy had yellow hair and was a year older. Nobody knew how old Jack was. He didn't know himself. He lived with his grandfather on a tumble-down farm, and worked as hard as a man, although he wasn't much bigger than Mike.

He had made friends with the children as they wandered through the fields. He knew how to catch rabbits. He knew how to catch fish in the river. He knew where the best nuts and blackberries were to be found. In fact, he knew everything, the children thought, even the names of all the birds that flew about the hedges, and the difference between a grass snake and an adder, and things like that.

Jack was always dressed in raggedy things, but the children didn't mind. His feet were bare, and his legs were scratched with brambles. He never grumbled; he never whined. He made a joke of everything, and he had been a good friend to the three miserable children.

"Ever since Aunt Harriet made up her mind that Mummy and Daddy wouldn't come back, she has been perfectly horrid," said Nora.

"And so has Uncle Henry," said Mike. "We none of us go to school now, and I have to help Uncle in the fields from morning to night. I don't mind that, but I do wish Aunt Harriet wouldn't treat the two girls so badly. They are not very old, and she makes them do all the work of the house for her."

"I do every bit of the washing now," said Nora. "I wouldn't mind the little things, but the sheets are so big and heavy."

6

"And I do all the cooking," said Peggy. "Yesterday I burnt a cake because the oven got too hot, and Aunt Harriet sent me to bed for the rest of the day without anything to eat at all."

"I climbed through the window and gave her some bread and cheese," said Mike. "And Uncle caught me and shook me so hard that I couldn't stand up afterwards. I had to go without my supper, and my breakfast this morning was only a small piece of bread."

"We haven't had any new clothes for months," said Peggy. "My shoes are dreadful. And I don't know what we shall do when the winter comes, because none of our coats will fit us."

"You are much worse off than I am," said Jack. "I have never had anything nice, so I don't miss it. But you have had everything you wanted, and now it is all taken away from you—you haven't even a father and mother you can go to for help."

"Do you remember *your* father and mother, Jack?" asked Mike. "Did you always live with your old grandfather?"

"I never remember anyone except him," said Jack. "He's talking of going to live with an aunt of mine. If he does I shall be left all alone, for she won't have me, too."

"Oh, Jack! Whatever will you do?" asked Nora.

"I shall be all right!" said Jack. "The thing is what are *you* three going to do? I hate to see you all unhappy. If only we could all run away together!"

"We should be found at once and brought back," said Mike gloomily. "I know that. I've read in the papers about boys and girls running away, and they are always found by the police and brought back. If I knew some place where we would never be found, I *would* run away—and take the two girls with me too. I hate to see them slappd and worked hard by Aunt Harriet."

"Now listen to me," said Jack suddenly, in such an earnest voice that all three children turned to him at once. "If I tell you a very great secret will you promise never to say a word about it to anyone?"

"Oh, yes, Jack, we promise," said all three.

"You can trust us, Jack," said Mike.

"I know I can," he said. "Well, listen. I know a place where nobody could find us—if we ran away!"

"Where is it, Jack?" they all cried in great excitement.

"I'll show you this evening," said Jack, getting up. "Be by the lakeside at eight o'clock, when all your work is done, and I'll meet you there. I must go now, or Grandpa will be angry with me, and perhaps lock me into my room so that I can't get out again to-day."

"Good-bye, Jack," said Nora, who was feeling much better now. "We'll see you this evening."

Jack ran off, and the three children made their way slowly back to Uncle Henry's farm. They had taken their dinner out into the fields to eat—now they had to go back to work. Nora had a great deal of ironing to do, and Peggy had to clean the kitchen. It was a big stone kitchen, and Peggy knew it would take her until supper-time—and, oh dear, how tired she would be then! Aunt Harriet would scold her all the time, she knew.

"I've got to go and clean out the barn," said Mike to the girls, "but I'll be in at supper-time, and afterwards we'll see about this great secret of Jack's."

They each began their work, but all the time they were thinking excitedly of the evening. What was Jack's secret? Where was the place he knew of? Could they really and truly run away?

They all got into trouble because they were thinking so hard of the evening that they did not do their work to Aunt Harriet's liking nor to Uncle Henry's either. Nora got a few more slaps, and Peggy was scolded so hard that

8

she cried bitterly into her overall. She was made to scrub the kitchen floor all over again, and this made her late for supper.

Mike was shouted at by Uncle Henry for spilling some corn in the barn. The little boy said nothing, but he made up his mind that if it was possible to run away in safety he would do so, and take the girls with him, too.

"Nora and Peggy ought to be going to school and wearing nice clothes that fit them, and having friends to tea," said Mike to himself. "This is no life for them. They are just very hard-worked servants for Aunt Harriet, and she pays them nothing."

The children ate their supper of bread and cheese in silence. They were afraid of speaking in case their aunt and uncle shouted at them. When they had finished Mike spoke to his aunt.

"Please may we go for a walk in the fields before we go to bed?" he asked.

"No, you can't," said Aunt Harriet in her sharp voice. "You'll just go to bed, all of you. There's a lot of work to do tomorrow, and I want you up early."

The children looked at one another in dismay. But they had to do as they were told. They went upstairs to the big bedroom they all shared. Mike had a small bed in the corner behind a screen, and the two girls had a bigger bed between them.

"I believe Aunt Harriet and Uncle Henry are going out tonight, and that's why they want us to go to bed early," said Mike. "Well, if they do go out, we'll slip down and meet Jack by the river."

"We won't get undressed then," said Nora. 'We'll just slip under the sheets, dressed—and then it won't take us long to run down to the lake."

The three children listened hard. They heard the front door close. Mike popped out of bed and ran to the front room. From there he could see the path to the gate. He saw his uncle and aunt walk down it, dressed to go out.

He ran back to the others. "We'll wait for five minutes," he said, "then we'll go."

They waited quietly. Then they all slipped downstairs and out of the back door. They ran down to the lake as fast as they could. Jack was there waiting for them.

"Hallo, Jack," said Mike. "Here we are at last. They sent us to bed, but when they went out we slipped down here to meet you."

"What's your great secret, Jack?" asked Nora; "we are longing to know."

"Well, listen," said Jack. "You know what a big lake this is, don't you, perfectly wild all round, except at the two ends where there are a few farmhouses and cottages. Now I know a little island, a good way up the south side of the lake, that I'm sure nobody knows at all. I don't think anyone but me has ever been there. It's a fine island, and would make the best hiding-place in the world!"

The three children listened, their eyes wide with astonishment. An island on the big lake! Oh, if only they could really go there and hide—and live by themselves— with no unkind aunt and uncle to slap them and scold them and make them work hard all day long!

"Are you too tired to walk down the lakeside to a place where you can see the island?" asked Jack. "I only found it quite by chance one day. The woods come right down to the lakeside opposite the island, and they are so thick that I don't think anyone has ever been through them, and so no one can have seen my island!"

"Jack! Jack! Take us to see your secret island!" begged Nora. "Oh, we must go. We're all tired—but we must, *must* see the secret island."

"Come on, then," said Jack, pleased to see how excited the others were. "Follow me. It's a good way."

The bare-footed boy took the three children across the fields to a wood. He threaded his way through the trees as if he were a rabbit. The wood thinned out and changed to a common, which, in turn, gave way to another wood, but this time the trees were so thick that it seemed as if there was no way through them at all.

But Jack kept on. He knew the way. He led the children without stopping, and at last they caught sight of the gleam of water. They had come back to the lakeside again. The evening was dim. The sun had sunk long since, and the children could hardly see.

Jack pushed his way through the trees that grew down to the waterside. He stood there and pointed silently to something. The children crowded round him.

"My secret island!" said Jack.

And so it was. The little island seemed to float on the dark lake-waters. Trees grew on it, and a little hill rose in the middle of it. It was a mysterious island, lonely and beautiful. All the children stood and gazed at it, loving it and longing to go to it. It looked so secret—almost magic.

"Well," said Jack at last. "What do you think? Shall we run away, and live on the secret island?"

"Yes!" whispered all the children. "Let's!"

An Exciting Day

The three children thought of nothing else but Jack's secret island all the next day. Could they possibly run away and hide there? Could they live there? How could they get food? What would happen if people came to look for them? Would they be found? How busy their minds were, thinking, thinking, planning, planning! Oh, the excitement of that secret island! It seemed so mysterious and lovely. If only, only they were all there, safe from slappings and scoldings!

The first time the children had a little time together to talk, they spoke about the island.

"Mike, we *must* go!" said Nora.

"Mike, let's tell Jack we'll go," said Peggy.

Mike scratched his curly black head. He felt old and worried. He wanted to go very badly—but would the three of them really be able to stand a wild life like that? No proper beds to sleep in—perhaps no proper food to eat—and suppose one of them was ill? Well, they would have to chance all that. They could always come back if things went too wrong.

"We'll go," said Mike. "We'll plan it all with Jack. He knows better than we do."

So that night, when they met Jack, the four of them laid their plans. Their faces were red with excitement, their eyes were shining. An adventure! A real proper adventure, almost like Robinson Crusoe—for they were going to live all by themselves on a lonely island.

"We must be careful in our plans," said Jack. "We

12

mustn't forget a single thing, for we ought not to go back to get anything, you know, or we might be caught."

"Could we go over to the island and just see what it's like before we go to live there?" asked Nora. "I would so love to see it."

"Yes," said Jack. "We'll go on Sunday."

"How can we go?" asked Mike. "Do we have to swim?"

"No," said Jack. "I have an old boat. It was one that had been left to fall to pieces, and I found it and patched it up. It still gets water in, but we can bale that out. I'll take you over in that."

The children could hardly wait for Sunday to come. They had to do a certain amount of work on Sundays, but usually they were allowed to take their dinner out and have a picnic afterwards.

It was June. The days were long and sunny. The farm garden was full of peas, broad beans, gooseberries, and ripening cherries. The children stole into it and picked as many pea-pods as they could find, and pulled up two big lettuces. Aunt Harriet gave them so little to eat that they always had to take something else as well. Mike said it wasn't stealing, because if Aunt Harriet had given them the food they earned by the hard work they did, they would have twice as much. They were only taking what they had earned. They had a loaf of bread between them, some butter, and some slices of ham, as well as the peas and lettuces. Mike pulled up some carrots, too. He said they would taste most delicious with the ham.

They hurried off to meet Jack. He was by the lakeside, carrying a bag on his back. He had his dinner in it. He showed them some fine red cherries, and a round cake.

"Mrs. Lane gave me those for hoeing her garden yesterday," he said. "We'll have a fine dinner between us."

"Where's the boat, Jack?" said Nora.

13

"You wait and see!" said Jack. "I don't leave my secret things out for everyone to see! No one else but you three knows about my boat!"

He set off in the hot June sunshine, and the three children followed him. He kept close to the lakeside and although the children kept a sharp look-out for the boat they did not see it until Jack stopped and showed it to them.

"See that great alder bush hanging over the lake just there?" he said. "Well, my boat's underneath it! It's well hidden, isn't it?"

Mike's eyes shone. He loved boats. He did hope Jack would let him help to row. The children pulled out the boat from under the thick tree. It was quite a big one, but very, very old. It had a good deal of water in, and Jack set everyone to work baling it out. There was an old pair of oars in the boat, and Jack put them in place.

"Now get in," he said. "I've a good way to row. Would you like to take an oar, Mike?"

Of course Mike would! The two boys rowed over the water. The sun shone down hotly, but there was a little breeze that blew every now and again. Soon the children saw the secret island in the distance. They knew it because of the little hill it had in the middle.

The secret island had looked mysterious enough on the night they had seen it before—but now, swimming in the hot June haze, it seemed more enchanting than ever. As they drew near to it, and saw the willow trees that bent over the water-edge and heard the sharp call of moorhens that scuttled off, the children gazed in delight. Nothing but trees and birds and little wild animals. Oh, what a secret island, all for their very own, to live on and play on.

"Here's the landing-place," said Jack, and he guided the boat to a sloping sandy beach. He pulled it up on the sand, and the children jumped out and looked round. The

14

They rowed across to the secret island

landing-place was a natural little cove—a lovely spot for a picnic—but picnickers never came here! Only a lonely otter lay on the sand now and again, and moorhens scuttled across it. No fire had ever been made on this little beach to boil a kettle. No bits of old orange peel lay about, or rusty tins. It was quite unspoilt.

"Let's leave our things here and explore a bit," said Mike, who was simply longing to see what the island was like. It seemed very big now they were on it.

"All right," said Jack, and he put his bag down.

"Come on," said Mike to the girls. "This is the beginning of a big adventure."

They left the little cove and went up through the thick trees. There were willows, alders, hazels, and elderberries at first, and then as they went up the hill that lay behind the cove there were silver birches and oaks. The hill was quite steep, and from the top the children could see a very long way—up the lake and down the lake.

"I say! If we come here to live, this hill will make an awfully good place to watch for enemies from!" said Mike excitedly. "We can see everything from here, all around!"

"Yes," said Jack. "Nobody would be able to take us by surprise."

"We *must* come here, we must, we must!" said Nora. "Oh, look at those rabbits, Peggy—they are as tame as can be, and that chaffinch nearly came on to my hand! Why are they so tame, Mike?"

"I suppose because they are not used to people," said Mike. "What's the other side of the hill, Jack? Shall we go down it?"

"There are caves on the other side of the hill," said Jack. "I haven't explored those. They would make good hiding-places if anyone ever came to look for us here."

They went down the hill on the other side. Gorse grew there and heather and bracken. Jack pointed out a big cave in the hillside. It looked dark and gloomy in the hot sunshine.

"We haven't time to go there now," said Jack. "But a cave would be an awfully good place to store anything in, wouldn't it? It would keep things nice and dry."

A little way down the hill the children heard a bubbling noise.

"What's that?" asked Peggy, stopping.

"Look! It's a little spring!" cried Mike. "Oh, Jack! This shall be our water-supply! It's as cold as can be, and as clear as crystal!"

"It tastes fine, too," said Jack. "I had a drink last time I was here. Lower down, another spring joins this one, and there is a tiny brook."

At the bottom of the hill was a thick wood. In clear patches great bushes of brambles grew. Jack pointed them out.

"There will be thousands of blackberries in the autumn," he said. "And as for hazel nuts, you should see them! And in another place I know here, on a warm slope, you can find wild raspberries by the score!"

"Oh, do show us!" begged Mike. But Jack said there was not time. Besides, the raspberries wouldn't be ripe yet.

"The island is too big to explore all over to-day," said Jack. "You've seen most of it—this big hill with its caves, the springs, the thick wood, and beyond the wood is a grassy field and then the water again. Oh, it is a glorious place!"

"Jack, where shall we live on this island?" said Peggy, who always liked to have everything well settled in her mind.

"We shall build a house of wood," said Jack. "I know how to. That will do finely for the summer, and for the winter we will have to find a cave, I think."

17

The children gazed at one another in glee. A house of wood, built by themselves—and a cave! How lucky they were to have a friend like Jack, who had a boat and a secret island!

They went back to the little landing-place, hungry and happy. They sat down and ate their bread and ham, carrots and peas, cherries and lettuces, and cake. It was the loveliest meal they had ever had in their lives, they thought. A little moorhen walked up to them and seemed surprised to see so many people in its home. But it did not run away. It ran round, pecking at the lettuce leaves, saying, "Fulluck, fulluck!" in its loud voice.

"If I could live here on this secret island always and always and always, and never grow up at all, I would be quite happy," said Nora.

"Well, we'll have a shot at living here for a good while at least!" said Jack. "Now, when shall we come?"

"And what shall we bring?" said Mike.

"Well, we don't really need a great deal at present," said Jack. "We can make soft beds of heather and bracken to lie on at night. What would be useful would be things like enamel mugs and plates and knives. I'll bring an axe and a very sharp woodman's knife. We'll need those when we build our house. Oh—and matches would be *most* useful for lighting fires. We shall have to cook our meals. I'll bring my fishing-line along, too."

The more the children talked about their plan, the more excited they got. At last they had arranged what to bring. They were gradually to hide things in a hollow tree by the lakeside, and then, when the time came, they could carry them to the boat and row off to the secret island, ready to set up house there.

"A frying-pan would be useful," said Nora.

"And a saucepan or two," said Peggy, "and a kettle. Oh! What fun it will be. I don't care how much we are

18

slapped or scolded now—I shall think of this exciting plan all day long!"

"We had better fix a day for starting off," said Jack. "What about a week from now? Sunday would be a good day for running away, because no one will come to look for us until night-time, when we don't go home!"

"Yes! A week to-day!" cried everyone. "Oooh! How happy we shall be!"

"Now we must go home," said Jack, setting off to the boat. "You can row if you like, Mike, and I'll bale out the water as we go. Get in, you girls."

"Ay, ay, Captain!" they sang out, full of joy to think they had such a fine leader as Jack! Off they all went, floating across the water in the evening light. What would they be doing next Sunday?

The Escape

All that week the three children carried out their plans. Aunt Harriet and Uncle Henry could not understand what was different about the children—they did not seem to mind being scolded at all. Even Nora took a slapping without tears. She was so happy when she thought of the secret island that she couldn't shed a tear!

The children took all the clothes they possessed down to the hollow tree by the lakeside. Mike took four enamel cups, some enamel plates, and two enamel dishes. Nora smuggled down an old kettle that Aunt Harriet had put away in a cupboard. She did not dare to take one of those on the stove. Peggy took a frying-pan and a saucepan to the hollow tree, and had to put up with a dreadful scolding when her aunt could not find them.

Jack took a saucepan too, and an axe and a fine sharp knife. He also took some small knives and forks and spoons, for the other children did not dare to take these. There were only just enough put out for them and their aunt and uncle to use. So they were glad when Jack found some and brought them along.

"Can you get some empty tins to store things in?" asked Jack. "I am trying to get sugar and things like that, because we must have those, you know. Grandad gave me some money the other day, and I'm buying a few things to store."

"Yes, I'll get some empty tins," said Mike. "Uncle has plenty in the shed. I can wash them out and dry them. And could you get matches, Jack? Aunt only leaves one box out, and that won't go far."

"Well, I've got a small magnifying glass," said Jack, and he showed it to the others. "Look, if I focus the rays of the sun on to that bit of paper over there, see what happens. It burns it, and, hey presto, there's a fire ready-made!"

"Oh, good!" said Mike. "We'll use that on a sunny day, Jack, and save our matches!"

"I'm bringing my work-basket in case we need to sew anything," said Peggy.

"And I've got a box of mixed nails and an old hammer," said Mike. "I found them in the shed."

"We're getting on!" said Jack, grinning, "I say—what a time we're going to have!"

"I wish Sunday would come!" sighed Nora.

"I shall bring our snap cards and our game of ludo and our dominoes," said Peggy. "We shall want to play games sometimes. And what about some books?"

"Good for you!" cried Mike. "Yes—books and papers we'll have, too—we shall love to read quietly sometimes."

The old hollow tree by the lakeside was soon full of the queerest collection of things. Not a day went by without something being added to it. One day it was a plank of wood. Another day it was half a sack of potatoes. Another day it was an old and ragged rug. Really, it was a marvel that the tree held everything!

At last Sunday came. The children were up long before their uncle and aunt. They crept into the kitchen garden and picked a basket of peas, pulled up six lettuces, added as many ripe broad beans as they could find, a bunch of young carrots, some radishes, and, putting their hands into the nest-boxes of the hens, they found six new-laid eggs!

Nora crept indoors and went to the larder. What could she take that Aunt Harriet would not notice that morning? Some tea? Yes! A tin of cocoa from the top shelf. A packet of currants and a tin of rice from the store

21

shelf, too. A big loaf, a few cakes from the cake-tin! The little girl stuffed them all into her basket and raced out to join the others. Long before Aunt Harriet was up all these things were safely in the hollow tree.

Peggy didn't quite like taking anything from the larder, but Mike said that as Aunt and Uncle wouldn't have to keep them after that day, they could quite well spare a few odds and ends for them.

"Anyway, if they paid us properly for our work, we would have enough to buy all these things and more," he said, as he stuffed them into the tree.

They went back to the farm for the last time, to breakfast. Peggy cooked the breakfast, and hoped Aunt would not notice that her long iron cooking spoon was gone. She also hoped that Aunt would not want to get another candle from the packet in the larder, for Peggy knew Mike had taken the rest of them, and had taken an old lantern of Uncle's, too!

The children ate their breakfast in silence.

Aunt Harriet looked at them. "I suppose you think you are going off for a picnic today!" she said. "Well, you are not! You can stay and weed the kitchen garden, Peggy and Nora. And I've no doubt Uncle Henry can set Mike something to do. *Someone* has been taking cakes out of my tin, and so you'll all stay in today!"

The hearts of the three children sank. Today of all days! As soon as the girls were washing up alone in the scullery, Mike looked in at the window.

"You girls slip off down to the lake as soon as you get a chance," he said. "Wait there for me. I won't be long!"

Peggy and Nora felt happier. They were to escape after all, then! They washed up a few more things and then saw their aunt going upstairs.

"She has gone to look out Uncle's Sunday suit and shirt," whispered Nora. "Quick! Now's our chance. We can slip out of the back door."

22

Peggy ran to the cupboard under the dresser and took out a long bar of soap. "We forgot all about soap!" she said. "We shall want some! I just remembered in time!"

Nora looked round for something to take, too. She saw a great slab of margarine on the dresser, and she caught it up.

"This will help us in our frying!" she said. "Come on, Peggy—we've no time to lose."

They raced out of the back door, down the path, and out into the fields. In five minutes' time they were by the hollow tree, well out of sight. Jack was not yet there. They did not know how long Mike would be. He would not find it so easy to get away!

But Mike had laid his plans. He waited for the moment when his aunt discovered that the girls had gone, and then walked into the kitchen.

"What's the matter, Aunt Harriet?" he asked, pretending to be very much surprised at her angry face and voice.

"Where have those two girls gone?" cried his aunt.

"I expect they have only gone to get in the clothes or something," said Mike. "Shall I go and find them for you?"

"Yes, and tell them they'll get well slapped for running off like this without finishing their work," said his aunt in a rage.

Mike ran off, calling to his uncle that he was on an errand for his aunt. So Uncle Henry said nothing, but let him go. Mike tore across the fields to the lakeside and met the two girls there. They hugged one another in joy.

"Now, where's Jack?" said Mike. "He said he would meet us as soon as he could."

"There he is!" said Nora; and sure enough, there was Jack coming across the field, waving to them. He carried a heavy bag into which he had crammed all sorts of things at

23

the very last moment—rope, an old mackintosh, two books, some newspapers, and other things. His face was shining with excitement.

"Good! You're here!" he said.

"Yes, but we nearly couldn't come," said Nora, and she told Jack what had happened.

"I say! I hope this won't mean that your uncle and aunt will start to look for you too soon," said Jack.

"Oh, no!" said Mike. "It only means that they will make up their minds to whip us well when we get back this evening, but we shan't go back! They'll think we've gone off on our usual Sunday picnic."

"Now we've got a lot to do," said Jack seriously. "This is all fun and excitement to us—but it's work, too—and we've got to get on with it. First, all these things must be carried from the hollow tree to the boat. Mike, you get out some of them and give them to the girls. Then we'll take the heavier things. I expect we shall have to come back to the tree three or four times before it's emptied."

The four of them set off happily, carrying as much as they could. The sun was hot, and they puffed and panted, but who cared? They were off to the secret island at last!

It was a good walk to the boat, and they had to make four journeys altogether, carrying things carefully. At last there was nothing left in the hollow tree. They need not come back again.

"I'm jolly glad," said Mike. "Every time I get back to that hollow tree I expect to find Aunt or Uncle hidden inside it, ready to pop out at us!"

"Don't say such horrid things," said Nora. "We're leaving Aunt and Uncle behind for ever!"

They were at the boat, and were stowing things there as well as they could. It was a good thing the boat was fairly big or it would never have taken everything. The children had had to bale out a good deal of water before they could put anything in the bottom. It leaked badly, but as long as someone could bale out with a tin it was all right.

"Now then," said Jack, looking round at the shore to see that nothing was left behind, "are we ready?"

"Ay, ay, Captain!" roared the other three. "Push off!"

The boat was pushed off. Mike and Jack took an oar each, for the boat was heavy and needed two people to pull it. It floated easily out on to the deeper water.

"We're off at last!" said Nora, in a little happy voice that sounded almost as if she were going to cry.

Nobody said anything more. The boat floated on and on, as Mike and Jack rowed strongly. Peggy baled out the water that came in through the leaks. She wondered what it would be like not to sleep in a proper bed. She wondered what it would be like to wake up under the blue sky—to have no one to make her do this, that and the other. How happy she felt!

It was a long way to the island. The sun rose higher and higher. The adventurers felt hotter and hotter. At last Nora pointed excitedly in front.

"The secret island!" she cried. "The secret island."

Mike and Jack stopped rowing for a moment and the boat floated on slowly by itself whilst the four gazed at the lonely little island, hidden so well on the heart of the lake. Their own island! It had no name. It was just the Secret Island!

Mike and Jack rowed on again. They came to the little sandy cove beneath the willow trees. Jack jumped out and pulled the boat in. The others jumped out too and gazed round.

"We're really here, we're really here, we're really here!" squealed Nora, jumping up and down and round and round in delight. "We've escaped. We've come to live on this dear little hidden island."

"Come on, Nora, give a hand," ordered Jack. "We've a lot to do before night, you know!"

Nora ran to help. The boat had to be unloaded, and that

was quite a job. All the things were put on the beach under the willow trees for the time being. By the time that was finished the children were hotter than ever and very hungry and thirsty.

"Oh, for a drink!" groaned Mike.

"Peggy, do you remember the way to the spring?" asked Jack. "You do? Well, just go and fill this kettle with water, will you? We'll all have a drink and something to eat!"

Peggy ran off up the hill and down the other side to the spring. She filled the kettle and went back. The others had put out enamel mugs ready to drink from. Mike was busy looking out something to eat, too. He had put out a loaf of bread, some young carrots, which they all loved to nibble, a piece of cheese each, and a cake.

What a meal that was! How they laughed and giggled and chattered! Then they lay back in the sun and shut their eyes. They were tired with all their hard work. One by one they fell asleep.

Jack awoke first. He sat up. "Hey!" he said. "This won't do! We've got to get our beds for the night and arrange a good sleeping-place! We've dozens of things to do! Come on, everyone, to work, to work!"

But who minded work when it was in such a pleasant place? Peggy and Nora washed up the mugs and dishes in the lake water and set them in the sun to dry. The boys put all the stores in a good place and covered them with the old mackintosh in case it should rain. To-morrow they would start to build their house.

"Now to get a sleeping-place and bedding," said Jack. "Won't it be fun to sleep for the first time on the Secret Island!"

26

The First Night On The Island

"Where do you think would be the best place to sleep?" said Peggy, looking round the little cove.

"Well," said Jack, "I think it would be best to sleep under some thick trees somewhere, then, if it rains tonight, we shall not get too wet. But I don't think it will rain; the weather is quite settled."

"There are two nice, big, thick oak trees just beyond the cove," said Mike, pointing. "Shall we find a place there?"

"Yes," said Jack. "Find a bramble bush or gorse bush near them to keep any wind off. Let's go and see what we think."

They all went to the two big oak trees. Their branches swung almost down to the ground in places. Below grew clumps of soft heather, springy as a mattress. To the north was a great growth of gorse, thick and prickly.

"This looks a fine place to sleep," said Jack. "Look. Do you see this little place here, almost surrounded by gorse, and carpeted with heather? The girls could sleep here, and we could sleep just outside their cosy spot, to protect them. The oak trees would shelter us nicely overhead."

"Oh, I do think this is fine; I do, I do!" cried Nora, thinking that their green, heathery bedroom was the nicest in the world. She lay down on the heather. "It is as soft as can be!" she said; "and oh! there is something making a most delicious smell. What is it?"

"It is a patch of wild thyme," said Jack. "Look, there

27

is a bit in the middle of the heather. You will smell it when you go to sleep, Nora!"

"All the same, Jack, the heather won't feel quite so soft when we have lain on it a few hours," said Mike. "We'd better get some armfuls of bracken too, hadn't we?"

"Yes," said Jack. "Come on up the hill. There is plenty of bracken there, and heaps of heather too. We will pick the bracken there, and put it in the sun to dry. The heather doesn't need drying. Pick plenty, for the softer we lie the better we'll sleep! Heyho for a starry night and a heathery bed!"

The four children gathered armfuls of bracken and put it out in the sun to wither and dry. The heather they carried back to their green bedroom under the oak tree. They spread it thickly there. It looked most deliciously soft! The thick gorse bushes kept off the breeze, and the oaks above waved their branches and whispered. What fun it all was!

"Well, there are our bedrooms ready," said Jack. "Now, we'd better find a place to put our stores in. We won't be too far from the water, because it's so useful for washing ourselves and our dishes in."

The children were hungry again. They got out the rest of the cakes, and finished up the bread, eating some peas with it, which they shelled as they ate.

"Are we going to have any supper?" asked Mike.

"We might have a cup of cocoa each and a piece of my cake," said Jack. "We must be careful not to eat everything at once that we've brought, or we'll go short! I'll do some fishing to-morrow."

"Shall we begin to build the house to-morrow?" asked Mike, who was longing to see how Jack meant to make their house.

"Yes," said Jack. "Now you two girls wash up the

mugs again, and Mike and I will find a good place for the stores."

The girls went to the water and washed the things. The boys wandered up the beach—and, at the back of the sandy cove, they found just the very place they wanted!

There was a sandy bank there, with a few old willows growing on top of it, their branches drooping down. Rain had worn away the sandy soil from their roots, and underneath there was a sort of shallow cave, with roots running across it here and there.

"Look at that!" said Jack in delight. "Just the place we want for our stores! Nora, Peggy, come and look here!"

The girls came running. "Oh," said Peggy, pleased, "we can use those big roots as shelves, and stand our tins and cups and dishes on them! Oh, it's a proper little larder!"

"Well, if you girls get the stores from the cove and arrange them neatly here," said Jack. "Mike and I will go and fill the kettle from the spring, and we'll see if there isn't a nearer spring, because it's a long way up the hill and down the other side."

"Can't we come with you?" asked Peggy.

"No, you arrange everything," said Jack. "It had better all be done as quickly as possible, because you never know when it's going to turn wet. We don't want our stores spoilt."

Leaving Peggy and Nora to arrange the tins, baskets, and odds and ends neatly in the root-larder, the two boys went up the hill behind the cove. They separated to look for a spring, and Mike found one! It was a very tiny one, gushing out from under a small rock, and it ran down the hill like a little waterfall, getting lost in the heather and grass here and there. Its way could be seen by the rushes that sprang up beside its course.

"I expect it runs down into the lake," said Mike. "It's a very small spring, but we can use it to fill our kettle, and it won't take us quite so long as going to the other spring. If we have to live in the caves during the winter, the other spring will be more useful then, for it will be quite near the cave."

They filled the kettle. It was lovely up there on the hillside in the June sun. Bees hummed and butterflies flew all round. Birds sang, and two or three moorhens cried "Fulluck, fulluck!" from the water below.

"Let's go to the top of the hill and see if we can spy anyone coming up or down the lake," said Jack. So they went right up to the top, but not a sign of anyone could they see. The waters of the lake were calm and clear and blue. Not a boat was on it. The children might have been quite alone in the world.

They went down to the girls with the full kettle. Nora and Peggy proudly showed the boys how they had arranged the stores. They had used the big roots for shelves, and the bottom of the little cave they had used for odds and ends, such as Jack's axe and knife, the hammer and nails, and so on.

"It's a nice dry place," said Peggy. "It's just right for a larder, and it's so nice and near the cove. Jack, where are we going to build our house?"

Jack took the girls and Mike to the west end of the cove, where there was a thicket of willows. He forced his way through them and showed the others a fine clear place right in the very middle of the trees.

"Here's the very place," he said. "No one would ever guess there was a house just here, if we built one! The willows grow so thickly that I don't suppose anyone but ourselves would ever know they could be got through."

They talked about their house until they were tired out. They made their way back to the little beach and Jack said they would each have a cup of cocoa, a piece of cake, and go to bed!

He and Mike soon made a fire. There were plenty of dry twigs about, and bigger bits of wood. It did look cheerful to see the flames dancing. Jack could not use his little magnifying glass to set light to the paper or twigs because the sun was not bright enough then. It was sinking down in the west. He used a match. He set the kettle on the fire to boil.

"It would be better tomorrow to swing the kettle over the flames on a tripod of sticks," he said. "It will boil more quickly then."

But nobody minded how slowly the kettle boiled. They lay on their backs in the sand, looking up at the evening sky, listening to the crackle of the wood, and smelling a mixture of wood-smoke and honeysuckle. At last the kettle sent out a spurt of steam, and began to hiss. It was boiling.

Nora made the cocoa, and handed it round in mugs. "There's no milk," she said. "But there is some sugar."

They munched their cake and drank their cocoa. Though it had no milk in it, it was the nicest they had ever tasted.

"I do like seeing the fire," said Nora. "Oh, Jack, why are you stamping it out?"

"Well," said Jack, "people may be looking for us to-night, you know, and a spire of smoke from this island would give our hiding-place away nicely! Come on, now, everyone to bed! We've hard work to do tomorrow!"

Peggy hurriedly rinsed out the mugs. Then all of them went to their green, heathery bedroom. The sun was gone. Twilight was stealing over the secret island.

"Our first night here!" said Mike, standing up and looking down on the quiet waters of the lake. "We are all alone, the four of us, without a roof over our heads even, but I'm so happy!"

"So am I!" said everyone. The girls went to their hidden

31

green room in the gorse and lay down in their clothes. It seemed silly to undress when they were sleeping out of doors. Mike threw them the old ragged rug.

"Throw that over yourselves," he said. "It may be cold tonight, sleeping out for the first time. You won't be frightened, will you?"

"No," said Peggy. "You two boys will be near, and, anyway, what is there to be frightened of?"

They lay down on the soft heather, and pulled the old rug over them. The springy heather was softer than the old hard bed the two girls had been used to at home. The little girls put their arms round one another and shut their eyes. They were fast asleep almost at once.

But the boys did not sleep so quickly. They lay on their heathery beds and listened to all the sounds of the night. They heard the little grunt of a hedgehog going by. They saw the flicker of bats overhead. They smelt the drifting scent of honeysuckle, and the delicious smell of wild thyme crushed under their bodies. A reed-warbler sang a beautiful little song in the reeds below, and then another answered.

"Is that a blackbird?" asked Mike.

"No, a reed-warbler," said Jack. "They sing as beautifully as any bird that sings in the daytime! Listen, do you hear that owl?"

"Oooo-ooo-ooo-oooo!" came a long, quivering sound; "ooo-ooo-ooo-ooo!"

"He's hunting for rats and voles," said Jack. "I say, look at the stars, Mike?"

"Don't they seem far away?" said Mike, looking up into the purple night sky, which was set with thousands of bright stars. "I say, Jack, it's awfully nice of you to come away with us like this and share your secret island."

"It isn't nice of me at all," said Jack. "I wanted to. I'm doing just exactly what I most want to do. I only hope we

32

shan't be found and taken back, but I'll take jolly good care no one finds us! I'm laying my plans already!"

But Mike was not listening. His eyes shut, he forgot the owls and the stars; he fell asleep and dreamt of building a house with Jack, a lovely house.

Jack fell asleep, too. And soon the rabbits that lived under their gorse-bush came slyly out and peeped at the sleeping children in surprise. Who were they?

But, as the children did not move, the rabbits grew bold and went out to play just as usual. Even when one ran over Mike by mistake, the little boy did not know it. He was *much* too fast asleep!

The Building Of The House

What fun it was to wake up that first morning on the island! Jack awoke first. He heard a thrush singing so loudly on a tree near by that he woke up with a jump.

"Mind how you do it," said the thrush, "mind how you do it!"

Jack grinned. "I'll mind how I do it all right!" he said to the singing thrush. "Hi, Mike! Wake up! The sun is quite high!"

Mike woke and sat up. At first he didn't remember where he was. Then a broad smile came over his face. Of course—they were all on the secret island! How perfectly glorious!

"Peggy, Nora! Get up!" he cried. The girls awoke and sat up in a hurry. Wherever were they? What was this green bedroom—oh, of course, it was their heathery bedroom on the secret island!

Soon all four children were up and about. Jack made them take off their things and have a dip in the lake. It was simply lovely, but the water felt cold at first. When they had dried themselves on an old sack—for they had no towels—the children felt terribly hungry. But Jack had been busy. He had set his fishing-line, and, even as they bathed, he had seen the float jerk up and down. It was not long before Jack proudly laid four fine trout on the sand of the cove, and set about to make a fire to cook them.

Mike went to fill the kettle to make some tea. Peggy got some big potatoes out of the sack and put them almost in the fire to cook in their skins. Jack found the frying-pan in their storeroom and put a piece of margarine in to fry the fish, which he knew exactly how to clean.

"I don't know what we should do without you," said Mike, as he watched Jack. "Goodness! How I shall enjoy my breakfast!"

They all did. The tea did not taste very nice without milk. "It's a pity we can't get milk," said Jack. "We shall miss that, I'm afraid. Now let's all wash up, and put everything away—and then we'll start on our house!"

In great excitement everything was washed up and put away. Then Jack led the way through the thick willow trees, and they came to the little clear place in the centre of them.

"Now, this is how I mean to build the house," he said. "Do you see these little willow trees here—one there —one there—two there—and two there. Well, I think you will find that if we climb up and bend down the top branches, they will meet each other nicely in the centre, and we can weave them into one another. That will make the beginning of a roof. With my axe I shall chop down some other young willow trees, and use the trunk and thicker branches for walls. We can drive the trunks and branches into the ground between the six willow trees we are using, and fill up any cracks with smaller branches woven across. Then if we stuff every corner and crevice with bracken and heather, we shall have a fine big house, with a splendid roof, wind-proof and rain-proof. What do you think of that?"

The other children listened in the greatest excitement. It sounded too good to be true. Could it be as easy as all that?

"Jack, can we really do it?" said Mike. "It sounds all right—and those willow trees are just the right distance from one another to make a good big house—and their top branches will certainly overlap well."

"Oh, let's begin, let's begin!" cried Nora, impatient as usual, dancing up and down.

"I'll climb up this first willow tree and swing the branches over with my weight," said Jack. "All you others must catch hold of them and hold them till I slip down. Then I'll climb another tree and bend those branches over too. We'll tie them together, and then I'll climb up the other trees. Once we've got all the top branches bending down touching one another, and overlapping nicely, we can cut long willow-sticks and lace our roof together. I'll show you how to."

Jack swung himself up into one of the little willow trees. It was only a young one, with a small trunk—but it had a head of long, fine branches, easy to bend. Jack swung them down, and the girls and Mike caught them easily. They held on to them whilst Jack slid down the tree and climbed another. He did the same thing there, bending down the supple branches until they reached and rested on top of those bent down from the other tree.

"Tie them together, Mike!" shouted Jack. "Peggy, go and find the rope I brought."

Peggy darted off. She soon came back with the rope. Mike twisted it round the branches of the two trees, and tied them firmly together.

"It's beginning to look like a roof already!" shouted Nora, in excitement. "Oh, I want to sit underneath it!"

She sat down under the roof of willow boughs, but Jack called to her.

"Get up, Nora! You've got to help! I'm up the third tree now—look, here come the top branches bending over with my weight—catch them and hold them!"

Nora and Peggy caught them and held on tightly. The branches reached the others and overlapped them. Mike was soon busy tying them down, too.

The whole morning was spent in this way. By

36

dinnertime all the six trees had been carefully bent over. Jack showed Mike and the girls how to weave the branches together, so that they held one another and made a fine close roof. "You see, if we use the trees like this, their leaves will still grow and will make a fine thick roof," said Jack. "Now, although our house has no walls as yet, we at least have a fine roof to shelter under if it rains!"

"I want something to eat," said Nora. "I'm so hungry that I feel I could eat snails!"

"Well, get out four eggs, and we'll have some with potatoes," said Jack. "We'll boil the eggs in our saucepan. There's plenty of potatoes, too. After the eggs are boiled we'll boil some potatoes and mash them up. That will be nice for a change. We'll nibble a few carrots, too, and have some of those cherries."

"We do have funny meals," said Peggy, going to get the saucepan and the eggs, "but I do like them! Come on, Nora, help me get the potatoes and peel them whilst the eggs are boiling. And Mike, get some water, will you? We haven't enough."

Soon the fire was burning merrily and the eggs were boiling in the saucepan. The girls peeled the potatoes, and Jack washed the carrots. He went to get some water to drink, too, for everyone was very thirsty.

"You'd better catch some more fish for tonight, Jack," said Peggy. "I hope our stores are going to last out a bit! We do seem to eat a lot!"

"I've been thinking about that," said Jack, watching the potatoes boiling. "I think I'll have to row to land occasionally and get more food. I can get it from Granddad's farm. There are plenty of potatoes there, and I can always get the eggs from the hen-house. Some of the hens are mine—and there's a cow that's really mine too, for Granddad gave her to me when she was a calf!"

"I wish we had hens and a cow here!" said Peggy. "We should have lots of milk then and plenty of eggs!"

"How would we get hens and a cow here?" said Mike, laughing. "I think Jack's idea of rowing across to land sometimes is a good one. He can go at night. He knows the way, and could get back before day breaks."

"It's dangerous, though," said Peggy. "Suppose he were caught? We couldn't do without Jack!"

The children ate their dinner hungrily. They thought that eggs and potatoes had never tasted so nice before. The sun shone down hotly. It was simply perfect weather. Nora lay down when she had finished her meal and closed her eyes. She felt lazy and sleepy.

Jack poked her with his foot. "You're not to go to sleep, Nora," he said. "We must get on with our house, now we've started. We've got to clear up as usual, and then we must get back to the house. We'll start on the walls this afternoon."

"But I'm sleepy," said Nora. She was rather a lazy little girl, and she thought it would be lovely to have a nap whilst the others got on with the work. But Jack was not the one to let anyone slack. He jerked Nora to her feet and gave her a push.

"Go on, lazy-bones," he said. "I'm captain here. Do as you're told."

"I didn't know you were captain," said Nora, rather sulkily.

"Well, you know now," said Jack. "What do the others say about it?"

"Yes, you're captain, Jack," said Mike and Peggy together. "Ay, ay, sir!"

Nobody said any more. They washed up in the lake and cleared the things away neatly. They put some more wood on the fire to keep it burning, because Jack said it was silly to keep on lighting it. Then they all ran off to the willow thicket.

Jack made himself busy. He chopped down some willow

saplings—young willow trees—with his axe, and cut off the longer branches.

"We'll use these to drive into the ground for walls," said Jack. "Where's that old spade, Mike? Did you bring it as I said?"

"Yes, here it is," said Mike. "Shall I dig holes to drive the sapling trunks into?"

"Yes," said Jack. "Dig them fairly deep."

So Mike dug hard in the hot sun, making holes for Jack to ram the willow wood into. The girls stripped the leaves off the chopped-down trees, and with Jack's knife cut off the smaller twigs. They trimmed up the bigger branches nicely.

Everyone worked hard until the sun began to go down. The house was not yet built—it would take some days to do that—but at any rate there was a fine roof, and part of the wall was up. The children could quite well see how the house would look when it was done—and certainly it would be big, and very strong. They felt proud of themselves.

"We'll do no more today," said Jack. "We are all tired. I'll go and see if there are any fish on my line."

But, alas! there were no fish that night!

"There's some bread left and a packet of currants," said Peggy. "And some lettuces and margarine. Shall we have those?"

"This food question is going to be a difficult one," said Jack thoughtfully. "We've plenty of water—we shall soon have a house—but we must have food or we shall starve. I shall catch rabbits, I think."

"Oh, no, Jack, don't do that," said Nora. "I do like rabbits so much."

"So do I, Nora," said Jack. "But if rabbits were not caught, the land would soon be overrun with them, you know. You have often had rabbit-pie, haven't you? And I guess you liked it, too!"

"Yes, I did," said Nora. "Well, if you are sure you can

39

catch them so that they are not hurt or in pain, Jack, I suppose you'll have to."

"You leave it to me," said Jack. "I don't like hurting things any more than you do. But I know quite well how to skin rabbits. If it makes you feel squeamish, you two girls can leave it to Mike and me. So long as you can cook the rabbits for dinner, that's all you need worry about. And ever since Peggy said she wished we had a cow and some hens, I've been thinking about it. I believe we could manage to get them over here on to the island—then we *would* be all right!"

Mike, Peggy, and Nora stared at Jack in amazement. What a surprising boy he was! However could they get a cow and hens?

"Let's hurry up and get the supper," said Jack, smiling at their surprised faces. "I'm hungry. We'll think about things tomorrow. We'll have our meal now and a quiet read afterwards, then to bed early. Tomorrow we'll go on with the house."

Soon they were munching bread and margarine, and eating lettuce. They saved the currants for another time. Then they got out books and papers and sprawled on the soft heather, reading whilst the daylight lasted. Then they had a dip in the lake, threw on their clothes again, and settled down for the night in their heathery beds.

"Good-night, everyone," said Mike. But nobody answered—they were all asleep!

Willow House Is Finished

The next day, after a meal of fish and lettuce, the children were ready to go on with the building of their house in the willow thicket. It was lucky that Jack had caught more fish on his line that morning, for stores were getting low. There were still plenty of potatoes, but not much else. Jack made up his mind that he would have to take the boat and see what he could bring back in it that night. There was no doubt but that food was going to be their great difficulty.

All morning the four children worked hard at the house. Jack cut down enough young willows to make the walls. Mike dug the holes to drive in the willow stakes. He and Jack drove them deeply in, and the girls jumped for joy to see what fine straight walls of willow the boys were making.

The willow stakes were set a little way apart, and Jack showed the girls how to take thin, supple willow branches and weave them in and out of the stakes to hold the walls in place, and to fill up the gaps. It was quite easy to do this when they knew how, but they got very hot.

Mike went up and down to the spring a dozen times that morning to fetch water! They all drank pints of it, and were glad of its coldness. The sun was really very hot, though it was nice and shady in the green willow thicket.

"It begins to look like a house now," said Jack, pleased. "Look, this front gap here is where we shall have the door. We can make that later of long stakes interwoven with willow strips, and swing it on some sort of a hinge so that it opens and shuts. But we don't need a door at present."

That day all the walls were finished, and the girls had gone a good way towards weaving the stakes together so that the walls stood firmly and looked nice and thick.

"In the olden days people used to fill up the gaps with clay and let it dry hard," said Jack. "But I don't think there's any clay on this island, so we must stuff up the cracks with dried bracken and heather. That will do nicely. And the willow stakes we have rammed into the ground will grow, and throw out leaves later on, making the wall thicker still."

"How do you mean—the stakes we have cut will grow?" asked Mike in surprise. "Sticks don't grow, surely!"

Jack grinned. "Willow sticks do!" he said. "You can cut a willow branch off the tree—strip it of all buds and leaves, and stick it in the ground, and you'll find that, although it has no roots, and no shoots—it will put out both and grow into a willow tree by itself! Willows are full of life, and you can't stamp it out of them!"

"Well—our house will be growing all the year round, then!" cried Nora. "How funny!"

"I think it's lovely!" said Peggy. "I like things to be as alive as that. I shall love to live in a house that's growing over me—putting out roots and shoots and buds and leaves! What shall we call our house, Jack?"

"Willow House!" said Jack. "That's the best name for it!"

"It's a good name," said Peggy. "I like it. I like everything here. It's glorious. Just us four—and our secret island. It's the loveliest adventure that ever was!"

"If only we had more to eat!" said Mike, who seemed to feel hungry every hour of the day. "That's the only thing I don't like about this adventure!"

"Yes," said Jack. "We'll have to put that right! Don't worry. We shall get over it somehow!"

That night there was nothing much to eat but potatoes. Jack said he would go off in the boat as soon as it was dark, to see what he could find at his old farm.

So he set off. He took with him a candle, set in the lantern, but he did not light it in case he should be seen.

"Wait up for me," he said to the others, "and keep a small fire going—not big, in case the glow could be seen."

The other three waited patiently for Jack to come back. He seemed a long, long time. Nora stretched herself out on the old rug and fell asleep. But Mike and Peggy kept awake. They saw the moon come up and light everything. The secret island seemed mysterious again in the moonlight. Dark shadows stretched beneath the trees. The water lapped against the sand, black as night, close by them, but silvered where the moon caught it beyond. It was a warm night, and the children were hot, even though they had no covering.

It seemed hours before they heard the splash of oars. Mike ran down to the edge of the water and waited. He saw the boat coming softly over the water in the moonlight. He called Jack.

"Hallo, there, Jack! Are you all right?"

"Yes," said Jack's voice. "I've got plenty of news too!"

The boat scraped on the sand and stones. Mike pulled it up the beach, and Jack jumped out.

"I've got something here for us!" said Jack, and they saw his white teeth in the moonlight as he grinned at them. "Put your hands down there in the boat, Nora."

Nora did—and squealed!

"There's something soft and warm and feathery there!" she said. "What is it?"

"Six of my hens!" said Jack. "I found them roosting in the hedges! I caught them and trussed them up so that

43

they couldn't move! My word, they were heavy to carry! But we shall have plenty of eggs now! They can't escape from the island!"

"Hurrah!" cried Peggy. "We can have eggs for breakfast, dinner, and tea!"

"What else have you brought?" asked Mike.

"Corn for the hens," said Jack. "And packets of seeds of all kinds from the shed. And some tins of milk. And a loaf of bread, rather stale. And lots more vegetables!"

"And here are some cherries," said Nora, pulling out handfuls of red cherries from the boat. "Did you pick these, Jack?"

"Yes," said Jack. "They are from the tree in our garden. It's full of them now."

"Did you see your grandfather?" asked Mike.

"Yes," grinned Jack, "but he didn't see me! He's going away—to live with my aunt. The farm is to be shut up, and someone is to feed the animals until it's sold. So I think I shall try and get my own cow somehow, and make her swim across the lake to the island!"

"Don't be silly, Jack," said Peggy. "You could never do that!"

"You don't know what I can do!" said Jack. "Well, listen—I heard my Granddad talking to two friends of his, and everyone is wondering where we've all gone! They've searched everywhere for us—in all the nearby towns and villages, and in all the country round about!"

"Oooh!" said the three children, feeling rather frightened. "Do you suppose they'll come here?"

"Well, they may," said Jack. "You never know. I've always been a bit afraid that the smoke from our fire will give the game away to someone. But don't let's worry about that till it happens."

"Are the police looking for us, too?" asked Peggy.

"Oh yes," said Jack. "Everyone is, as far as I can make

44

Mike shone the lantern onto the hens

45

out. I heard Granddad tell how they've searched barns and stacks and ditches, and gone to every town for twenty miles round, thinking we might have run away on a lorry. They don't guess how near we are!"

"Is Aunt Harriet very upset?" asked Peggy.

"Very!" grinned Jack. "She's got no one to wash and scrub and cook for her now! But that's all she cares, I expect! Well, it's good news about my Granddad going to live with my aunt. I can slip to and fro and not be seen by him now. My word, I wished you were with me when I got these hens. They did peck and scratch and flap about. I was afraid someone would hear them."

"Where shall we put them?" said Mike, helping Jack to carry them up the beach.

"I vote we put them into Willow House till the morning," said Jack. "We can stop up the doorway with something."

So they bundled the squawking hens into Willow House, and stopped up the doorway with sticks and bracken. The hens fled to a corner and squatted there, terrified. They made no more noise.

"I'm jolly tired," said Jack. "Let's have a few cherries and go to bed."

They munched the ripe cherries, and then went to their green bedroom. The bracken which they had picked and put on the hillside to dry had been quite brown and withered by that afternoon, so the girls had added it to their bed and the boys', and tonight their beds seemed even softer and sweeter-smelling than usual. They were all tired. Mike and Jack talked for a little while, but the girls went to sleep quickly.

They slept late the next morning. Peggy woke first, and sat up, wondering what the unusual noise was that she heard. It was a loud cackling.

"Of course! The hens!" she thought. She slipped off her

46

bracken-and-heather bed, jumped lightly over the two sleeping boys and ran to Willow House. She pulled aside the doorway and squeezed inside. The hens fled to a corner when they saw her, but Peggy saw a welcome sight!

Four of the hens had laid eggs! Goody! Now they could have a fine breakfast! The little girl gathered them up quickly, then, stopping up the doorway again, she ran out. She soon had a fire going, and, when the others sat up, rubbing their eyes, Peggy called them.

"Come on! Breakfast! The hens have laid us an egg each!"

They ran to breakfast. "We'll have a dip afterwards," said Mike. "I feel so hungry."

"We must finish Willow House properly today," said Jack. "And we must decide what to do with the hens, too. They can't run loose till they know us and their new home. We must put up some sort of enclosure for them."

After breakfast the four of them set to work to make a tiny yard for the hens. They used willow stakes again and quickly built a fine little fence, too high for the hens to jump over. Jack made them nesting-places of bracken, and hoped they would lay their eggs there. He scattered some seed for them, and they pecked at it eagerly. Peggy gave them a dish of water.

"They will soon know this is their home and lay their eggs here," said Jack. "Now, come on, let's get on with Willow House! You two girls stuff up the cracks with heather and bracken, and Mike and I will make the door."

Everyone worked hard. The girls found it rather a nice job to stuff the soft heather and bracken into the cracks and make the house rain- and wind-proof. They were so happy in their job that they did not notice what a fine door Jack and Mike had made of woven willow twigs. The boys called the girls, and proudly showed them what they had done.

47

The door had even been fixed on some sort of a hinge, so that it swung open and shut! It looked fine! It did not quite fit at the top, but nobody minded that. It was a door—and could be shut or opened, just as they pleased. Willow House was very dark inside when the door was shut—but that made it all the more exciting!

"I'm so hungry and thirsty now that I believe I could eat all the food we've got!" said Mike at last.

"Yes, we really must have something to eat," said Jack. "We've got plenty of bread and potatoes and vegetables. Let's cook some broad beans. They are jolly good. Go and look at my fishing-line, Mike, and see if there are any fish on it."

There was a fine trout, and Mike brought it back to cook. Soon the smell of frying rose on the air, and the children sniffed hungrily. Fish, potatoes, bread, beans, cherries, and cocoa with milk from one of Jack's tins. What a meal!

"I'll think about getting Daisy the cow across next," said Jack, drinking his cocoa. "We simply must have milk."

"And, Jack, we could store some of our things in Willow House now, couldn't we?" said Peggy. "The ants get into some of the things in the cave-larder. It's a good place for things like hammers and nails, but it would be better to keep our food in Willow House. Are we going to live in Willow House, Jack?"

"Well, we'll live in the open air mostly, I expect," said Jack, "but it will be a good place to sleep in when the nights are cold and rainy, and a fine shelter on bad days. It's our sort of home."

"It's a lovely home," said Nora; "the nicest there ever was! What fun it is to live like this!"

The Cow Comes To The Island

A day or two went by. The children were busy, for there seemed lots of things to do. The door of Willow House came off and had to be put on again more carefully. One of the hens escaped, and the four children spent nearly the whole morning looking for it. Jack found it at last under a gorse bush, where it had laid a big brown egg.

They made the fence of the hen-yard a bit higher, thinking that the hen had been able to jump over. But Mike found a hole in the fence through which he was sure the hen had squeezed, and very soon it was blocked up with fronds of bracken. The hens squawked and clucked, but they seemed to be settling down, and always ran eagerly to Nora when she fed them twice a day.

Mike thought it would be a good idea to make two rooms inside Willow House, instead of one big room. The front part could be a sort of living-room, with the larder in a corner, and the back part could be a bedroom, piled with heather and bracken to make soft lying. So they worked at a partition made of willow, and put it up to make two rooms. They left a doorway between, but did not make a door. It was nice to have a two-roomed house!

One evening Jack brought something unusual to the camp-fire on the little beach. Mike stared at what he was carrying.

"You've caught some rabbits!" he said, "and you've skinned them, too, and got them ready for cooking!"

"Oh, Jack!" said Nora. "Must you catch those dear

little rabbits? I do love them so much, and it is such fun to watch them playing about round us in the evenings."

"I know," said Jack, "but we must have meat to eat sometimes. Now, don't worry, Nora—they did not suffer any pain and you know you have often eaten rabbit-pie at home."

All the same, none of the children enjoyed cooking the rabbits, though they couldn't help being glad of a change of food. They were getting a little tired of fish. Nora said she felt as if she couldn't look a rabbit in the face that evening!

"In Australia, rabbits are as much of a pest as rats are here," said Jack, who seemed to know all sorts of things. "If we were in Australia we would think we had done a good deed to get rid of a few pests."

"But we're not in Australia," said Peggy. Nobody said any more, and the meal was finished in silence. The girls washed up as usual, and the boys went to get some water from the spring ready to boil in the morning. Then they all had a dip in the lake.

"I think I'll have a shot at getting my cow along tonight," said Jack, as they dressed themselves again.

"You can't, Jack!" cried Nora. "You'd never get a cow here!"

"I'll come with you, Jack," said Mike. "You'll want someone to help you."

"Right!" said Jack. "We'll start off as soon as it's dark."

"Oh, Jack!" said the girls, excited to think of a cow coming. "Where shall we keep it?"

"It had better live on the other side of the island," said Jack. "There is some nice grass there. It won't like to eat heather."

"How will you bring it, Jack?" asked Mike. "It will be difficult to get it into the boat, won't it?"

"We shan't get it into the boat, silly!" said Jack, laughing. "We shall make it swim *behind* the boat!"

The other three stared at Jack in surprise. Then they began to laugh. It was funny to think of a cow swimming behind the boat to their secret island!

When it was dark, the two boys set off. The girls called good-bye, and then went to Willow House, for the evening was not quite so warm as usual. They lighted a candle and talked. It was fun to be on the secret island alone.

The boys rowed down the lake and came to the place where Jack usually landed—a well-hidden spot by the lake-side, where trees came right down to the water. They dragged the boat in and then made their way through the wood. After some time they came to the fields that lay round the house of Jack's grandfather. Jack looked at the old cottage. There was no light in it. No one was there. His grandfather had gone away. In the field nearby some cows and horses stood, and the boys could hear one of the horses saying, "Hrrrumph! Hrrrrumph!"

"Do you see that shed over there, Mike?" said Jack, in a low voice. "Well, there are some lengths of rope there. Go and get them whilst I try to find which is my own cow. The rope is in the corner, just by the door."

Mike stumbled off over the dark field to the tumble-down shed in the corner. Jack went among the cows, making a curious chirrupy noise. A big brown and white cow left the others and went lumbering towards Jack.

Jack cautiously struck a match and looked at it. It was Daisy, the cow he had brought up from a calf. He rubbed its soft nose, and called to Mike:

"Hurry up with that rope! I've got the cow."

Mike had been feeling about in the shed for rope and had found a great coil of it. He stumbled over the field to Jack.

"Good," said Jack, making a halter for the patient

animal. "Now, before we go, I'd like to pop into the old cottage and see if I can find anything we'd be glad of."

"Could you find some towels, do you think?" asked Mike. "I do hate having to dry myself with old sacks."

"Yes, I'll see if there are any left," said Jack, and he set off quietly towards the old cottage. He found the door locked, but easily got in at a window. He struck a match and looked round. There were only two rooms in the cottage, a living-room and a bedroom. All the furniture had gone. Jack looked behind the kitchen door, and found what he had hoped to see—a big roller-towel still hanging there. It was very dirty, but could easily be washed. He looked behind the bedroom door—yes, there was a roller-towel there, too! Good! His grandfather hadn't thought of looking behind the doors and taking those when he went. Jack wondered if the old carpet left on the floor was worth taking, too, but he thought not. Good clean heather made a better carpet!

Jack wandered out to the little shed at the back of the cottage—and there he did indeed make a find! There was an old wooden box there, and in it had been put all the clothes he possessed! His grandfather had not thought it worth while to take those with him. There they were, rather ragged, it is true, but still, they were clothes! There were three shirts, a few vests, an odd pair of trousers, an overcoat, a pair of old shoes, and a ragged blanket!

Jack grinned. He would take all these back with him. They might be useful when the cold weather came. He thought the best way to take them back would be to wear them all—so the boy put on all the vests, the shirts, the trousers, the shoes, and the overcoat over his own clothes, and wrapped the blanket round him, too! What a queer sight he looked!

Then he went out to the garden and filled his many pockets with beans and peas and new potatoes. After that he thought it was time to go back to Mike and the cow. Mike would be tired of holding the animal by now!

So, carrying the two dirty towels, Jack made his way slowly over the field to Mike.

"I thought you were never coming!" said Mike, half-cross. "Whatever happened to you? This cow is getting tired of standing here with me."

"I found a lot of my clothes," said Jack, "and an old blanket and two towels. The cow will soon get some exercise! Come on! You carry the towels and this blanket, and I'll take Daisy."

They went back over the fields and through the thick wood to the boat. The cow did not like it when they came to the wood. She could not see where they were going and she disliked being pulled through the close-set trees. She began to moo.

"Oh, don't do that!" said Jack, scared. "You will give us away, Daisy."

"Moo-oo-oo!" said Daisy sorrowfully, trying her hardest to stand still. But Jack and Mike pulled her on.

It was hard work getting her down to the boat. It took the boys at least two hours before they were by the lake, panting and hot. Daisy had mooed dozens of times, each time more loudly than before, and Jack was beginning to think that his idea of taking her across to the island was not such a good one after all. Suppose her mooing gave them away, and people came after them? Suppose she mooed a great deal on the island? Whatever would they do?

Still, they had at last got her to the boat. Jack persuaded the poor, frightened cow to step into the water. She gave such a moo that she startled even the two boys. But at last she was in the water. The boys got into the boat, and pushed off. Jack had tied the cow's rope to the stern of the boat. The boys bent to their oars, and poor Daisy found that she was being pulled off her feet into deeper water!

It was a dreadful adventure for a cow who had never been out of her field before, except to be milked in a nearby shed! She waggled her long legs about, and began to swim in a queer sort of way, holding her big head high out of the water. She was too frightened to moo.

Jack lighted the lantern and fixed it to the front of the boat. It was very dark and he wanted to see where he was going. Then off they rowed up the lake towards the secret island, and Daisy the cow came after them, not able to help herself.

"Well, my idea is working," said Jack after a bit.

"Yes," said Mike, "but I'm jolly glad it's only *one* cow we're taking, not a whole herd!"

They said no more till they came in sight of the island, which loomed up near by, black and solid. The girls had heard the splashing of the oars, and had come down to the beach with the candle.

"Have you got the cow, Jack?" they called.

"Yes," shouted back the boys. "She's come along behind beautifully. But she doesn't like it, poor creature!"

They pulled the boat up the beach and then dragged out the shivering, frightened cow. Jack spoke to her kindly and she pressed against him in wonder and fear. He was the one thing she knew, and she wanted to be close to him. Jack told Mike to get a sack and help him to rub the cow down, for she was cold and wet.

"Where shall we put her for tonight?" asked Mike.

"In the hen-yard," said Jack. "She's used to hens and hens are used to her. There is a lot of bracken and heather there and we can put some more armfuls in for her to lie on. She will soon be warm and comfortable. She will like to hear the clucking of the hens, too."

So Daisy was pushed into the hen-yard, and there she

lay down on the warm heather, comforted by the sound of the disturbed hens.

The girls were so excited at seeing the cow. They asked the boys over and over again all about their adventure till Mike and Jack were tired of telling it.

"Jack! You do look awfully fat tonight!" said Nora suddenly, swinging the lantern so that its light fell on Jack. The others looked at him in surprise. Yes, he did look enormous!

"Have you swollen up, or something?" asked Peggy anxiously. Jack laughed loudly.

"No!" he said, "I found some clothes of mine in a box and brought them along. As the easiest way to carry them was to wear them, I put them on. That's why I look so fat!"

It took him a long time to take all the clothes off, because they were all laughing so much. Peggy looked at the holes in them and was glad she had brought her work-basket along. She could mend them nicely! The blanket, too, would be useful on a cold night.

"What's that funny light in the sky over there?" said Nora, suddenly, pointing towards the east. "Look!"

"You silly! It's the dawn coming" said Jack. "It must be nearly daylight! Come on, we really must go to sleep. What a night we've had!"

"Moo-oo-oo!" said Daisy, from the hen-yard, and the children laughed.

"Daisy thinks so, too!" cried Peggy.

A Lazy Day—With A Horrid Ending

The next morning the children slept very late indeed. The sun was high in the sky before anyone stirred, and even then they might not have awakened if Daisy the cow hadn't decided that it was more than time for her to be milked. She stood in the hen-yard and bellowed for all she was worth.

Jack sat up, his heart thumping loudly. Whatever was that awful noise? Of course—it was Daisy! She wanted to be milked!

"Hi, you others!" he shouted. "Wake up! It must be about nine o'clock! Look at the sun, it's very high! And Daisy wants to be milked!"

Mike grunted and opened his eyes. He felt very sleepy after his late night. The girls sat up and rubbed their eyes. Daisy bellowed again, and the hens clucked in fright.

"Our farmyard wants its breakfast," grinned Jack. "Come on, lazy-bones, come and help. We'll have to see to them before we get our own meal."

They scrambled up. They were so very sleepy that they simply had to run down to the lake and dip their heads into the water before they could do anything!

Then they all went to gloat over their cow. How pretty she was in her brown and white coat! How soft and brown her eyes were! A cow of their own! How lovely!

"And what a voice she has!" said Jack, as the cow mooed again. "I must milk her."

"But I say—we haven't a pail!" said Mike.

The children stared at one another in dismay. It was true—they had no pail.

"Well, we must use the saucepans," said Jack firmly. "And we can all do with a cup or two of milk to start the day. I'll use the biggest saucepan, and when it's full I'll have to pour it into the bowls and jugs we've got—and the kettle, too. We must certainly get a pail. What a pity I didn't think of it last night!"

There was more than enough milk to fill every bowl and jug and saucepan. The children drank cupful after cupful. It was lovely to have milk after drinking nothing but tea and cocoa made with water. They could not have enough of it!

"I say! Daisy has trodden on a hen's egg and smashed it," said Nora, looking into the hen-yard. "What a pity!"

"Never mind," said Jack. "We won't keep her here after to-day. She shall go and live on that nice grassy piece, the other side of the island. Nora, feed the hens. They are clucking as if they'd never stop. They are hungry."

Nora fed them. Then they all sat down to their breakfast of boiled eggs and creamy milk. Daisy the cow looked at them as they ate, and mooed softly. She was hungry, too.

Jack and Mike took her to the other side of the island after they had finished their meal. She was delighted to see the juicy green grass there and set to work at once, pulling mouthfuls of it as she wandered over the field.

"She can't get off the island, so we don't need to fence her in," said Jack. "We must milk her twice a day, Mike. We must certainly get a pail from somewhere."

"There's an old milking-pail in the barn at Aunt Harriet's farm," said Peggy. "I've seen it hanging there often."

"Has it got a hole in it?" asked Jack. "If it has it's no use to us. We'll have to stand our milk in it all day and we don't want it to leak away."

"No, it doesn't leak," said Peggy. "I filled it with water one day to take to the hens. It's only just a very old one and not used now."

"I'll go and get it tonight," said Mike.

"No, I'll go," said Jack. "You might be caught."

"Well, so might you," said Mike. "We'll go together."

"Can't we come, too?" asked the girls.

"Certainly not," said Jack, at once. "There's no use the whole lot of us running into danger."

"How shall we keep the milk cool?" wondered Peggy. "It's jolly hot on this island."

"I'll make a little round place to fit the milk-pail into, just by one of the springs," said Jack, at once. "Then, with the cool spring water running round the milk-pail all day, the milk will keep beautifully fresh and cool."

"How clever you are, Jack!" said Nora.

"No, I'm not," said Jack. "It's just common sense, that's all. Anyone can think of things like that."

"I do feel tired and stiff today," said Mike, stretching out his arms. "It was pretty hard work pulling old Daisy along last night!"

"We'd better have a restful day," said Jack, who was also feeling tired. "For once in a while we won't do anything. We'll just lie about and read and talk."

The children had a lovely day. They bathed three times, for it was very hot. Nora washed the two big roller towels in the lake, and made them clean. They soon dried in the hot sun, and then the two boys took one for themselves and the two girls had the other. How nice it was to dry themselves on towels instead of on rough sacks!

"Fish for dinner," said Jack, going down to look at his lines.

"And custard!" said Nora, who had been doing some cooking with eggs and milk.

"Well, I feel just as hungry as if I'd been hard at work building all morning!" said Mike.

The afternoon passed by lazily. The boys slept. Nora read a book. Peggy got out her work-basket and began on the long, long task of mending up the old clothes Jack had brought back the night before. She thought they would be very useful indeed when the cold weather came. She wished she and Nora and Mike could get some of their clothes, too.

The hens clucked in the hen-yard. Daisy the cow mooed once or twice, feeling rather strange and lonely—but she seemed to be settling down very well.

"I hope she won't moo too much," thought Peggy, her needle flying in and out busily. "She might give us away with her mooing if anyone came up the lake in a boat. But thank goodness no one ever does!"

Everyone felt very fresh after their rest. They decided to have a walk round the island. Nora fed the hens and then they set off.

It was a fine little island. Trees grew thickly down to the water-side all round. The steep hill that rose in the middle was a warm, sunny place, covered with rabbit runs and burrows. The grassy piece beyond the hill was full of little wild flowers, and birds sang in the bushes around. The children peeped into the dark caves that ran into the hillside, but did not feel like exploring them just then, for they had no candles with them.

"I'll take you to the place where wild raspberries grow," said Jack. He led them round the hill to the west side, and there, in the blazing sun, the children saw scores of raspberry canes, tangled and thick.

"Jack! There are some getting ripe already!" cried Nora, in delight. She pointed to where spots of bright red dotted the canes. The children squeezed their way through and began to pick the raspberries. How sweet and juicy they were!

"We'll have some of these with cream each day," said

"Look," cried Jack alarmingly, *"some people in a boat."*

Peggy. "I can skim the cream off the cow's milk, and we will have raspberries and cream for supper. Oooh!"

"Oooh!" said everyone, eating as fast as they could.

"Are there any wild strawberries on the island, too?" asked Nora.

"Yes," said Jack, "but they don't come till later. "We'll look for those in August and September."

"I do think this is a lovely island," said Peggy happily. "We've a spendid house of our own—hens—a cow, wild fruit growing—fresh water each day!"

"It's all right now it's warm weather," said Jack. "It won't be quite so glorious when the cold winds begin to blow! But winter is a long way off yet."

They climbed up the west side of the hill, which was very rocky. They came to a big rock right on the very top, and sat there. The rock was so warm that it almost burnt them. From far down below the blue spire of smoke rose up from the fire.

"Let's play a game," said Jack. "Let's play . . ."

But what game Jack wanted the others never knew—for Jack suddenly stopped, sat up very straight, and stared fixedly down the blue, sparkling lake. The others sat up and stared, too. And what they saw gave them a dreadful shock!

"Some people in a boat!" said Jack. "Do you see them? Away down there!"

"Yes," said Mike, going pale. "Are they after us, do you think?"

"No," said Jack, after a while. "I think I can hear a radio playing—and if it was anyone after us they surely wouldn't bring that! They are probably just trippers, from the village at the other end of the lake."

"Do you think they'll come to the island?" asked Peggy.

"I don't know," said Jack. "They may—but anyway it would only be for a little while. If we can hide all traces of our being here they won't know a thing about us."

"Come on, then," said Mike, slipping off the rock. "We'd better hurry. It won't be long before they're here."

The children hurried down to the beach. Jack and Mike stamped out the fire, and carried the charred wood to the bushes. They scattered clean sand over the place where they had the fire. They picked up all their belongings and hid them.

"I don't think anyone would find Willow House," said Jack. "The trees really are too thick all round it for any tripper to bother to squeeze through."

"What about the hens?" said Peggy.

"We'll catch them and pop them into a sack just for now," said Jack. "The hen-yard will have to stay. I don't think anyone will find it—it's well hidden. But we certainly couldn't have the hens clucking away there!"

"And Daisy the cow?" said Peggy, looking worried.

"We'll watch and see which side of the island the trippers come," said Jack. "As far as I know, there is only one landing-place, and that is our beach. As Daisy is right on the other side of the island, they are not likely to see her unless they go exploring. And let's hope they don't do that!"

"Where shall *we* hide?" said Nora.

"We'll keep a look-out from the hill, hidden in the bracken," said Jack. "If the trippers begin to wander about, we must just creep about in the bracken and trust to luck they won't see us. There's one thing—they won't be *looking* for us, if they are trippers. They won't guess there is anyone else here at all!"

"Will they find the things in the cave-larder?" asked Nora, helping to catch the squawking hens.

"Peggy, get some heather and bracken and stuff up the opening to the cave-larder," said Jack. Peggy ran off at once. Jack put the hens gently into the sack one by one and ran up the hill with them. He went to the other side of

62

the hill and came to one of the caves he knew. He called to Nora, who was just behind him.

"Nora! Sit at the little opening here and see that the hens don't get out! I'm going to empty them out of the sack into the cave!"

With much squawking and scuffling and clucking the scared hens hopped out of the sack and ran into the little cave. Nora sat down at the entrance, hidden by the bracken that grew there. No hen could get out whilst she was there.

"The boat is going round the island," whispered Jack as he parted the bracken at the top of the hill and looked down to the lake below. "They can't find a place to land. They're going round to our little beach! Well—Daisy the cow is safe, if they don't go exploring! Hope she doesn't moo!"

The Trippers Come To The Island

Nora sat crouched against the entrance of the little cave. She could hear the six hens inside, clucking softly as they scratched about. Jack knelt near her, peering through the bracken, trying to see what the boat was doing.

"Mike has rowed our own boat to where the brambles fall over the water, and has pushed it under them," said Jack, in a low voice. "I don't know where he is now. I can't see him."

"Where's Peggy?" whispered Nora.

"Here I am," said a low voice, and Peggy's head popped up above the bracken a little way down the hill. "I say — isn't this horrid? I do wish those people would go away."

The sound of voices came up the hillside from the lake below.

"Here's a fine landing-place!" said one voice.

"They've found our beach," whispered Jack.

"Pull the boat in," said a woman's voice. "We'll have our supper here. It's lovely!"

There was the sound of a boat being pulled a little way up the beach. Then the trippers got out.

"I'll bring the radio," said someone. "You bring the supper things, Eddie."

"Do you suppose anyone has ever been on this little island before?" said a man's voice.

"No!" said someone else. "The countryside round about is quite deserted—no one ever comes here, I should think."

The three children crouched down in the bracken and

listened. The trippers were setting out their supper. One of the hens in the cave began to cluck loudly. Nora thought it must have laid an egg.

"Do you hear that noise?" said one of the trippers. "Sounds like a hen to me!"

"Don't be silly, Eddie," said a woman's voice scornfully. "How could a hen be on an island like this! That must have been a blackbird or something."

Jack giggled. It seemed very funny to him that a hen's cluck should be thought like a blackbird's clear song.

"Pass the salt," said someone. "Thanks. I say! Isn't this a fine little island! Sort of secret and mysterious. What about exploring it after supper?"

"That's a good idea," said Eddie's voice. "We will!"

The children looked at one another in dismay. Just the one thing they had hoped the trippers wouldn't do!

"Where's Mike, do you suppose?" said Peggy, in a low voice. "Do you think he's hiding in our boat?"

"I expect so," whispered Jack. "Don't worry about him. He can look after himself all right."

"Oh, my goodness! There's Daisy beginning to moo!" groaned Peggy, as a dismal moo reached her ears. "She knows it is time she was milked."

"And just wouldn't I like a cup of milk!" said Jack, who was feeling very thirsty.

"Can you hear that cow mooing somewhere?" said one of the trippers, in surprise.

"I expect it's a cow in a field on the mainland," said another lazily. "You don't suppose there is a cow wandering loose on this tiny island, do you, Eddie?"

"Well, I don't know," said Eddie, in a puzzled voice. "Look over there. Doesn't that look like a footprint in the sand to you?"

The children held their breath. Could it be true that they had left a footprint on the sand?

"And see here," went on the tripper, holding up something. "Here's a piece of string I found on the beach. String doesn't grow, you know."

"You are making a great mystery about nothing," said one of the women crossly. "Other trippers have been here, that's all."

"Perhaps you are right," said Eddie. "But all the same, I'm going to explore the island after supper!"

"Oh, put on the radio, Eddie," said someone. "I'm tired of hearing you talk so much."

Soon loud music blared through the air, and the children were glad, for they knew it would drown any sound of Daisy's mooing or the hens' clucking. They sat in the bracken, looking scared and miserable. They did not like anyone else sharing their secret island. And what would happen if the trippers did explore the island and found the children?

Nora began to cry softly. Tears ran down her cheeks and fell on her hands. Jack looked at her and then crept silently up. He slipped his arm round her.

"Don't cry, Nora," he said. "Perhaps they won't have time to explore. It is getting a bit dark now. Do you see that big black cloud coming up? It will make the night come quickly, and perhaps the trippers will think there's a storm coming and row off."

Nora dried her eyes and looked up. There certainly was a big black cloud.

"It looks like a thunderstorm," said Peggy, creeping up to join them.

"Oooh!" said Nora suddenly, almost squealing out loud. "Look! Someone's coming up the hill! I can see the bracken moving! It must be one of the trippers creeping up to find us!"

The children went pale. They looked to where Nora pointed—and sure enough they could see first one frond

66

of bracken moving, and then another and another. Someone was certainly creeping up the hill hidden under the fronds.

Nora clutched hold of Jack. "Don't make a sound," he whispered. "No one can possibly know we're here. Keep quiet, Nora. We'll slip inside the cave if he comes much nearer."

They sat silently watching the swaying of the tall bracken as the newcomer crept through it. It was a horrid moment. Was someone going to spring out on them?

"Get inside the cave, you two girls," whispered Jack. "I think you'll be safe there. I'm going to slip round the hill and come up behind this person, whoever he is."

The girls crept just inside the cave and parted the bracken that grew around it to see what Jack was going to do. He was just slipping away when the person creeping up the hillside stopped his crawling. The bracken kept still. This was worse than seeing it move! Oh dear!

Then a head popped out of the bracken, and Nora gave a loud squeal.

"Mike!" she said. "Mike!"

"Sh, you silly chump!" hissed Peggy, shaking her. "You'll be heard by the trippers!"

Fortunately the radio was going loudly, so Nora's squeal was not heard. The three children stared in delight at Mike. It was he who had been creeping up through the bracken after all! What a relief! He grinned at them and put his head down again. Once more the bracken fronds began to move slightly as Mike made his way through them up to the cave.

"Oh, Mike," said Nora, when he came up to them. "You did give us such a fright. We thought you were a tripper coming after us!"

"I got a good view of them," said Mike, sitting down beside the others. "There are three men and two women. They are tucking into an enormous supper."

"Do you think they'll explore the island as they said?" asked Peggy anxiously.

"Perhaps this thunderstorm will put them off," said Mike, looking up at the black sky. "My word, it's brought the bats out early! Look at them!"

Certainly the little black bats were out in their hundreds. The hot, thundery evening had brought out thousands of insects, and the bats were having a great feast, catching the flies and beetles that flew through the air.

It was the bats that sent the trippers away. One of the women caught sight of two or three bats darting round under the trees, and she gave a shriek.

"Ooh! Bats! Ooh! I can't bear bats! I'm frightened of them. Let's pack up and go quickly!"

"I can't bear bats either!" squealed the other woman. "Horrid little creatures!"

"They won't hurt you," said a man's voice. "Don't be silly."

"I can't help it; I'm frightened of them," said a woman. "I'm going!"

"But I wanted to explore the island," said Eddie.

"Well, you'll have to explore it another day," said the woman. "Just look at the sky, too—there's going to be a dreadful storm."

"All right, all right," said Eddie, in a sulky voice. "We'll go. Fancy being frightened of a few bats!"

The children on the hillside stared at one another in delight. The trippers were really going. And no one had discovered them. Goody, goody!

"Good old bats!" whispered Jack. "Would you think anyone would be scared of those little flitter-mice, Nora?"

68

"Aunt Harriet was," said Nora. "I don't know why. I think they are dear little creatures, with their funny black wings. Anyway, I shall always feel friendly towards them now. They have saved us from being found!"

Daisy the cow mooed loudly. Jack frowned. "If only we had milked Daisy before the trippers came!" he said.

"Did you hear that?" said one of the trippers. "That was thunder in the distance!"

The four children giggled. Nora rolled over and stuffed her hands into her mouth to stop laughing loudly.

"Good old Daisy!" whispered Mike. "She's pretending to be a thunderstorm now, to frighten them away!"

Nora gave a squeal of laughter, and Jack punched her. "Be quiet," he said. "Do you want us to be discovered just when everything is going so nicely?"

The trippers were getting into their boat. They pushed off. The children heard the sound of oars, and peeped out. They could see the boat, far down below, being rowed out on to the lake. A big wind sprang up and ruffled the water. The boat rocked to and fro.

"Hurry!" cried a woman's voice. "We shall get caught in the storm. Oh! Oh! There's one of those horrid bats again! I'll never come to this nasty island any more!"

"I jolly well hope you won't!" said Jack, pretending to wave good-bye.

The children watched the boat being rowed down the lake. The voices of the people came more and more faintly on the breeze. The last they heard was the radio being played once again. Then they saw and heard no more. The trippers were gone.

"Come on," said Jack, standing up and stretching himself. "We've had a very narrow escape—but thank goodness, no one saw us or our belongings."

"Except that footprint and a bit of string," said Mike.

"Yes," said Jack, thoughtfully. "I hope that man called

69

Eddie doesn't read anywhere about four runaway children and think we might be here because of what he heard and found. We must be prepared for that, you know. We must make some plans to prevent being found if anyone comes again to look for us."

A distant rumble of thunder was heard. Jack turned to the others. "Not Daisy mooing this time!" he grinned. "Come on, there's a storm coming. We've plenty to do. I'll go and get Daisy, to milk her. Nora and Mike, you catch the hens and take them back to the hen-yard—and Mike, make some sort of shelter for them with a couple of sacks over sticks, or something, so that they can hide there if they are frightened. Peggy, see if you can light the fire before the rain comes."

"Ay, ay, Captain!" shouted the children joyfully, full of delight to think they had their island to themselves once more!

A Stormy Night In Willow House

There was certainly a thunderstorm coming. The sky was very black indeed, and it was getting dark. Nora and Mike caught the six hens in the little cave, bundled them gently into the sack, and raced off to the hen-yard with them. Mike stuck two or three willow sticks into the ground at one end of the hen-yard and draped the sack over them.

"There you are, henny-pennies!" said Nora. "There is a nice little shelter for you!"

Plop! Plop! Plop! enormous drops of rain fell down and the hens gave a frightened squawk. They did not like the rain. They scuttled under the sack at once and lay there quietly, giving each other little pecks now and again.

"Well, that settles the hens," said Mike. "I wonder how Peggy is getting on with the fire."

Peggy was not getting on at all well. The rain was now coming down fast, and she could not get the fire going. Jack arrived with Daisy the cow and shouted to Peggy:

"Never mind about the fire! Now that the rain's coming down so fast you won't be able to light it. Get into Willow House, all of you, before you get too wet."

"The girls can go," said Mike, running to help Jack. "I'll get the things to help you milk. My goodness—we haven't drunk all the milk yet that Daisy gave us this morning!"

"Put it into a dish and pop it in the hen-yard," said Jack. "Maybe the hens will like it!"

In the pouring rain Jack milked Daisy the cow. Soon all the saucepans and the kettle and bowls were full! Really, thought Jack, he simply *must* get that old milking-pail that

71

the girls had told him of at their Aunt's farm. It was such a tiring business milking a cow like this.

When the milking was finished, Jack took Daisy back to her grassy field on the other side of the island. Mike went to Willow House where the two girls were. It was dark there, and the sound of rain drip-drip-dripping from the trees all around sounded rather miserable.

Mike and the two girls sat in the front part of Willow House and waited for Jack. Mike was very wet, and he shivered.

"Poor old Jack will be wet through, too," he said. "Feel this milk, girls. It's as warm as can be. Let's drink some and it will warm us up. We can't boil any, for we haven't a fire."

Jack came to Willow House dripping wet. But he was grinning away as usual. Nothing ever seemed to upset Jack.

"Hallo, hallo!" he said. "I'm as wet as a fish! Peggy, where did we put those clothes of mine that I brought to the island last night?"

"Oh yes!" cried Peggy, in delight. "Of course! You and Mike can change into those."

"Well, I don't know about that," said Mike. "Jack only brought three old vests, a shirt or two, and an overcoat."

"Well, we can wear a vest each, and a shirt, and I'll wear the overcoat, and you can wrap the old blanket I brought all round you!" said Jack.

The boys took off their wet clothes and changed into the dry ones. "I'll hang your wet ones out to dry as soon as the rain stops," said Peggy, squeezing the rain out of them.

"I can't see a thing here," said Mike, buttoning up his shirt all wrong.

"Well, light the lantern, silly," said Jack. "What do you suppose the candles are for? Nora, find the lantern and light it. It may want a new candle inside. You know where

72

you put the candles, don't you? Over in that corner somewhere."

Nora found the lantern. It did want a new candle inside. She found a box of matches and lighted the candle. Mike hung the lantern up on a nail he had put in the roof. It swung there, giving a dim but cheerful light to the little party huddled inside Willow House.

"This really feels like a house now," said Nora, pleased. "I do like it. It's very cosy. Not a drop of rain is coming through our roof or the walls."

"And not a scrap of wind!" said Jack. "That shows how well we packed the walls with heather and bracken. Listen to the wind howling outside! We shouldn't like to be out in that! What a good thing we've got Willow House to live in! Our outdoor bedroom wouldn't be at all comfortable tonight!"

The thunderstorm broke overhead. The thunder crashed around as if someone were moving heavy furniture up in the sky.

"Hallo! Someone's dropped a wardrobe, I should think!" said Jack, when an extra heavy crash came!

"And there goes a grand piano tumbling down the stairs!" said Mike, at another heavy rumble. Everyone laughed. Really, the thunderstorm *did* sound exactly like furniture being thrown about.

The lightning flashed brightly, lighting up the inside of Willow House. Nora was not sure that she liked it. She cuddled up to Mike. "I feel a bit frightened," she said.

"Don't be silly!" said Mike. "You're as bad as those women trippers over the bats! There's nothing to be frightened of. A storm is a grand thing. We're perfectly safe here."

"A storm is just a bit of weather being noisy!" laughed Jack. "Cheer up, Nora. We're all right. You can think you're lucky you're not Daisy the cow. After all, we do know that a storm is only a storm, but she doesn't."

73

Crash! Rumble! Crash! The thunder roared away, and the children made a joke of it, inventing all kinds of furniture rumbling about the sky, as each crash came. The lightning flashed, and each time Jack said. "Thanks very much! The sky keeps striking matches, and the wind keeps blowing them out!"

Even Nora laughed, and soon she forgot to be frightened. The rain pelted down hard, and the only thing that worried Jack was whether or not a rivulet of rain might find its way into Willow House and run along the floor on which they were sitting. But all was well. No rain came in at all.

Gradually the storm died away, and only the pitter-patter of raindrops falling from the trees could be heard, a singing, liquid sound. The thunder went farther and farther away. The lightning flashed for the last time. The storm was over.

"Now we'll have something to eat and a cup of milk to drink, and off to bed we'll go," said Jack. "We've had quite enough excitement for today! And Mike and I were so late last night that I'm sure he's dropping with sleep. I know I am."

Peggy got a small meal for them all, and they drank Daisy's creamy milk. Then the girls went into the back room of Willow House and snuggled down on the warm heather there, and the boys lay down in the front room. In half a minute everyone was asleep!

Again Daisy the cow awoke them with her mooing. It was strange to wake up in Willow House instead of in their outdoor sleeping-place among the gorse, with the sky above them. The children blinked up at their green roof, for leaves were growing from the willow branches that were interlaced for a ceiling. It was dim inside Willow House. The door was shut, and there were no windows. Jack had thought it would be too difficult to make

74

windows, and they might let in the wind and the rain too much. So Willow House was rather dark and a bit stuffy when the door was shut—but nobody minded that! It really made it all the more exciting!

The children ran out of Willow House and looked around—all except Nora. She lay lazily on her back, looking up at the green ceiling, thinking how soft the heather was and how nice Willow House smelt. She was always the last out of bed!

"Nora, you won't have time for a dip before breakfast if you don't come now," shouted Peggy. So Nora ran out, too. What a lovely morning it was! The thunderstorm had cleared away and left the world looking clean and newly washed. Even the pure blue sky seemed washed, too.

The lake was as blue as the sky. The trees still dripped a little with the heavy rain of the night before, and the grass and heather were damp to the foot.

"The world looks quite new," said Mike. "Just as if it had been made this very morning! Come on—let's have our dip!"

Splash! Into the lake they went. Mike and Jack could both swim. Jack swam like a fish. Peggy could swim a little way, and Nora hardly at all. Jack was teaching her, but she was a bit of a baby and would not get her feet off the sandy bed of the lake.

Peggy was first out of the water and went to get the breakfast—but when she looked round their little beach, she stood still in disgust!

"Look here, boys!" she cried. "Look, Nora! How those trippers have spoilt our beach!"

They all ran out of the cold water, and, rubbing themselves down with their two towels, they stared round at their little beach, which was always such a beautiful place, clean and shining with its silvery sand.

But now, what a difference! Orange-peel lay every-

75

where. Banana skins, brown, slippery, and soaked with rain, lay where they had been thrown. A tin that had once had canned pears in, and two cardboard cartons that had been full of cream, rolled about on the sand, empty. A newspaper, pulled into many pieces by the wind, blew here and there. An empty cigarette packet joined the mess.

The children felt really angry. The little beach was theirs and they loved it. They had been careful to keep it clean, tidy, and lovely, and had always put everything away after a meal. Now some horrid trippers had come there just for one meal and had left it looking like a rubbish-heap!

"And they were grown-up people, too!" said Jack, in disgust. "They ought to have known better. Why couldn't they take their rubbish away with them?"

"People that leave rubbish about in beautiful places like this are just rubbishy people themselves!" cried Peggy fiercely, almost in tears. "Nice people never do it. I'd like to put those people into a big dustbin with all their horrid rubbish on top of them—and wouldn't I bang on the lid, too!"

The other laughed. It sounded so funny. But they were all angry about their beach being spoilt.

"I'll clear up the mess and burn it," said Mike.

"Wait a minute!" said Jack. "We might find some of the things useful."

"What! Old banana skins and orange-peel!" cried Mike. "You're not thinking of making a pudding or something of them, Jack!"

"No," said Jack, with a grin, "But if we keep the tin and a carton and the empty cigarette packet in our cave-cupboard, we might put them out on the beach if anyone else ever comes—and then, if they happen to find the remains of our fire, or a bit of string or anything like that—why, they won't think of looking for us—they'll just think trippers have been here!"

"Good idea, Jack!" cried everyone.

"You really are good at thinking out clever things," said Peggy, busy getting the fire going. Its crackling sounded very cheerful, for they were all hungry. Peggy put some milk on to boil. She meant to make cocoa for them all to drink.

Mike picked up the cigarette packet, the tin, and one of the cardboard cartons. He washed the carton and the tin in the lake, and then went to put the three things away in their little cave-cupboard. They might certainly come in useful some day!

Nora brought in five eggs for breakfast. Peggy fried them with two trout that Jack had caught on his useful lines. The smell was delicious!

"I say! Poor old Daisy *must* be milked!" said Jack, gobbling down his breakfast and drinking his hot cocoa.

Suddenly Nora gave a squeal and pointed behind him. Jack turned—and to his great astonishment he saw the cow walking towards him!

"You wouldn't go to milk her in time so she has come to you!" laughed Peggy. "Good old Daisy! Fancy her knowing the way!"

Nora Gets Into Trouble

There seemed quite a lot of jobs always waiting to be done each day on the island. Daisy had to be milked. The hens had to be seen to. The fishing-lines had to be baited and looked at two or three times a day. The fire had to be kept going. Meals had to be prepared and dishes washed up. Willow House had to be tidied up each day, for it was surprising how untidy it got when the four children were in it even for an hour.

"I'll milk Daisy each morning and Mike can milk her in the evenings," said Jack, as they sat eating their breakfast that morning. "Nora, you can look after the hens. It won't only be your job to feed them and give them water and collect the eggs, but you'll have to watch the fence round the hen-yard carefully to see that the hens don't peck out the heather we've stuffed into the fence to stop up the holes. We don't want to lose our hens!"

"What is Peggy going to do?" asked Nora.

"Peggy had better do the odd jobs," said Jack. "She can look after the fire, think of meals and tidy up. I'll see to my fishing-lines. And every now and again one or other of us had better go to the top of the hill to see if any more trippers are coming. Our plans worked quite well last time—but we were lucky enough to spot the boat coming. If we hadn't seen it when we did, we would have been properly caught!"

"I'd better go and get the boat out from where I hid it under the overhanging bushes, hadn't I?" said Mike, finishing his cocoa.

"No," said Jack. "It would be a good thing to keep it always hidden there except when we need it. Now I'm off to milk Daisy!"

He went off, and the children heard the welcome sound of the creamy milk splashing into a saucepan, for they still had no milking-pail. Mike and Jack were determined to get one that night! It was so awkward to keep milking a cow into saucepans and kettles!

Peggy began to clear away and wash up the dishes. Nora wanted to help her, but Peggy said she had better go and feed the hens. So off she went, making the little clucking noise that the hens knew. They came rushing to her as she climbed over the fence of their little yard.

Nora scattered the seed for them, and they gobbled it up, scratching hard with their strong clawed feet to find any they had missed. Nora gave them some water, too. Then she took a look round the fence to see that it was all right.

It seemed all right. The little girl didn't bother to look very hard, because she wanted to go off to the raspberry patch up on the hillside and see if there were any more wild raspberries ripe. If she had looked carefully, as she should have done, she would have noticed quite a big hole in the fence, where one of the hens had been pecking out the bracken and heather. But she didn't notice. She picked up a basket Peggy had made of thin twigs, and set off.

"Are you going to find raspberries, Nora?" called Peggy.

"Yes!" shouted Nora.

"Well, bring back as many as you can, and we'll have them for pudding at dinner-time with cream!" shouted Peggy. "Don't eat them all yourself!"

"Come with me and help me!" cried Nora, not too pleased at the thought of having to pick raspberries for everyone.

"I've got to get some water from the spring," called back Peggy; "and I want to do some mending."

79

So Nora went alone. She found a patch of raspberries she hadn't seen yesterday, and there were a great many ripe. The little girl ate dozens and then began to fill her basket with the sweet juicy fruit. She heard Jack taking Daisy the cow back to her grassy field on the other side of the island. She heard Mike whistling as he cut some willow stakes down in the thicket, ready for use if they were wanted. Everyone was busy and happy.

Nora sat down in the sun and leaned against a warm rock that jutted out from the hillside. She felt very happy indeed. The lake was as blue as a forget-me-not down below her. Nora lazed there in the sun until she heard Mike calling:

"Nora! Nora! Wherever are you! You've been hours!"

"Coming!" cried Nora, and she made her way through the raspberry canes, round the side of the hill, through the heather and bracken, and down to the beach, where all the others were. Peggy had got the fire going well, and was cooking a rabbit that Jack had produced.

"Where are the raspberries?" asked Jack. "Oh, you've got a basketful! Good! Go and skim the cream off the milk in that bowl over there, Nora. Put it into a jug and bring it back. There will be plenty for all of us."

Soon they were eating their dinner. Peggy was certainly a good little cook. But nicest of all were the sweet juicy raspberries with thick yellow cream poured all over them! How the children did enjoy them!

"The hens are very quiet today," said Jack, finishing up the last of his cream. "I haven't heard a single cluck since we've been having dinner!"

"I suppose they're all right?" said Peggy.

"I'll go and have a look," said Mike. He put down his plate and went to the hen-yard. He looked here—and he looked there—he lifted up the sack that was stretched over one corner of the yard for shelter—but no hens were there!

"Are they all right?" called Jack.

Mike turned in dismay. "No!" he said. "They're not here! They've gone!"

"Gone!" cried Jack, springing up in astonishment. "They can't have gone! They must be there!"

"Well, they're not," said Mike. "They've completely vanished! Not even a cluck left!"

All the children ran to the hen-yard and gazed in amazement and fright at the empty space.

"Do you suppose someone has been here and taken them?" asked Peggy.

"No," said Jack sternly, "look here! This explains their disappearance!"

He pointed to a hole in the fence of the hen-yard. "See that hole! They've all escaped through there—and now goodness knows where they are!"

"Well, I never heard them go," said Peggy. "I was the only one left here. They must have gone when I went to get water from the spring!"

"Then the hole must have been there when Nora fed the hens this morning," said Jack. "Nora, what do you mean by doing your job as badly as that? Didn't I tell you this morning that you were to look carefully round the fence each time the hens were fed to make sure it was safe? And now, the very first time, you let the hens escape! I'm ashamed of you!"

"Our precious hens!" said Peggy, in dismay.

"You might do your bit, Nora," said Mike. "It's too bad of you."

Nora began to cry, but the others had no sympathy for her. It was too big a disappointment to lose their hens. They began to hunt round to see if by chance the hens were hidden anywhere near.

Nora cried more and more loudly, till Jack got really angry with her. "Stop that silly baby noise!" he said. "Can't you help to look for the hens, too?"

81

"You're not to talk to me like that!" wept Nora.

"I shall talk to you how I like," said Jack. "I'm the captain here, and you've got to do as you're told. If one of us is careless we all suffer, and I won't have that! Stop crying, I tell you, and help to look for the hens."

Nora started to hunt, but she didn't stop crying. She felt so unhappy and ashamed and sad, and it was really dreadful to have all the others angry with her, and not speaking a word to her. Nora could hardly see to hunt for the hens.

"Well, they are nowhere about here!" said Jack, at last. "We'd better spread out and see if we can find them on the island somewhere. They may have wandered right to the other side. We'll all separate and hunt in different places. Peggy, you go that way, and I'll go over to Daisy's part."

The children separated and went different ways, calling to the hens loudly. Nora went where Jack had pointed. She called to the hens, too, but none came in answer. Wherever could they be?

What a hunt there was that afternoon for those vanished hens! It was really astonishing that not one could be found. Jack couldn't understand it! They were nowhere on the hill. They were not even in the little cave where Jack had hidden them the day before, because he looked. They were not among the raspberry canes. They were not in Daisy's field. They were not under the hedges. They were not anywhere at all, it seemed!

Nora grew more and more unhappy as the day passed. She felt that she really couldn't face the others if the hens were not found. She made a hidey-hole in the tall bracken and crouched there, watching the others returning to the camp for supper. They had had no tea and were hungry and thirsty. So was Nora—but nothing would make her go and join the others! No—she would rather stay where she was, all alone, than sit down with Mike, Jack and Peggy while they were still so cross and upset.

"Well, the hens are gone!" said Mike, as he joined Jack going down the hill to the beach.

"It's strange," said Jack. "They can't have flown off the island, surely!"

"It's dreadful, I think," said Peggy; "we did find their eggs so useful to eat."

Nora sat alone in the bracken. She meant to sleep there for the night. She thought she would never, never be happy again.

The others sat down by the fire, whilst Peggy made some cocoa, and doled out a rice pudding she had made. They wondered where Nora was.

"She'll be along soon, I expect," said Peggy.

They ate their meal in silence—and then—then oh, what a lovely sound came to their ears! Yes, it was "cluck, cluck, cluck!" And walking sedately down to the beach came all six hens! The children stared and stared and stared!

"Where *have* you been, you scamps?" cried Jack. "We've looked for you everywhere!"

"Cluckluck, cluckluck!" said the hens.

"You knew it was your meal-time, so you've come for it!" said Jack. "I say, you others! I wonder if we could let the hens go loose each day—oh no—we couldn't—they'd lay their eggs away and we'd never be able to find them!"

"I'll feed them," said Peggy. She threw them some corn and they pecked it up eagerly. Then they let Mike and Jack lift them into their mended yard and they settled down happily, roosting on the perch made for them at one end.

"We'd better tell Nora," said Jack. So they went up the hillside calling Nora. "Nora! Nora! Where are you?"

But Nora didn't answer! She crouched lower in the

83

bracken and hoped no one would find her. But Jack came upon her suddenly and shouted cheerfully. "Oh, there you are! The hens have all come back, Nora! They knew it was their meal-time, you see! Come and have your supper. We kept some for you."

Nora went with him to the beach. Peggy kissed her and said, "Now don't worry any more. It's all right. We've got all the hens safely again."

"Had I better see to the hens each day, do you think, instead of Nora?" Mike asked Jack. But Jack shook his head.

"No," he said. "That's Nora's job—and you'll see, she'll do it splendidly now, won't you, Nora?"

"Yes, I will, Jack," said Nora, eating her rice pudding, and feeling much happier. "I do promise I will! I'm so sorry I was careless."

"That's all right," said the other three together—and it *was* all right, for they were all kind-hearted and fond of one another.

"But what *I'd* like to know," said Peggy, as she and Nora washed the dirty things, "is *where* did those hens manage to hide themselves so cleverly?"

The children soon knew—for when, in a little while, Mike went to fetch something from Willow House he saw three shining eggs in the heather there! He picked them up and ran back to the others.

"Those cunning hens walked into Willow House and hid there!" he cried, holding up the eggs.

"Well, well, well!" said Jack, in surprise. "And to think how we hunted all over the island—and those rascally hens were near by all the time!"

84

The Caves In The Hillside

The days slipped past, and the children grew used to their happy, carefree life on the island. Jack and Mike went off in the boat one night and fetched the old milking-pail from Aunt Harriet's farm, and a load of vegetables from the garden. The plums were ripening, too, and the boys brought back as many as would fill the milking-pail! How pleased the girls were to see them!

Now it was easy to milk Daisy, for they had a proper pail. Peggy cleaned it well before they used it, for it was dusty and dirty. When Jack or Mike had milked Daisy they stood the pail of milk in the middle of the little spring that gushed out from the hillside and ran down to the lake below. The icy-cold water kept the milk cool, and it did not turn sour, even on the hottest day.

Jack got out the packets of seeds he had brought from his grandfather's farm, and showed them to the others. "Look," he said, "here are lettuce seeds, and radish seeds, and mustard and cress, and runner beans! It's late to plant the beans, but in the good soil on this island I daresay they will grow quickly and we shall be able to have a crop later in the year."

"The mustard and cress and radish will grow very quickly!" said Peggy. "What fun! The lettuces won't be very long, either, this hot weather, if we keep them well watered."

"Where shall we plant them?" asked Mike.

"Well, we'd better plant them in little patches in different corners of the island," said Jack. "If we dig out a big patch and have a sort of vegetable garden, and anyone comes here to look for us, they will see our garden and know someone is here! But if we just plant out tiny patches, we can easily throw heather over them if we see anyone coming."

"Jack's always full of good ideas," said Nora. "I'll help to dig and plant, Jack."

"We'll all do it," said Jack. So together they hunted for good places, and dug up the ground there, and planted their precious seeds. It was Peggy's job to water them each day and see that no weeds choked the seeds when they grew.

"We're getting on!" said Nora happily. "Milk and cream each day, eggs each day, wild raspberries when we want them, and lettuces, mustard and cress, and radishes soon ready to be pulled!"

Jack planted the beans in the little bare places at the foot of a brambly hedge. He said they would be able to grow up the brambles, and probably wouldn't be noticed if anyone came. The bean seedlings were carefully watched and nursed until they were strong and tall, and had begun to twist themselves round any stem near. Then Peggy left them to themselves, only watering them when they needed it.

It was sometimes difficult to remember which day it was. Jack had kept a count as best he could, and sometimes on Sundays the children could hear a church bell ringing if the wind was in the right direction.

"We ought to try and keep Sunday a day of rest and peace," said Mike. "We can't go to church, but we could make the day a *good* sort of day, if you know what I mean."

So they kept Sunday quietly, and the little island always seemed an extra peaceful day then. They hardly ever knew what the other days were—whether it was Tuesday

86

or Thursday or Wednesday! But Jack always told them when it was Sunday, and it was the one day they really knew. Nora said it had a different feel, and certainly the island seemed to know it was Sunday, and was a dreamier, quieter place then.

One day Jack said they must explore the caves in the hillside.

"If anyone does come here to look for us, and it's quite likely," he said, "we must really have all our plans made as to what to do, and know exactly where to hide. People who are really looking for us won't just sit about on that beach as the trippers did, you know—they will hunt all over the island."

"Well, let's go and explore the cave today," said Mike. "I'll get the lantern."

So, with the lantern swinging in his hand, and a box of matches ready in his pocket to light it, Jack led the way to the caves. The children had found three openings into the hillside—one where the hens had been put, another larger one, and a third very tiny one through which they could hardly crawl.

"We'll go in through the biggest entrance," said Jack. He lighted the lantern, and went into the dark cave. It seemed strange to leave the hot July sunshine. Nora shivered. She thought the caves were rather queer. But she didn't say anything, only kept very close to Mike.

Jack swung the lantern round and lit up all the corners. It was a large cave—but not of much use for hiding in, for every corner could be easily seen. Big cobwebs hung here and there, and there was a musty smell of bats.

Mike went all round the walls, peeping and prying—and right at the very back of the cave he discovered a curious thing. The wall was split from about six feet downwards, and a big crack, about two feet across, yawned there. At first it seemed as if the crack simply showed rock behind

In great excitement they explored the cave

it—but it didn't. There was a narrow, winding passage there, half hidden by a jutting-out piece of rock.

"Look here!" cried Mike, in excitement. "Here's a passage right in the very rock of the hillside itself. Come on, Jack, bring your lantern here. I wonder if it goes very far back."

Jack lifted up his lantern and the others saw the curious half-hidden passage, the entrance to which was by the crack in the wall. Jack went through the crack and walked a little way down the passage.

"Come on!" he cried. "It's all right! The air smells fresh here, and the passage seems to lead to somewhere."

The children crowded after him in excitement. What an adventure this was!

The passage wound here and there, and sometimes the children had to step over rocks and piles of fallen earth. Tree-roots stretched over their heads now and again. The passage was sometimes very narrow, but quite passable. And at last it ended—and Jack found that it led to an even larger cave right in the very middle of the hill itself! He lifted his lantern and looked round. The air smelt fresh and sweet. Why was that?

"Look!" cried Nora, pointing upwards. "I can see daylight!"

Sure enough, a long way up, a spot of bright daylight came through into the dark cave. Jack was puzzled. "I think some rabbits must have burrowed into the hill, and come out unexpectedly into this cave," he said. "And their hole is where we can see that spot of daylight. Well—the fresh air comes in, anyhow!"

From the big cave a low passage led to another cave on the right. This passage was so low that the children had to crawl through it—and to their surprise they found that this second cave led out to the hillside itself, and was no other than the cave into which it was so hard to crawl because of the small entrance.

"Well, we are getting on," said Jack. "We have discovered that the big cave we knew leads by a passage to an even bigger one—and from that big one we can get into this smaller one, which has an opening on to the hillside —and that opening is too small for any grown-up to get into!"

"What about the cave we put the hens into?" asked Nora.

"That must be just a little separate cave by itself," said Jack. "We'll go and see."

So they squeezed themselves out of the tiny entrance of the last cave, and went to the hen-cave. But this was quite ordinary—just a little low, rounded cave smelling strongly of bats.

They came out and sat on the hillside in the bright sunshine. It was lovely to sit there in the warmth after the cold, dark caves.

"Now listen," said Jack thoughtfully. "Those caves are going to be jolly useful to us this summer if anyone comes to get us. We could get Daisy into that big inner cave quite well, for one thing."

"Oh, Jack! She'd never squeeze through that narow, winding passage," said Peggy.

"Oh yes, she would," said Jack. "She'd come with me all right—and what's more, Daisy is going to practise going in and out there, so that if the time comes when she has really got to hide for a few hours, she won't mind. It wouldn't be any good putting her into that cave, and then having her moo fit to lift off the top of the hill!"

Everyone laughed. Mike nodded his head. "Quite right," he said. "Daisy will have to practise! I suppose the hens can go there quite well, too?"

"Easily," said Jack. "And so can we!"

"The only things we can't take into the cave are our boat and our house," said Mike.

"The boat would never be found under those brambles by the water," said Jack. "And I doubt if anyone would ever find Willow House either, for we have built it in the very middle of that thicket, and it is all *we* can do to squeeze through to it! Grown-ups could never get through. Why, we shall soon have to climb a tree and drop down to Willow House if the bushes and trees round it grow any more thickly!"

"I almost wish someone *would* come!" said Peggy. "It would be so exciting to hide away!"

"A bit *too* exciting!" said Jack. "Remember, there's a lot to be done as soon as we see anyone coming!"

"Hadn't we better plan it all out now?" said Mike. "Then we shall each know what to do."

"Yes," said Jack. "Well, I'll manage Daisy the cow, and go straight off to fetch her. Mike, you manage the hens and get them into a sack, and take them straight up to the cave. Peggy, you stamp out the fire and scatter the hot sticks. Also you must put out the empty cigarette packet, the tin, and the cardboard carton that the trippers left, so that it will look as if trippers have been here, and nobody will think it's funny to find the remains of a fire, or any other odd thing."

"And what shall I do?" asked Nora.

"You must go to the spring and take the pail of milk from there to the cave," said Jack. "Before you do that scatter heather over our patches of growing seeds. And Peggy, you might make certain the cave-cupboard is hidden by a curtain of bracken or something."

"Ay, ay, Captain!" said Peggy. "Now we've all got our duties to do—but you've got the hardest, Jack! I wouldn't like to hide Daisy away down that narrow passage! What will you do if she gets stuck?"

91

"She won't get stuck," said Jack. "She's not as fat as all that! By the way, we'd better put a cup or two in the cave, and some heather, in case we have to hide up for a good many hours. We can drink milk then, and have somewhere soft to lie on."

"We'd better keep a candle or two in the entrance," said Peggy. "I don't feel like sitting in the dark there."

"I'll tell you what we'll do," said Jack thoughtfully. "We won't go in and out of that big inner cave by the narrow passage leading from the outer cave. We'll go in and out by that tiny cave we can hardly squeeze in by. It leads to the inner cave, as we found out. If we keep using the other cave and the passage to go in, we are sure to leave marks, and give ourselves away. I'll have to take Daisy that way, but that can't be helped."

"Those caves will be cosy to live in in the winter-time," said Peggy. "We could live in the outer one, and store our things in the inner one. We should be quite protected from bad weather."

"How lucky we are!" said Nora. "A nice house made of trees for the summer—and a cosy cave-home for the winter!"

"Winter's a long way off yet," said Jack. "I say!—I'm hungry! What about frying some eggs, Peggy, and sending Mike to get some raspberries?"

"Come on!" shouted Peggy, and raced off down the hillside, glad to leave behind the dark, gloomy caves.

The Summer Goes By

No one came to interfere with the children. They lived together on the island, playing, working, eating, drinking, bathing—doing just as they liked, and yet having to do certain duties in order to keep their farmyard going properly.

Sometimes Jack and Mike went off in the boat at night to get something they needed from either Jack's farm or Aunt Harriet's. Mike managed to get into his aunt's house one night and get some of his and the girls' clothes—two or three dresses for the girls, and a coat and shorts for himself. Clothes were rather a difficulty, for they got dirty and ragged on the island, and as the girls had none to change into, it was difficult to keep their dresses clean and mended.

Jack got a good deal of fruit and a regular amount of potatoes and turnips from his grandfather's farm, which still had not been sold. There was always enough to eat, for there were eggs, rabbits, and fish, and Daisy gave them more than enough milk to drink.

Their seeds grew quickly. It was a proud day when Peggy was able to cut the first batch of mustard and cress and the first lettuce and mix it up into a salad to eat with hard-boiled eggs! The radishes, too, tasted very good, and were so hot that even Jack's eyes watered when he ate them! Things grew amazingly well and quickly on the island.

The runner beans were now well up to the top of the bramble bushes, and Jack nipped the tips off, so that they would flower well below.

"We don't want to have to make a ladder to climb up and pick the beans," he said. "My word, there are going to be plenty—look at all the scarlet flowers!"

"They smell nice!" said Nora, sniffing them.

"The beans will taste nicer!" said Jack.

The weather was hot and fine, for it was a wonderful summer. The children all slept out of doors in their "green bedroom," as they called it, tucked in the shelter of the big gorse bushes. They had to renew their beds of heather and bracken every week, for they became flattened with the weight of their bodies and were uncomfortable. But these jobs were very pleasant, and the children loved them.

"How brown we are!" said Mike one day, as they sat round the fire on the beach, eating radishes, and potatoes cooked in their jackets. They all looked at one another.

"We're as brown as berries," said Nora.

"What berries?" said Mike. "I don't know any brown berries. Most of them are red!"

"Well, we're as brown as oak-apples!" said Nora. They certainly were. Legs, arms, faces, necks, knees—just as dark as could be! The children were fat, too, for although their food was a queer mixture, they had a great deal of creamy milk.

Although life was peaceful on the island, it had its excitements. Each week Jack solemnly led poor Daisy to the cave and made her squeeze through the narrow passage into the cave beyond. The first time she made a terrible fuss. She mooed and bellowed, she struggled and even kicked—but Jack was firm and kind and led her inside. There, in the inner cave, he gave her a juicy turnip, fresh-pulled from his grandfather's farm the night before. Daisy was pleased. She chewed it all up, and was quite good when she was led back through the passage once more.

The second time she made a fuss again, but did not kick, nor did she bellow quite so loudly. The third time she seemed quite pleased to go, because she knew by now that a fine turnip awaited her in the cave. The fourth time she even went into the cave by herself and made her way solemnly to the passage at the far end.

"It's an awfully tight squeeze," said Mike, from the back. "If Daisy grows any fatter she won't be able to get through, Jack."

"We won't meet our troubles half-way," said Jack cheerfully. "The main thing is, Daisy likes going into the cave now, and won't make a fuss if ever the time comes when she has to be put there in a hurry."

July passed into August. The weather was thundery and hot. Two or three thunderstorms came along, and the children slept in Willow House for a few nights. Jack suggested sleeping in the cave, but they all voted it would be too hot and stuffy. So they settled down in Willow House, and felt glad of the thick green roof above them, and the stout, heather-stuffed walls.

The wild raspberries ripened by the hundred. Wild strawberries began to appear in the shady parts of the island—not tiny ones, such as the children had often found round the farm, but big, sweet, juicy ones, even nicer than garden ones. They tasted most delicious with cream. The blackberries grew ripe on the bushes that rambled all over the place, and the children's mouths were always stained with them, for they picked them as they went about their various jobs.

Jack picked them on his way to milk Daisy, and so did Mike. Peggy picked them as she went to get water from the spring. Nora picked them as she went to feed the hens.

Nuts were ripening, too, but were not yet ready. Jack looked at the heavy clusters on the hazel-trees and longed for them to be ripe. He went to have a look at the beans.

They were ready to be picked! The runners grew up the brambles, and the long green pods were mixed up with the blackberry flowers and berries.

"Beans for dinner today!" shouted Jack. He went to fetch one of the many baskets that Peggy knew how to weave from willow twigs, and soon had it full of the juicy green beans.

Another time Jack remembered the mushrooms that used to grow in the field at the end of his grandfather's farm. He and Mike set off in the boat one early morning at the end of August to see if they could find some.

It was a heavenly morning. Mike wished they had brought the girls, too, but it would not do to take a crowd. Someone might see them. It was just sunrise. The sun rose up in the east and the whole sky was golden. A little yellow-hammer sang loudly on a nearby hedge, "Little bits of bread and no cheese!" A crowd of young sparrows chirruped madly in the trees. Dew was heavy on the grass, and the boys' bare feet were dripping wet. They were soaked to the knees, but they didn't mind. The early sun was warm, and all the world was blue and gold and green.

"Mushrooms!" said Jack, in delight, pointing to where two or three grew. "Look—fresh new ones, only grown up last night. Come on! Fill the sack!"

There were scores in the field. Jack picked the smaller ones, for he knew the bigger ones did not taste so nice and might have maggots in them. In half an hour their sack was full and they slipped away through the sunny fields to where they had moored their boat.

"What a breakfast we'll have!" grinned Jack. And they did! Fried mushrooms and fried eggs, wild strawberries and cream! The girls had gone out strawberry hunting whilst the boys had gone to look for mushrooms.

Nora learnt to swim well. She and Peggy practised every day in the lake till Jack said they were as good as he and

Mike were. They were soon like fish in the water, and tumbled and splashed about each day with yells and shrieks. Jack was clever at swimming under water and would disappear suddenly and come up just beside one of the others, clutching hard at their legs! What fun they had!

Then there came a spell of bad weather—just a few days. The island seemed very different then, with the sun gone, a soft rain-mist driving over it, soaking everything, and the lake-water as cold as ice.

Nora didn't like it. She didn't like feeding the hens in the rain. She asked Peggy to do it for her. But Jack heard her and was cross.

"You're not to be a fair-weather person," he told her. "It's all very well to go about happily when the sun is shining and do your jobs with a smile—but just you be the same when we get bad weather!"

"Ay, ay, Captain!" said Nora, who was learning not to be such a baby as she had been. And after that she went cheerfully out to feed the hens, even though the rain trickled down her neck and ran in a cold stream down her brown back.

They were rather bored when they had to keep indoors in Willow House when it rained. They had read all their books and papers by that time, and although it was fun to play games for a while, they couldn't do it all day long. Peggy didn't mind—she had always plenty of mending to do.

She showed the boys and Nora how to weave baskets. They needed a great many, for the baskets did not last very long, and there were always raspberries, strawberries, or blackberries to pick. Mike, Jack and Nora thought it was fun to weave all kinds and shapes of baskets, and soon they had a fine selection of them ready for sunny weather.

Then the sun came back again and the children lay

about in it and basked in the hot rays to get themselves warm once more. The hens fluffed out their wet feathers and clucked happily. Daisy came out from under the tree which gave her shelter, and gave soft moos of pleasure. The world was full of colour again and the children shouted for joy.

The beans, radishes, lettuces, and mustard and cress grew enormously in the rain. Jack and Mike picked a good crop, and everyone said that never had anything tasted so delicious before as the rain-swollen lettuces, so crisp, juicy, and sweet.

All sorts of little things happened. The hole in the boat grew so big that one day, when Mike went to fetch the boat from its hiding-place, it had disappeared! It had sunk into the water! Then Jack and Mike had to use all their brains and all their strength to get it up again and to mend it so that it would not leak quite so badly.

The corn for the hens came to an end, and Jack had to go and see if he could find some more. There was none at his grandfather's farm, so he went to Mike's farm—and there he found some in a shed, but was nearly bitten by a new dog that had been bought for the farm. The dog bit a hole in his trousers, and Peggy had to spend a whole morning mending them.

Another time there was a great alarm, because Nora said she had heard the splashing of oars. Jack rushed off to get Daisy, and Mike bundled the hens into a sack—but, as nothing more seemed to happen, Peggy ran to the top of the hill and looked down the lake.

No boat was in sight—only four big white swans, quarrelling among themselves, and slashing the water with their feet and wings!

"It's all right, boys!" she shouted. "It's only the swans! It isn't a boat!"

So Daisy was left in peace and the hens were emptied

out of the sack again. Nora was teased, and made up her mind that she would make quite certain it *was* a boat next time she gave the alarm!

One day Jack slipped down the hillside when he was reaching for raspberries and twisted his ankle. Mike had to help him back to the camp on the beach. Jack was very pale, for it was a bad twist.

Peggy ran to get some clean rags and soaked them in the cold spring water. She bound them tightly round Jack's foot and ankle.

"You mustn't use it for a while," she said. "You must keep quiet. Mike will do your jobs."

So Jack had to lie about quietly for a day or two, and he found this very strange. But he was a sensible boy, and he knew that it was the quickest way to get better. Soon he found that he could hop about quite well with a stout hazel stick Mike cut for him from the hedges—and after a week or so his foot was quite all right.

Another time poor Peggy overbalanced and fell into a gorse bush below her on the hill. She was dreadfully scratched, but she didn't even cry. She went to the lake and washed her scratches and cuts, and then got the supper just as usual. Jack said he was very proud of her. "Anybody else would have yelled the place down!" he said, looking at the scratches all over her arms and legs.

"It's nothing much," said Peggy, boiling some milk. "I'm lucky not to have broken my leg or something!"

So, with these little adventures, joys, and sorrows, the summer passed by. No one came to the island, and gradually the children forgot their fears of being found, and thought no more of it.

Jack Does Some Shopping

The summer passed away. The days grew gradually shorter. The children found that it was not always warm enough to sit by the camp-fire in the evenings, and they went to Willow House, where they could light the lantern and play games. Willow House was always cosy.

They had had to stuff the walls again with heather and bracken, for some of it crumbled away and then the wind blew in. All the willow stakes they had used in the making of the walls had put out roots, and now little tufts of green, pointed leaves jutted out here and there up the sticks! The children were pleased. It was fun to have walls and a roof that grew!

One day Mike got a shock. He went to get another candle for the lantern—and found that there was only one left! There were very few matches left, too, for although the children were careful with these, and only used one when the fire had gone out, they had to use them sometimes.

"I say, Jack, we've only got one candle left," said Mike.

"We'll have to get some more, then," said Jack.

"How?" asked Mike. "They don't grow on trees!"

"Jack means he'll go and get some from somewhere," said Peggy, who was mending a hole in Jack's shirt. She was so glad she had been sensible enough to bring her work-basket with her to the secret island. She could stop their clothes from falling to pieces by keeping an eye on them, and stitching them as soon as they were torn.

"But where could he get candles except in a shop?" said Mike.

"Well, I've been thinking," said Jack seriously. "I've been thinking very hard. The autumn is coming, when we shall need a better light in the evenings. We shall need another blanket, too. And there are all sorts of little things we want."

"I badly want some more mending wool and some black cotton," said Peggy. "I had to mend your grey trousers with blue wool yesterday, Jack."

"And I'll have to have some more corn for the hens soon," said Nora.

"And it *would* be nice if we could get some flour," said Peggy. "Because if I had a bag of flour I could make you little rolls of bread sometimes—I just long for bread, don't you!"

"It would be nice," said Jack. "Well, listen, everyone. Don't you think it would be a good idea if I took the boat and went to the village at the other end of the lake and bought some of the things we badly need?"

The others all cried out in surprise.

"You'd be caught!"

"You haven't any money to buy things with!"

"Oh, don't go, Jack!"

"I shouldn't be caught," said Jack. "I'd be very careful. No one knows me at that village. Anyway, if you're afraid, I'll go on to the next village—only it's five miles away and I'd be jolly tired carrying back all the things we want."

"But what about money, Jack?" said Peggy.

"I'd thought of that," said Jack. "If Mike will help me to pick a sackful of mushrooms early one moning, I could bring them back here, arrange them in the willow baskets we make, and then take them to the village to sell. With the money I get I'll buy the things we want."

"Oh, that *is* a good idea, Jack," said Peggy. "If only you don't get caught!"

101

"Don't worry about that, silly," said Jack. "Now we'd better make out a list of things we want, and I'll try and get them when I go."

"I wish we could have a book or two," said Peggy.

"And a pencil would be nice," said Nora. "I like drawing things."

"And a new kettle," said Peggy. "Ours leaks a bit now."

"And a few more nails," said Mike.

"And the flour and the wool and the black cotton," said Peggy.

So they went on, making up a list of things they would like to have. Jack said them all over, and counted them up so that he wouldn't forget them.

"Mike and I will get the mushrooms from the field over the water tomorrow morning," he said.

"And I say, Jack—do you suppose you could sell some wild strawberries if you took them?" asked Nora eagerly. "I know where there are lots. I found a whole patch yesterday, ever so big, and very sweet!"

"That's a splendid idea," said Jack, pleased. "Look here, we'll make lots of little baskets today, and then we will arrange the mushrooms and strawberries neatly in them and I'll take them in the boat to sell. We should make a lot of money!"

The children were really excited. Mike went off to get a supply of thin willow twigs, and Peggy ran to get some rushes. She had discovered that she could make dainty baskets from the rushes, too, and she thought those would be nice for the strawberries.

Soon all four children were sitting on the sunny hillside among the heather, weaving the baskets. The boys were as good at it as the girls now, and by the time the sun was sinking there was a fine array of baskets. Peggy counted them. There were twenty-seven!

102

"I say! If we can fill and sell all those, Jack, you will have plenty of money to buy everything," said Mike.

The children went to bed early, for they knew they would have to be up at dawn the next day. They had no watches or clocks, and the only way to wake up early was to go to bed early! They knew that. It was a warm night, so they slept in their outdoor bedroom among the gorse bushes, lying cosily on their heather beds. Nothing ever woke them now, as it had done at first. A hedgehog could crawl over Jack's legs and he wouldn't stir! A bat could flick Mike's face and he didn't even move.

Once a little spider had made a web from Peggy's nose to her shoulder, and when Nora awoke and saw it there she called the boys. How they laughed to see a web stretching from Peggy's nose, and a little spider in the middle of it! They woke Peggy up and told her—but she didn't mind a bit!

"Spiders are lucky!" she said. "I shall have some luck today!" And so she did—for she found her scissors, which she had lost the week before!

The children awoke early, just as the daylight was putting a sheet of silver over the eastern sky. A robin was tick-tick-ticking near by and burst into a little creamy song when the children awoke. He was not a bit afraid of them, for they all loved the birds and fed them with crumbs after every meal. The robin was very tame and would often sit on Peggy's shoulder whilst she prepared the meals. She liked this very much.

They all got up and had their dip in the lake. Peggy thought of one more thing they wanted—a bar of soap! Their one piece was finished—and it was difficult to rub dirt off with sand, which they had to do now they had no soap. Jack added that to the list in his mind—that made twenty-one things wanted! What a lot!

"Mike and I won't be very long picking mushrooms," he

103

said, as he got into the boat and pushed off. "You and Nora go and pick the strawberries, Peggy. Have a kettle boiling on the fire when we come back so that we can have something hot to drink. It's rather chilly this morning."

How busy the four children were as the sun rose! Mike and Jack were away in the mushroom field, picking as many mushrooms as they could, and stuffing them into the big sack they carried. Nora and Peggy were picking the wild strawberries on the island. Certainly the patch Nora had found was a wonderful one. Deep red strawberries glowed everywhere among the pretty leaves, and some of the berries were as big as garden ones.

"Don't they look pretty in our little green baskets?" said Peggy, pleased. The girls had taken some of their baskets with them, and had lined them with strawberry leaves first. Then neatly and gently they were putting the ripe strawberries in.

"I should think Jack could sell these baskets of strawberries for sixpence each," said Peggy. "They are just right for eating."

The girls filled twelve of the rush baskets, and then went back to light the camp-fire. It was soon burning well, and Peggy hung the kettle over the flames to boil. Nora went to feed the hens.

"I'll milk Daisy, I think," said Peggy. "It is getting about milking-time, and the boys won't have time this morning. Watch the fire, Nora, and take the kettle off when it boils."

Soon the boys were back, happy to show the girls such a fine collection of white mushrooms. Peggy had finished milking Daisy and there was soon hot tea for everyone. The tin of cocoa had long been finished, and was added to the list that Jack had in his mind.

Whilst the boys were having breakfast of fried eggs and mushrooms, with a few wild strawberries and cream to follow, the two girls were busy arranging the fine mushrooms in the willow baskets, which were bigger and stronger than the rush strawberry ones. There were more than enough to fill the baskets.

Peggy and Nora carried the full baskets carefully to the boat. They put them safely at the far end and covered them with elder leaves so that the flies would not get at them. The flies did not like the smell of the elder leaves.

The boys set off in the boat. It had been arranged that they should both go to the far end of the lake, but that only Jack should go to sell their goods and to shop. One boy alone would not be so much noticed. Mike was to wait in the boat, hidden somewhere by the lakeside, till Jack returned. Mike had some cold cooked fish and some milk, for it might be some hours before Jack came back.

"Here's a good place to put the boat," said Jack, as he and Mike rowed up the lake, and came in sight of the village at the far end. An alder tree leaned over the water by the lakeside, and Mike guided the boat there. It slid under the drooping tree and Jack jumped out.

"I can easily find my way to the village from here," he said. "I'll be as quick as I can, Mike."

Jack had two long sticks, and on them he threaded the handles of the baskets of mushrooms and strawberries. In this way he could carry them easily, without spilling anything. Off he went with his goods through the wood, and Mike settled down in the boat to wait for his return.

Jack was not long in finding the road that led to the little village—and to his great delight he found that it was market-day there! A small market was held every Wednesday, and it happened to be Wednesday that day!

"Good!" thought Jack. "I shall not be so much noticed if there is a crowd of people—and I should be able to sell my goods easily!"

The boy went to the little market-place, calling "Fine

mushrooms! Ripe wild strawberries!" at the top of his voice.

When people saw the neat and pretty baskets of mushrooms and strawberries they stopped to look at them. Certainly they were excellent goods, and very soon Jack was selling them fast. Shillings and sixpences clinked into his pocket, and Jack felt very happy. What a fine lot of things he would be able to buy!

At last his sticks held no more baskets. The people praised him for his goods and the cleverly woven baskets, and told him to come again. Jack made up his mind that he would. It was a pleasant way of earning money, and he could buy all the things he needed if only he could get the money!

He went shopping. He bought a very large bag of flour. He bought wool and cotton for Peggy. He bought scores of candles and plenty of matches. He bought a new kettle and two enamel plates. Peggy was always wishing she had more dishes. He bought some storybooks, and two pencils and a rubber. A drawing-book was added to his collection, some nails, soap, butter for a treat, some bars of chocolate, some tins of cocoa, tea, rice—oh, Jack had a load to carry before he had done!

When he could carry no more, and his money was all gone, he staggered off to the boat. He kept thinking what fun everyone would have that night when he unpacked the bags and boxes!

Mike was waiting for him impatiently. He was delighted to see Jack, and helped him to dump the things into the boat. Then off they rowed, home to the secret island.

Jack Nearly Gets Caught

What fun it was that evening, unpacking all the things Jack had brought! Mike helped Jack to take everything to the beach, and Nora and Peggy jumped up and down and squealed with excitement.

"Flour! What a lot! I can make you rolls now to eat with your fish and eggs!" cried Peggy in delight. "And here's my wool—and my cotton!"

"And *two* pencils for me—and a rubber—and a drawing-book!" cried Nora.

"And butter—oh, and *chocolate*!" yelled Mike. "I've forgotten what chocolate tastes like!"

"Oh, Jack, you are clever," said Peggy. "Did you sell all the mushrooms and strawberries?"

"Every single basket," said Jack. "And what is more, the people told me to bring more next week—so I shall earn some more money, and lay in a good stock of things for the winter! What do you say to that?"

"Fine, Captain!" shouted everyone joyfully. "We shall be as cosy as can be with candles to see by, nice things to eat, books to read, chocolate to nibble! Hurrah!"

"Have you brought the corn for my hens, Jack?" asked Nora anxiously.

"Yes, there it is!" said Jack. "And what about this new kettle and enamel dishes, Peggy? I thought you'd like those."

"Oh, Jack, isn't it all exciting?" cried Peggy. "Look here—shall we have supper now—and look at all the things again afterwards—and then put them away carefully? You and Mike will have to put up shelves in Willow House for all these new stores!"

Talking all at once and at the tops of their voices the children set to work to get supper. This was a rabbit stew, with runner beans picked by Nora and a baked potato each, with raspberries and cream afterwards. And as a special treat Jack gave everyone half a bar of the precious chocolate! The children were so happy—they really felt that they couldn't be any happier! The girls had been lonely all day without the two boys, and it was lovely to be all together again.

After supper they cleared away and washed the dishes, and then stamped out the fire. They took everything to Willow House, and lighted the lantern that hung from the roof. Jack also lighted another candle to make enough light to see clearly all the treasures he had brought.

"I say! What a nice lot of matches!" said Mike. "We'll have to store those carefully in a dry place."

"And look at the books!" squealed Peggy. "Jack can read them out loud to us in the evening. *Robinson Crusoe*, and *Stories from the Bible* and *Animals of the World* and *The Boy's Book of Aeroplanes*. What a lovely lot! It will be fun to read about Robinson Crusoe, because he was alone on the island, just as we are. I guess we could teach him a few things, though!"

Everyone laughed. "He could teach *us* a few things, too!" said Jack.

Jack had really shopped very well. He had even bought a tin of treacle, so that sometimes, for a treat, Peggy could make toffee! He had got sugar, too, which would be nice in their tea and cocoa. Their own sugar had been finished long ago.

"And we needn't be too careful now of all our things," said Jack, "because I can go each week and sell mushrooms and strawberries and earn money to buy more."

"But what will you do when the mushrooms and strawberries are over?" asked Peggy.

"Then there will be blackberries and nuts," said Jack. "They won't fetch so much money, but at any rate I can get enough to store up plenty of things for the winter. If we can get flour, potatoes, rice, cocoa, and things like that, we shall be quite all right. Daisy can always give us milk and cream, and we get lots of eggs from the hens, fish from the lake, and a rabbit or two. We are really very lucky."

"Jack, read to us tonight," begged Nora. "It's so long since I heard a story."

"We'll begin *Robinson Crusoe* first, then," said Jack. "That seems sort of suitable. By the way, Nora, can you read yourself?"

"Well, I wasn't very good at it," said Nora.

"I think it would be a good idea if we all took a night each to read out loud," said Jack. "It's no good forgetting what we learnt. I'll read tonight—and you shall read tomorrow night, Nora."

So, by the light of the two candles, Jack began reading the tale of Robinson Crusoe to the others. They lay on the heather, listening, happy to be together, enjoying the tale. When Jack shut up the book they sighed.

"That was lovely," said Peggy. "My goodness, Jack, I guess we could write an exciting book if we wrote down all our adventures on the island!"

"Nobody would believe them!" laughed Jack. "Yet it's all true—here we are, living by ourselves, feeding ourselves, having a glorious time on a secret island that nobody knows!"

The next day Jack and Mike rigged up some shelves on which to keep some of their new stores. It was fun arranging everything. The children soon began to make out their next list of things for Jack to buy when he went to market.

"We shall have to keep the days pretty carefully in future," said Jack. "I don't want to miss Wednesdays now because Wednesday is market-day at the village. I shall get better prices then."

So, the next Wednesday, once again there was a great stir just about dawn, and the four children hurried to their tasks of picking mushrooms and strawberries. They had made plenty of baskets again, and Jack and Mike set off two or three hours later with the boat, taking the full baskets with them.

For three or four weeks Jack went to market, sold all his goods, and bought a great many stores for the winter. He and Mike decided to store the bags and sacks of goods in the inner cave of the hillside, as there they would be quite dry—and, as the children would probably have to live in the caves in the winter, the stores would be quite handy there.

As the weeks went by there were not so many wild strawberries to be found. Mushrooms stopped growing in the field, and other market goods had to take their place. The children went nutting in the hazel trees and struck down great clusters of ripe nuts, lovely in their ragged green coats and brown shells. The girls picked baskets of big ripe blackberries, and Jack took these to the market instead of mushrooms and strawberries.

People soon grew to know him at the market. They wondered where he came from, but Jack never told them anything about himself.

"I just live by the lakeside," he said, when people asked him where he lived. They thought he meant somewhere by the lake—they did not know he meant by the lakeside on the secret island—and certainly Jack was not going to tell them!

110

One day, for the first time, Jack saw a policeman in the village. This struck him as strange, for he had never seen one there before, and he knew that the village was too small to have a policeman of its own. It shared one with the village five miles away. Jack's heart sank—could the policeman have been told that a strange boy was about—and could he be wondering if the boy was one of the lost children! Jack began to edge away, though his baskets of nuts and blackberries were only half sold.

"Hi, you!" called the policeman suddenly. "Where do you come from, boy?"

"From the lakeside, where I've been gathering blackberries and nuts to sell," said Jack, not coming near the policeman.

"Is your name Mike?" said the policeman.

And then Jack knew for certain that the policeman had been told that maybe he, Jack, *was* one of the four runaway children—and he had come to find out.

"No, that's not my name," said Jack, looking very innocent. "Buy some nuts, Mister Policeman?"

"No," said the policeman, getting a strip of paper out of his pocket, and looking at a photograph there. "Come you here, my lad. I think you're one of the runaway children —let's have a look at you."

Jack turned pale. If the policeman had a picture of him, he was caught! Quick as lightning the boy flung down the two sticks on which he had a dozen or so baskets strung, and darted off through the crowd that had gathered. Hands were put out to stop him, but he struggled away, tearing his jacket, but not caring for anything but to escape.

He slipped round a corner and into a garden. He darted round the cottage there and peered into the back garden. There was no one there—but there was a little henhouse at the side. Jack made up his mind quickly. He opened the door of the henhouse, slipped inside, and crouched down in the straw there, hardly daring to breathe. There were no hens there—they were scratching about in the little run outside.

Jack heard the sound of shouting and running feet, and he knew that people were looking for him. He crouched lower, hoping that no one had seen him dart into the cottage garden.

The running feet went by. The shouting died down. No one had seen him! Jack let out a big breath, and his heart thumped loudly. He was really frightened.

He stayed in the henhouse all day long. He did not dare to move out. He was hungry and thirsty and very cramped, but he knew quite well that if he slipped out he might be seen. He must stay there till night. He wondered what Mike would think. The girls would be anxious, too.

A hen came in, sat on a nesting-box and laid an egg. She cackled and went out again. Another came in and laid an egg. Jack hoped that no one would see him if they came looking for eggs that afternoon!

Someone did come for the eggs—but it was after tea and the henhouse was very dark. The door was opened and a head came round. A hand was stretched out and felt in all the boxes. The eggs were lifted out—the door was shut again! Jack hadn't been seen! He was crouching against the other side of the house, well away from the nesting-boxes!

The henhouse did not smell nice. Jack felt miserable as he sat there on the floor. He knew that by running away he had as good as told the policeman that he was one of the runaways. And now the whole countryside would be searched again, and the secret island would probably be explored, too.

"But if I hadn't run away the policeman would have caught me and made me tell where the others were," thought the boy. "If only I can get back to where Mike is waiting with the boat, and get back safely to the island, we can make preparations to hide everything."

When it was dark, and the hens were roosting in the house beside him, Jack opened the door and slipped out. He stood listening. Not a sound was to be heard except the voices of people in the kitchen of the cottage near by.

He ran quietly down the path to the gate. He slipped out into the road—and then ran for his life to the road that led to the wood by the lakeside where Mike was waiting.

But would Mike be waiting there? Suppose people had begun to hunt already for the four children—and had found Mike and the boat! What then? How would he get back to the girls on the island?

Jack forgot his hunger and thirst as he padded along at top speed to where he had left Mike. No one saw him. It was a dark night, for the moon was not yet up. Jack made his way through the trees to the lakeside.

And then his heart leapt for joy! He heard Mike's voice! "Is that you, Jack? What a time you've been! Whatever's happened?"

The Great Hunt Begins

Jack scrambled into the boat, panting. "Push off, quickly, Mike!" he said. "I was nearly caught today, and if anyone sees us we shall all be discovered!"

Mike pushed off, his heart sinking. He could not bear the idea of being caught and sent back to his uncle's farm. He waited till Jack had got back his breath and then asked him a few questions. Jack told him everything. Mike couldn't help smiling when he thought of poor Jack sitting with the hens in the hen-house—but he felt very frightened. Suppose Jack had been caught!

"This is the end of my marketing," said Jack gloomily. "I shan't dare to show my nose again in any village. They will all be on the look-out for me. Why can't people run away if they want to? We are not doing any harm—only living happily together on our secret island!"

After a bit Jack helped Mike to row, and they arrived at the island just as the moon was rising. The girls were on the beach by a big fire, waiting anxiously for them.

"Oh Jack, oh Mike!" cried Nora, hugging them both, and almost crying with delight, at seeing them again. "We thought you were never coming! We imagined all kinds of dreadful things! We felt sure you had been caught!"

"I jolly nearly *was*," said Jack.

"Where is your shopping" asked Peggy.

"Haven't got any," said Jack. "I had only sold a few baskets when a policeman spotted me. I've got the money for the ones I sold—but what's the good of money on this island, where you can't buy anything!"

Mike and Jack pulled hard at the oars

Soon Jack had told the girls his story. He sat by the fire, warming himself, and drinking a cup of hot cocoa. He was dreadfully hungry, too, for he had had nothing to eat all day. He ate a whole rice pudding, two fishes, and a hard-boiled egg whilst he talked.

Everyone was very grave and solemn. They knew things were serious. Nora was really scared. She tried her hardest not to cry, but Jack heard her sniffing and put his arm round her. "Don't be a baby," he said. "Things may not be so bad after all. We have all our plans laid. There is no real reason why anyone should find us if we are careful. We are all upset and tired. Let's go to bed and talk tomorrow."

So to bed in Willow House they went. Jack took off his clothes and wrapped himself in the old rug because he said he smelt like hens. Peggy said she would wash his things the next day. They did not get to sleep for a long time because first one and then another of them would say something, or ask a question—and then the talking would all begin again.

"Now, nobody is to say another word!" said Jack at last, in his firmest voice.

"Ay, ay, Captain!" said everyone sleepily. And not another word was spoken.

In the morning the children awoke early, and re-membered what had happened the day before. Nobody felt like singing or shouting or joking as they usually did. Peggy solemnly got the breakfast. Jack went off in his old overcoat to milk the cow, for his things were not yet washed. Mike got some water from the spring, and Nora fed the hens. It was not a very cheerful party that sat down to breakfast.

When the things were cleared away, and Peggy had washed Jack's clothes and set them out to dry, the children held a meeting.

116

"The first thing to do," said Jack, "is to arrange that someone shall always be on watch during the day, on the top of the hill. You can see all up the lake and down from there, and we should get good warning then if anyone were coming—we should have plenty of time to do everything."

"Shall we have someone on guard during the night?" asked Nora.

"No," said Jack. "People are not likely to come at night. We can sleep in peace. I don't think anyone will come for a few days, anyhow, because I think they will search around the lake-side first, and will only think of the island later."

"I think, as we are not going to the mainland for some time, we had better make a big hole in the boat and let her sink," said Mike. "I've always been afraid she might be found, although she is well hidden under the brambles. After all, Jack, if she is sunk, no one could possibly find her!"

"That's a good idea, Mike," said Jack. "We can't be too careful now. Sink her this morning. We can easily get her up again and mend her if we want her. Peggy, will you see that every single thing is cleared away that might show people we are here? Look, there's some snippings of wool, there—that sort of thing must be cleared up, for it tells a tale!"

"I'll see to it," promised Peggy. Jack knew she would, for she was a most dependable girl.

"Every single thing must be taken to the caves today," said Jack, "except just those few things we need for cooking, like a saucepan and kettle and so on. We can easily slip those away at the last minute. We will leave ourselves a candle or two in Willow House, because we can sleep there till we have to go to the caves."

"Jack, what about the hen-yard?" asked Nora. "It really

117

does look like a yard now, because the hens have scratched about so much."

"That's true," said Jack. "Well, as soon as we know we've got to hide, Mike can pull up the fence round the hen-yard and store it in Willow House. Then he can scatter sand over the yard and cover it with heather. It's a good thing you thought of that, Nora."

"There's one thing, even if we have to hide away for days, we've enough food!" said Peggy.

"What about Daisy, though?" said Mike. "She won't have anything to eat. A cow eats such a lot."

"We should have to take her out to feed at night," said Jack. "And by the way, Peggy, don't light the fire for cooking until the very last minute and stamp it out as soon as you have finished. A spire of smoke gives us away more than anything!"

"What about someone hopping up to the hill-top now?" said Mike. "The sun is getting high. We ought to keep a watch from now on."

"Yes, we ought," said Jack. "You take first watch, Mike. I'll give you a call when it's time to come down. We'll take turns all day long. Keep watch all round. We don't know from which end of the lake a boat might come, though it's more likely to be from the end I was at yesterday."

Mike sped up the hill and sat down there. The lake lay blue below him. Not a swan, not a moorhen disturbed its surface. Certainly no boat was in sight. Mike settled down to watch carefully.

The others were busy. Everything was taken up to the caves in the hillside and stored there. Nora left a sack by the hen-yard ready to bundle the hens into when the time came. She also put a pile of sand by the yard, ready for Mike to scatter after the fences had been pulled up. Nora was no longer the careless little girl she had been. Nor was

118

she lazy any more. She had learned that when she did badly everyone suffered, so now she did her best—and it was a very good best too.

After a while Jack went up to take Mike's place on the hill-top. Mike set to work to sink the boat. She soon sank to the bottom of the water, under the bramble bushes. Mike felt sure that no one would ever know she was there.

Peggy went hunting round looking for anything that might give them away. She did not find very much, for all the children tidied up after any meal or game. Broken egg-shells were always buried, uneaten food was given to the hens, and it was only things like snippings of wool or cotton that the wind had blown away that could be found.

Peggy went on guard next and then Nora. It was dull work, sitting up on the hill-top doing nothing but watch, so Nora took her pencil and drawing-book and drew what she could see. That made the time go quickly. Peggy took her mending. She always had plenty of that to do, for every day somebody tore their clothes on brambles. After every stitch Peggy looked up and down the lake, but nothing could be seen.

That evening Mike was on guard, and he was just about to come down to get his supper when he saw something in the distance. He looked carefully. Could it be a boat? He called Jack.

"Jack! Come quickly! I can see something. Is it a boat, do you think?"

Everyone tore up the hill. Jack looked hard. "Well, if it's a boat, it's very small," he said.

"It's something black," said Nora. "Whatever is it? Oh, I do hope it isn't anyone coming now."

The children watched, straining their eyes. And suddenly the thing they thought might be a small boat flew up into the air!

"It's that black swan we saw the other day!" said Jack,

119

with a squeal of laughter. "What a fright it gave us! Look, there it goes! Isn't it a beauty?"

The children watched the lovely black swan flying slowly towards them, its wings making a curious whining noise as it came. Nora went rather red, for she remembered how frightened she had been the first time she had heard a swan flying over the island—but nobody teased her about it. They were all too thankful it was only a swan, not a boat.

"There's no need to keep watch any more tonight," said Jack, and they all went down the hill. Evening was almost on them. They sat by their fire and ate their supper, feeling happier than the day before. Perhaps after all no one would come to look for them—and anyway, they had done all they could now to get things ready in case anyone *did* come.

The next day the children kept watch in turn again, and the next. The third day, when Nora was on guard, she thought she saw people on the far side of the lake, where a thick wood grew. She whistled softly to Jack, and he came up and watched, too.

"Yes, you're right, Nora," he said at last. "There *are* people there—and they are certainly hunting for something or someone!"

They watched for a while and then they called the others. There was no fire going, for Peggy had stamped it out. They all crowded on to the hill-top, their heads peeping out of the tall bracken that grew there.

"See over there!" said Jack. "The hunt is on! It will only be a day or two before they come over here. We must watch very carefully indeed!"

"Well, everything is ready," said Peggy. "I wish they would come soon, if they are coming—I hate all this waiting about. It gives me a cold feeling in my tummy."

"So it does in mine," said Mike. "I'd like a hot-water bottle to carry about with me!"

That made everyone laugh. They watched for a while longer and then went down, leaving Jack on guard.

For two days nothing happened, though the children thought they could see people on the other side of the lake, beating about in the bushes and hunting. Mike went on guard in the morning and kept a keen watch. Nora fed the hens as usual and Jack milked Daisy.

And then Mike saw something! He stood up and looked—it was something at the far end of the lake, where Jack had gone marketing. It was a boat! No mistaking it this time—a boat it was, and a big one, too!

Mike called the others and they scrambled up. "Yes," said Jack at once. "That's a boat all right—with about four people in, too. Come on, there's no time to be lost. There's only one place a boat can come to here—and that's our island. To your jobs, everyone, and don't be frightened!"

The children hurried off. Jack went to get Daisy. Mike went to see to the hens and the hen-yard. Peggy scattered the dead remains of the fire, and caught up the kettle and the saucepan and any odds and ends of food on the beach to take to the cave. Nora ran to cover up their patches of growing seeds with bits of heather. Would they have time to do everything? Would they be well hidden before the boatload of people came to land on their secret island?

The Island Is Searched

Now that people had really come at last to search the island the children were glad to carry out their plans, for the days of waiting had been very upsetting. They had laid their plans so well that everything went smoothly. Daisy, the cow, did not seem a bit surprised to have Jack leading her to the inner cave again, and went like a lamb, without a single moo!

Jack got her safely through the narrow passage to the inner cave and left her there munching a turnip whilst he went to see if he could help the others. Before he left the outer cave he carefully rubbed away any traces of Daisy's hoofmarks. He arranged the bracken carelessly over the entrance so that it did not seem as if anyone went in and out of it.

Mike arrived with the hens just then, and Jack gave him a hand. Mike squeezed himself into the little tiny cave that led by the low passage to the inner cave, for it had been arranged that only Jack and the cow should use the other entrance for fear that much use of it should show too plainly that people went in and out.

Jack passed him the sack of hens, and Mike crawled on hands and knees through the low passage and into the big inner cave where Daisy was. The hens did not like being pulled through the tiny passage and squawked dismally. But when Mike shook them out of the sack, and scattered grain for them to eat, they were quite happy again. Jack had lighted the lantern in the inner cave, and it cast its dim light down. Mike thought he had better stay in the cave, in case the hens found their way out again.

So he sat down, his heart thumping, and waited for the others. One by one they came, carrying odds and ends. Each child had done his or her job, and with scarlet cheeks and beating hearts they sat down together in the cave and looked at one another.

"They're not at the island yet," said Jack. "I took a look just now. They've got another quarter-mile to go. Now, is there anything we can possibly have forgotten?"

The children thought hard. The boat was sunk. The cow and the hens were in. The fire was out and well scattered. The hen-yard was covered with sand and heather. The yard-fence was taken up and stored in Willow House. The seed-patches were hidden. The milk-pail was taken from the spring.

"We've done *every*thing!" said Peggy.

And then Mike jumped up in a fright. "My hat!" he said. "Where is it? I haven't got it on! I must have left it somewhere!"

The others stared at him in dismay. His hat was certainly not on his head nor was it anywhere in the cave.

"You had it on this morning," said Peggy. "I remember seeing it, and thinking it was getting very dirty and floppy. Oh, Mike dear! Where can you have left it? Think hard, for it is very important."

"It might be the one thing that gives us away," said Jack.

"There's just time to go and look for it," said Mike. "I'll go and see if I can find it."

He crawled through the narrow passage and out into the cave with the low entrance. He squeezed through that and went out into the sunlight. He could see the boat from where he was, being rowed through the water some distance away. He ran down the hill to the beach. He hunted there. He hunted round about the hen-yard. He hunted by the spring. He hunted everywhere! But he could *not* find that hat!

123

And then he wondered if it was anywhere near Willow House, for he had gone there that morning to store the hen-yard fences. He squeezed through the thickly growing trees and went to Willow House. There, beside the doorway, was his hat! The boy pushed it into his pocket, and made his way back up the hillside. Just as he got to the cave-entrance he heard the boat grinding on the beach below. The searchers had arrived.

He crawled into the big inner cave. The others greeted him excitedly.

"Did you find it, Mike?"

"Yes, thank goodness," said Mike, taking his hat out of his pocket. "It was just by Willow House—but I don't expect it would have been seen there, because Willow House is too well hidden among those thick trees to be found. Still, I'm glad I found it—I'd have been worried all the time if I hadn't. The boat is on the beach now, Jack; I heard it being pulled in. There are four men in it."

"I'm just a bit worried about the passage to this inner cave from the outer cave," said Jack. "If that is found it's all up with us. I was wondering if we could find a few rocks and stones and pile them up half-way through the passage, so that if anyone *does* come through there, he will find his way blocked and won't guess there is another cave behind, where *we* are hiding!"

"That's a fine idea, Jack" said Mike. "It doesn't matter about the other entrance, because no grown-up could possibly squeeze through there. Come on, everyone. Find rocks and stones and hard clods of earth and stop up the passage half-way through!"

The children worked hard, and before half an hour had gone by the passage was completely blocked up. No one could possibly guess there was a way through. It would be quite easy to unblock when the time came to go out.

"I'm going to crawl through to the cave with the small entrance and peep out to see if I can hear anything," said Jack. So he crawled through and sat just inside the tiny, low-down entrance, trying to hear.

The men were certainly searching the island! Jack could hear their shouts easily.

"*Some*one's been here!" shouted one man. "Look where they've made a fire."

"Trippers, probably!" called back another man. "There's an empty tin here, too—and a carton—just the sort of thing trippers leave about."

"Hi! Look at this spring here!" called another voice. "Looks to me as if people have been tramping about here."

Jack groaned. Surely there were not many footmarks there!

"Well, if those children are here we'll find them all right!" said a fourth voice. "It beats me how they could manage to live here, though, all alone, with no food, except what that boy could buy in the village!"

"I'm going over to the other side to look there," yelled the first man. "Come with me, Tom. You go one side of the hill and I'll go the other—and then, if the little beggars are dodging about to keep away from us, one of us will find them!"

Jack felt glad he was safely inside the cave. He stayed where he was till a whisper reached him from behind.

"Jack! We can hear voices. Is everything all right?"

"So far, Mike," said Jack. "They are all hunting hard — but the only thing they seem to have found is a few footmarks round the spring. I'll stay here for a bit and see what I can hear."

The hunt went on. Nothing seemed to be found. The children had cleared everything up very well indeed.

But, as Jack sat just inside the cave, there came a shout from someone near the beach.

"Just look here! What do you make of this?"

Jack wondered whatever the man had found. He soon knew. The man had kicked aside the heather that had hidden the hen-yard—and had found the newly scattered sand!

"This looks as if something had been going on here," said the man. "But goodness knows what! You know, I think those children *are* here somewhere. It's up to us to find them. Clever little things, too, they must be, hiding away all traces of themselves like this!"

"We'd better beat through the bushes and the bracken," said another man. "They may be hiding there. That'd be the likeliest place."

Then Jack heard the men beating through the bracken, poking into every bush, trying their hardest to find a hidden child. But not one could they find.

Jack crawled back to the cave after two or three hours and told the others what had happened. They listened, alarmed to hear that the hen-yard had been discovered even though they had tried so hard to hide it.

"It's time we had something to eat," said Peggy. "We can't light a fire in here, for we would be smoked out, but there are some rolls of bread I made yesterday, some wild strawberries, and a cold pudding. And lots of milk, of course."

They sat and ate, though none of them felt hungry. Daisy lay down behind them, perfectly good. The hens clucked, quietly, puzzled at finding themselves in such a strange dark place, but quite happy with the children there.

When the meal was over Jack went back to his post again. He sat just inside the cave-entrance and listened.

The men were getting puzzled and disheartened. They were sitting at the foot of the hill, eating sandwiches and drinking beer. Jack could hear their voices quite plainly.

126

"Well, those children *may* have been on this island, and I think they were—but they're not here now," said one man. "I'm certain of that."

"We've hunted every inch," said another man. "I think you're right, Tom; those kids have been here all right — who else could have planted those runner beans we found?—but they've gone. I expect that boy the policeman saw last Wednesday gave the alarm, and they've gone off in the boat."

"Ah yes, the boat!" said a third man. "Now, if the children were here we'd find a boat, wouldn't we? Well, we haven't found one—so they can't be here!"

"Quite right," said the first man. "I didn't think of that. If there's no boat here, there are no children! What about going back now? I'm sure it's no good hunting any more."

"There's just one place we haven't looked," said the quiet voice of the fourth man. "There are some caves in this hillside—it's possible those children may have hidden there."

"Caves!" said another man. "Yes—just the place. We'll certainly look there. Where are they?"

"I'll show you in a minute," said the fourth man. "Got a torch?"

"No, but I've got plenty of matches," said the other man. "But look here—they can't be there if there's no boat anywhere to be seen. If they are here, there must be a boat somewhere!"

"It's possible for a boat to be sunk so that no searcher could find it," said the fourth man.

"Children would never think of that!" said another.

"No, I don't think they would," was the answer.

Jack, who could hear everything, thought gratefully of Mike. It had been Mike's idea to sink the boat. If he hadn't sunk it, it would certainly have been found, for

127

the seach had been much more thorough than Jack had guessed. Fancy the men noticing the runner beans!

"Come on," said a man. "We'll go to those caves now. But it's a waste of time. I don't think the children are within miles! They've gone off up the lakeside somewhere in their boat!"

Jack crawled silently back to the inner cave, his heart thumping loudly.

"They don't think we're on the island," he whispered, "because they haven't found the boat. But they're coming to explore the caves. Put out the lantern, Mike. Now everyone must keep as quiet as a mouse. Is Daisy lying down? Good! The hens are quiet enough, too. They seem to think it's night, and are roosting in a row! Now nobody must sneeze or cough—everything depends on the next hour or two!"

Not a sound was to be heard in the big inner cave. Daisy lay like a log, breathing quietly. The hens roosted peacefully. The children sat like mice.

And then they heard the men coming into the cave outside. Matches were struck—and the passage that led to their cave was found!

"Look here, Tom," said a voice. "Here's what looks like a passage—shall we see where it goes?"

"We'd better, I suppose," said a voice. And then there came the sound of footsteps down the blocked-up passage!

The End Of The Search

The children sat in the inner cave as though they were turned into stone. They did not even blink their eyes. It seemed almost as if they did not even breathe! But how their hearts thumped! Jack thought that everyone must hear his heart beating, even the searchers outside, it bumped against his ribs so hard.

The children could hear the sound of someone fumbling his way along the narrow passage. He found it a tight squeeze, by his groanings and grumblings. He came right up to the place where the children had piled rocks, stones, and earth to block up the passage.

"I say!" the man called back to the others, "the passage ends here in what looks like loose rocks. Shall I try to force my way through—pull the rocks to see if they are just a fall from the roof?"

"No!" cried another man. "If you can't get through, the children couldn't! This is a wild-goose chase—we'll never find the children in these caves. Come back, Tom."

The man turned himself round with difficulty and began to squeeze back—and at the very moment a dreadful thing happened!

Daisy the cow let out a terrific moo!

The children were not expecting it, and they almost jumped out of their skins with fright. Then they clutched at one another, expecting the men to come chasing along at once, having heard Daisy.

There was an astonished silence. Then one of the men said, "Did you hear that?"

"Of course!" said another. "What in the wide world was it?"

"Well, it wasn't the children, that's certain!" said the first, with a laugh. "I never in my life heard a child make a noise like *that*!"

"It sounded like a cow," said another voice.

"A cow!" cried the first man, "what next? Do you mean to say you think there's a cow in the middle of this hill, Tom?"

"Of course there can't be," said Tom, laughing. "But it sounded mighty like one! Let's listen and see if we hear anything again."

There was a silence, as if the men were listening—and at that moment Daisy most obligingly gave a dreadfull hollow cough, that echoed mournfully round and round the cave.

"I don't like it," said a man's voice. "It sounds too queer for anything. Let's get out of these dark caves into the sunshine. I'm perfectly certain, since we heard those noises, that no children would be inside those caves! Why, they'd be frightened out of their lives!"

Jack squeezed Nora's hand in delight. So old Daisy had frightened the men! What a glorious joke! The children sat as still as could be, glad now that Daisy had given such a loud moo and such a dreadful cough.

There was the sound of scrambling about in the outer cave and then it seemed as if the men were all outside again. "We'd better just hunt about and see if there are any more caves," said one man. "Look that seems like one!"

"That's the cave where we put the hens when the trippers came!" whispered Jack. "It's got no passage leading to our inner cave here. They can explore that all they like."

The men did explore it, but as it was just a cave and

nothing else, and had no passage leading out of it, they soon left it. Then they found the cave with the low-down, tiny entrance—the one the childen used to squeeze into when they wanted to go to their inner cave—but, as Jack had said, the entrance was too small for any grown up to use, and, after trying once or twice, the men gave it up.

"No one could get in there except a rabbit," said a man's voice.

"Children could," said another.

"Now look here, Tom, if we find children on this island now, I'll eat my hat!" said the first man. "There's no boat, to begin with—and we really haven't found anything except runner beans, which might have been dropped by birds, and a funny sort of sandy yard—and you can't tell me children are clever enough to live here day after day, and yet vanish completely, leaving no trace behind, as soon as we come! No, no—no children are as clever as that!"

"I think you're right," said Tom. "Come on, let's go. I'm tired of this island with its strange noises. The sooner we get back home, the better I'll be pleased. Where those children have gone just beats me. I wish we could find them. There's such a surprise waiting for them!"

The voices grew distant as the men went down the hill to the beach, where they had put their boat. Jack crept quietly through the low passage into the small cave with the tiny entrance. He put his ear down to the entrance and listened. The sound of voices floated up to him. He heard the sound of oars being put ready. He heard the sound of the boat being pushed on to the water. Then came the sound of splashing.

"They're going!" he called. "They really are!"

The others crowded round Jack. Then, when he thought it was safe, they all squeezed out of the tiny cave entrance and crept out on the hillside. Well hidden in the tall bracken, they watched the boatful of men being rowed away—away—away! The splashing of the oars, and the men's voices, came clearly to the four children as they stood there.

Nora suddenly began to cry. The excitement had been so great, and she had been so brave, that now she felt as if she must cry and cry and cry. And then Peggy began—and even Mike and Jack felt their eyes getting wet! This was dreadful—but oh, it was such a glorious feeling to know they had not been discovered, and that their dear little island, their secret island, was their very own again.

A low and mournful noise came from the inside of the hill—it was poor old Daisy the cow, sad at being left alone in the cave.

The children couldn't help laughing now! "Do you remember how Daisy frightened those men!" chuckled Jack.

"She frightened me too," said Peggy. "Honestly, I nearly jumped out of my skin—if my dress hadn't been well buttoned up I believe I would have jumped *right* out of myself!"

That made the others laugh still more—and half-laughing, half-crying, they sat down on the hillside to wait till the boat was out of sight.

"I really thought they'd found us when that men got up to the part we had blocked up," said Jack.

"Yes—it was a jolly good thing we *did* block it up!" said Peggy. "We would most certainly have been found if we hadn't!"

"And it was a good thing Mike sank the boat," said Nora. "If they had found a boat here they would have gone on looking for us till they'd found us."

"I wonder what they meant when they said that such a surprise was waiting for us," said Mike. "It couldn't have been a nice surprise, I suppose?"

"Of course not!" said Peggy.

"They're almost out of sight," said Nora. "Do you think it's safe to get up and do a dance or something, Jack? I'm just longing to shout and sing and dance after being shut up in the cave for so long!"

"Yes, we're safe enough now," said Jack. "They won't come back. We can settle into the caves for the winter quite happily."

"Shall we light a fire on the beach and have a good hot meal?" said Peggy. "I think we could all do with one!"

"Right," said Jack, and they set to work. Nora sang and danced about as she helped to fetch things. She felt so happy to think that they were safe, and that their secret island was their very own once more.

Soon they were eating as if they had never had a meal in their lives before. Then a loud moo from the hillside reminded them that Daisy was still there. So, leaving the girls to clear up, Jack sped off with Mike to get out Daisy and the hens.

"You're a good old cow, Daisy," Jack said to her, rubbing her soft nose. "We hoped you wouldn't moo when those men were hunting for us—but you knew better, and you mooed at them—and sent them off!"

The days were much shorter now, and night came early. It did not seem long before the sun went and the stars shone out in the sky. The children fetched the lantern from the cave and, taking their book, they went to Willow House. It was Nora's turn to read, and they all lay and listened to her. It was pleasant in Willow House with the lantern shining down softly, and the smell of the heather and bracken rising up. It was nice to be together and to know that the great hunt was over and they were safe.

"I'm sleepy," said Jack, at last. "Let's have some chocolate and a last talk and go to bed. You know, we

133

shall soon have to think seriously of going to live in the caves. It won't be nice weather much longer!"

"We'll decide everything tomorrow," said Mike sleepily, munching his chocolate.

They were soon asleep, for the day's excitement had quite tired them out. But how lovely it was to wake the next day and know that the hunt was over and that they were safe for the winter. How they sang and joked and teased one another as they went down to bathe!

"Oooh!" said Nora, as she slipped into the water. "It's getting jolly cold to bathe in the lake, Jack. Have we got to do this all the winter?"

"Of course not," said Jack. "We'll have to give it up soon—but it's nice whilst it's warm enough."

That week the weather became really horrid. Storms swept over the lake and the children thought it looked just like the sea, with its big waves curling over and breaking on the beach with a crash. The waves ran right up the beach and it was impossible to make a fire there. The children got soaked with rain, and they had to dry their clothes as best they could by a fire they lighted outside the big cave. This was a good place for a fire, because the wind usually blew from the other direction and the fire was protected by the hill itself.

"I think we'll have to give up Willow House now and go to live in the caves," said Jack one morning, after a very wild night. The wind had slashed at the trees all night long, the rain had poured down, and, to the children's dismay, a little rivulet of rain had actually come into Willow House from the back and had soaked the heather bed Peggy and Nora were lying on. The girls had had to get up in the middle of the night and go to the front room, where the boys slept. This was a squash, but the front room was dry.

The leaves were falling from the trees. Every tree and

134

bush had flamed out into yellow, crimson, pink, brown or orange. The island was a lovely sight to see when the sun came out for an hour or two, for then its rays lighted up all the brilliant leaves, and they shone like jewels. But now the leaves were falling.

Leaves were dropping down in Willow House from the branches that made the roof. It was funny to lie in bed at night and feel a leaf drop lightly on to your cheek. Willow House looked different now that there were so few green or yellow leaves growing on the roof and walls. It was bare and brown.

Nora caught a cold and began to sneeze. Jack said they must move to the caves at once, or they would all get cold—and if they were ill, what would happen? There was no doctor to make them well!

They dosed Nora with hot milk and wrapped her up in the two new blankets Jack had bought in the village one week when he had been marketing. They set her at the back of the outer cave, with a candle beside her, for it was dim in that corner. She soon got better, and was able to help the others when they made their plans for living in the cave.

"We'll make this outer cave our living-room and bedroom!" Jack said, "and the inner one shall be our storeroom. We'll always have a fire burning at the entrance, and that will warm us and cook our food. This is going to be rather fun! We shall be cave-people this winter!"

Days In The Cave

That week the children made all their plans for passing the winter in the cave. Already all their stores were safely placed in the inner cave. It was just a question of getting the outer cave comforable and home-like. Peggy was wonderful at this sort of thing.

"You two boys must make a few shelves to put round the cave," she said. "You can weave them out of stout twigs, and put them up somehow. We will keep our books and games there, and any odd things we want. You must somehow manage to hang the lantern from the middle of the roof. Then, in the corner over here we will have our beds of heather and bracken. You boys can bring that in, too. If it's wet we'll dry it by the fire. The bracken is getting old and dry now—it should make a fine bed."

Peggy swept up the floor of the cave with a brush made of heather twigs, and then she and Nora threw fine sand on it which they had brought from the beach. It looked very nice. The boys brought in the heather and bracken for the beds. Peggy arranged them comfortably, and then threw a blanket over each bed but one. There were only three blankets—two new ones and one old one—so it looked as if someone must go without.

"What's the fourth bed going to have for a blanket?" asked Jack.

And then Peggy brought out a great surprise! It was a fur rug, made of rabbit skins that she had carefully cleaned, dried, and sewn together! How the others stared!

"But how lovely, Peggy!" said Jack. "It's a most

beautiful fur rug, and will be as warm as toast. We'll take it in turns to have it on at night."

"Yes, that's what I thought," said Peggy, pleased to find the others admired her rabbit rug so much. "It was very hard to sew the skins together, but I did it at last. I thought it would be a nice surprise for when the cold weather came!"

Soon the cave began to look very homely indeed. The shelves were weighed down with the books and games. The lantern swung in the middle, and they all knocked their heads against it before they became used to it there! The beds lay neatly in the corners at the back, covered with blankets and the rabbit rug. In another corner stood the household things that Peggy was always using—the kettle, the saucepans, and so on.

And then Jack brought out a surprise—a nice little table he had made by himself! He had found the old plank the children had brought with them months ago when they first came to the island, and had managed, by means of a saw he had bought during his marketing, to make a good little table for Peggy!

It was a bit wobbly. The four legs were made of tree branches, the straightest Jack could find, but it was difficult to get them just right. He had sawn the plank into pieces, and nailed them together to make a square top to the table, and this was very good. Peggy was delighted!

"Now we can have meals on the table!" she cried. "Oh, that will be nice! And I can do my mending on the table, too—it will be much easier than crouching on the floor!"

"But what about chairs?" asked Nora. "You can't sit up to the table without chairs!"

"I'm making stools," said Jack—and so he was! He had found an old tree broken in two by the wind on the other side of the hill. With his saw he was sawing up the trunk, and each piece he sawed out was like a solid stool—just a piece of tree-trunk, but nice and smooth to sit on!

The days passed very happily as they made the cave into a home. It was fun to sit on their little stools beside Jack's table and eat their meals properly there. It was fun to watch the fire burning at the entrance of the cave, getting brighter and brighter as night came on. It was lovely to lie on a soft heathery bed at the back of the cave, covered by a warm blanket or rabbit rug, and watch the fire gradually die down to a few glowing embers.

It was very cosy in the cave when the wind howled round the hillside. The light from the lantern shone down, and sometimes Peggy had an extra candle beside her when she sewed. The boys scraped at a bit of wood, carving something, or played a game with Nora. Sometimes they read out loud. The fire burnt brightly and lighted up the cave brilliantly every now and again when extra big flames shot up. It was great fun.

There was always plenty to do. Daisy still had to be milked each morning and evening. She seemed quite happy living in the grassy field, and the boys had built her a sort of shelter where she went at night. There were the hens to feed and look after. They were in a yard near the cave now. They were not laying so many eggs, but the children had plenty of stores and did not worry about eggs.

There was the usual cooking, washing, and clearing-up to do. There was water to be got from the spring. There was firewood to hunt for and pile up. Peggy liked to find pine-cones because they burnt up beautifully and made such a nice smell.

November passed by. Sometimes there were lovely fine days when the children could sit out on the hillside and bask in the sun. Sometimes there were wind-swept days when the rain pelted down and the clouds raced across the sky, black and ragged. Then the lake was tossed into white-topped waves.

Mike and Jack had got the boat up again and mended it. They had pulled it up the beach as far as they could to be out of reach of the waves.

When December came, the children began to think of Christmas. It would be strange to have Christmas on the island!

"We'll have to decorate the cave with holly," said Jack. "There are two holly-trees on the island, and one has red berries on. But there is no mistletoe."

"Christmas will be funny with only just ourselves," said Peggy. "I don't know if I will like it. I like hearing carols sung, and seeing the shops all full of lovely things, and looking forward to Christmas stockings and crackers, and things like that."

"Before our Daddy and Mummy flew off in their aeroplane and got lost, we used to have Christmas with them," Nora said to Jack. "It was lovely then. I remember it all!"

"I wish Daddy and Mummy hadn't gone away and got lost for ever," said Mike. "I did love them—they were so jolly and happy."

Jack listened as the three children told him all they had done at Christmas time when their father and mother had been with them. He had always lived with his old grandfather, who had never bothered about Christmas. To Jack this all seemed wonderful. How Mike, and Nora, and Peggy must miss all the happy and lovely things they used to do when they had their father and mother with them!

The boy listened and made up his mind about something. He would take the boat and row off to the end of the lake just before Christmas. He still had some money —and with that he would buy crackers, a doll for Nora, a new work-box for Peggy, something for Mike, and some oranges and sweets! They should have a fine Christmas!

139

He said nothing to the others about it. He knew that they would be terribly afraid that he might be caught again. But he did not mean to go to the same village as before. He meant to walk to the one five miles away, where he would not be known, and buy what he wanted there. He was sure he would be safe, for he meant to be very careful indeed!

December crept on. The days were dull and dreary. Jack planned to go off in the boat one morning. He would tell the others he was just going for a row to get himself warm. He would not tell them about his great surprise for them!

A good day came when the pale wintry sun shone down, and the sky was a watery blue. Peggy was busy clearing up after breakfast. Mike meant to rebuild Daisy's shelter, which had been rather blown about by the wind. Nora was going to look for pine-cones.

"What are *you* going to do, Jack?" asked Peggy.

"Oh," said Jack, "I think I'll take the old boat out and go for a row to get myself warm. I haven't rowed for ages!"

"I'll come with you, Jack," said Nora.

But Jack didn't want anyone with him! "No, Nora," he said, "you go out and look for cones. I shall be gone a good while. Peggy, could you let me have some food to take with me?"

"Food!" said Peggy in amazement. "However long are you going for, Jack?"

"Oh, just a few hours," said Jack. "Some exercise will do me good. I'll take my fishing-line, too."

"Well, put on your overcoat, then," said Peggy; "you'll be cold out on the windy lake."

She put some rolls and a hard-boiled egg into a basket, together with a bottle of milk. Jack said goodbye and set off down the hillside. Nora came with him, half sulky at not being allowed to go in the boat.

"You might let me come, Jack," she said.

"You can't come today, Nora," said Jack. "You will know why when I come back!"

He pushed off and rowed out on to the lake, which was not very rough that day. He rowed hard, and Nora soon left the beach and went to seek for cones. She thought she would try and see where Jack was fishing, after a time, and went to the top of the hill—but, try as she would, she could see no sign of the boat. She thought that very strange.

Hours went by, and Jack did not come back. The others waited for him, wondering why he had gone off alone and why he had not come back.

"Do you think he's gone to the village again to get anything?" asked Peggy at last. "Nora says she couldn't see his boat anywhere on the lake when she looked—and if he was fishing anywhere near, we should easily see him!"

"Oh, dear!" said Mike, worried. "If he goes to that village he'll be caught again!"

But Jack hadn't been caught. Something else had happened—something very extraordinary!

141

Jack Has A Great Surprise

We must go back to Jack and find out what had been happening to him. He had been such a long time away from the island—far longer than he would have been if he had just gone shopping. What could have kept him?

Well, he had got safely in the boat to the far end of the lake, and had tied the boat up to a tree. Then he had slipped through the wood, and taken the road that led to the distant village, five miles away. It would take him nearly an hour and a half to get there, but what fun it would be to do a bit of shopping again!

The boy padded along the wintry road. It was muddy and cold, but he was as warm as toast. He jingled his money in his pocket and wondered if he could buy all he wanted to. He did badly want to get a doll for Nora, for he knew how much she would love it!

He carried the food Peggy had given him, and, when he got near the village, he sat up on a gate and ate it. Then off he went again. He did not think anyone would know him to be one of the runaways, for surely people had forgotten all about them by now! It was half a year since they had first run off to the island! But he was keeping a sharp look out in case he saw anyone looking at him too closely!

He went into the village. It was a big, straggling one, with a small High Street running down the middle. There were about six shops there. Jack went to look at them. He left the toy and sweet shop till last. He looked at the turkeys in the butcher's shop, some with red ribbons on.

He looked into the draper's shop and admired the gay streamers that floated all about it to decorate it for Christmas. It was fun to see shops again.

And then he came to the toy shop. It was lovely! Dolls stood in the window with their arms stretched out as if they were asking people to buy them. A railway train ran on lines. A little Father Christmas stood in the middle, carrying a sack. Boxes of chocolate, tins of toffee, and big bottles of brightly-coloured sweets were in the shop, too.

Jack stood gazing, wondering which doll to buy for Nora. He had already seen a nice little work-basket for Peggy, and had spied a book for Mike about boats. There was a box of red crackers at the back of the window, too, which he thought would do well for Nora. It would be such fun to pull them on Christmas Day in the cave, and wear paper hats there!

Jack went into the shop. It had two or three other people there, for the shop was a post office, too, and people were sending off Christmas parcels. The shop assistant was weighing them—and it was a long business. Jack waited patiently, looking round at all the toys.

The people in the shop were talking to one another. At first Jack did not listen—and then he heard something that made him prick up his ears.

This is what he heard:

"Yes, it's a great pity those children were never found," said one woman. "Their father and mother are quite ill with grief, I've heard."

"Poor things," said the second woman. "It's bad enough to come down in an aeroplane on a desert island, and not be found for two years—and then to come back safe to see your children—and learn that they've disappeared!"

Jack's eyes nearly dropped out of his head. What did this mean? Could it possibly—possibly—mean that Mike's father and mother had turned up again. Forgetting all about being careful, Jack caught hold of the arm of the first woman.

"Please" he said, "please tell me something. Were the three children you are talking about called Mike, Peggy and Nora—and is it *their* father and mother that have come back?"

The woman in the shop stared at the excited boy in astonishment. "Yes," said the first woman. "Those were the children's names. They disappeared in June with another boy, called Jack, and have never been found. And in August the missing father and mother were found far away on a Pacific Island, and brought back safely here. Their aeroplane had come down and smashed, and they had been living there until a ship picked them up."

"But their children had gone," said the shop assistant joining in, "and it almost broke their hearts, for they had been worrying about them for months and longing to see them."

"What do *you* know about all this?" suddenly said one of the women. "You're not one of the children, are you?"

"Never mind about that," said Jack impatiently. "Just tell me one thing—where are the father and mother?"

"They are not far away," said the shop assistant. "They are staying at a hotel in the next town, hoping that the children will still be heard of."

"What hotel?" said Jack eagerly.

"The Swan Hotel," said the shop assistant, and then the women stared in amazement as Jack tore out of the shop at top speed, his eyes shining, and a look of the greatest excitement on his brown face!

He ran to the bus-stop. He knew that buses went to the town, and he had only one thought in mind—to get to the Swan Hotel and tell Mike's father and mother that their children were safe! Never in his life had Jack been

144

so excited. To think that things would all come right like this, and he, Jack, was the one to tell the father and mother!

He jumped into the bus, and could not keep still. He leapt out of it when it rumbled into the town and ran off to the Swan Hotel. He rushed into the hall and caught hold of the hall-porter there.

"Where are Captain and Mrs. Arnold?" he cried. Mike had often told him that his father was a captain, and he knew the children's surname was Arnold—so he knew quite well whom to ask for.

"Here, here, not so fast, young man," said the porter, not quite liking the look of the boy in the old overcoat, and worn-out shoes. "What do you want the Captain for?"

"Oh, tell me, please, where are they?" begged Jack—at that moment a man's voice said:

"Who's this asking for me? What do you want, boy?"

Jack swung round. He saw a tall, brown-faced man looking down at him, and he liked him at once, because he was so like Mike to look at.

"Captain Arnold! I know where Mike and Peggy and Nora are!" he cried.

The Captain stared as if he had not heard aright. Then he took Jack's arm and pulled him upstairs into a room where a lady sat, writing a letter. Jack could see she was the children's mother, for she had a look of Peggy and Nora about her. She looked kind and strong and wise, and Jack wished very much that she was his mother, too.

"This boy says he knows where the children are, Mary," said the Captain.

What excitement there was then! Jack poured out his story and the two grown-ups listened without saying a word. When he had finished, the Captain shook hands with Jack, and his wife gave him a hug.

"You're a fine friend for our children to have!" said the

145

Captain, his face shining with excitement. "And you really mean to say that you have all been living together on that little island and nobody has found you?"

"Yes," said Jack, "and oh, sir, is it true that you and Mrs. Arnold have been living on an island, too, till a ship picked you up?"

"Quite true," said Captain Arnold, with a laugh. "Our plane came down and smashed—and there we were, lost on an island in the Pacific Ocean! Little did we know that our children were going to live alone on an island, too! This sort of thing must be in the family!"

"John, we must go at once to them," said Mrs. Arnold, who was almost crying with joy. "Quickly, this very minute. I can't wait!"

"We'd better get a proper boat," said Jack. "Our old boat is a leaky old thing now."

It wasn't long before a car was brought round to the door, and Jack, Captain and Mrs. Arnold were motoring to the lakeside. They hired a big boat from a fisherman there, and set off to the secret island. Jack wondered and wondered what the children would say!

Meanwhile the three children were getting more and more worried! It was past tea-time now, and getting dark. Where *could* Jack be?

"I can hear the splash of oars!" cried Peggy at last. They ran down to the beach, and saw the outline of the boat in the twilight coming near to the island. And then Mike saw that it was a bigger boat than their own—and there were three people in it, instead of one!

"That means Jack's been caught—and these people have been sent to get us!" he thought, and his heart sank. But then, to his amazement, he heard Jack's clear voice ringing out over the darkening water.

"Mike! Peggy! Nora! It's all right! I've brought a Christmas present for you!"

146

The three children stared. Whatever could Jack mean? But when the boat landed, and Captain and Mrs. Arnold sprang out, they soon knew!

"Mummy! Oh, Mummy! And Daddy!" shrieked the children, and flung themselves at their father and mother. You couldn't tell which were children and which were grown-ups, because they were all so mixed up. Only Jack was alone. He stood apart, looking at them—but not for long. Nora stretched out her hand and pulled him into the crowd of excited, happy people.

"You belong, too, Jack," she said.

Everyone seemed to be laughing and crying at the same time. But at last it was so dark that no one could see anyone else. Jack lighted the lantern that Mike had brought down to the beach, and led the way to the cave. He badly wanted Captain and Mrs. Arnold to see how lovely it was.

They all crowded inside. There was a bight fire crackling just outside, and the cave was warm and cosy. Jack hung the lantern up and placed two wooden stools for the children's parents. Peggy flew to heat some milk, and put out rolls of bread and some potted meat she had been saving up for Christmas. She did so want her mother to see how nicely she could do things, even though they all lived in a cave!

"What a lovely home!" said Mrs. Arnold, as she looked round and saw the shelves, the stools, the table, the beds, and everything. The cave was very neat and tidy, and looked so cosy and friendly. How they all talked! How they jumped up and down and laughed and told first this thing and then the other! Only one thing made Captain and Mrs. Arnold angry—and that was the tale of how unkind Aunt Harriet and Uncle Henry had been.

"They shall be punished," said Captain Arnold, and that was all he said about them.

147

Daisy chose to moo loudly that night, and Captain Arnold laughed till the tears came into his eyes when he heard about the night that poor Daisy had had to swim behind the boat to the island! And when he heard how she had mooed and frightened away the people who had come to look for them, he laughed still more!

"Someone will have to write a book about your adventures," he said. "I never in my life heard anything like them. *We* didn't have such thrilling adventures on *our* island! We just lived with the native people there till a boat picked us up! Very dull indeed!"

Jack disappeared at that moment, and when he came back he carried a great load of heather. He flung it down in a corner.

"You'll stay with us tonight, won't you, Captain?" he said. "We'd love to have you. Please do."

"Of course!" said Captain Arnold. And Mrs. Arnold nodded her dark head. "We will all be together in the cave," she said. "Then we shall share a bit of your secret island, children, and know what it is like."

So that night the children had visitors! They all fell asleep on their heather beds at last, happy, excited, and very tired. What fun to wake up tomorrow with their own father and mother beside them!

The End Of The Adventure

Mike awoke first in the morning. He sat up and remembered everything. There were his father and mother, fast asleep on their heathery bed in the corner of the cave! It was true then—he hadn't dreamt it all! They were alive and well, and had got their children again—everything was lovely.

Mike crept out to light the fire. He could not possibly go to sleep again. The day was just creeping in at the cave entrance. The sky was a very pale blue, and the sun was trying to break through a thin mist in the east. It was going to be fine!

When the fire was crackling merrily everyone woke up. Nora flung herself on her mother, for she could not believe she really had a mother again, and had to keep hugging her and touching her. Soon the cave was filled with talk and laughter.

Peggy and Nora got the breakfast. Mike showed his father the inner cave and their stores. Jack flew off to milk Daisy. The hens clucked outside, and Nora fetched in four brown eggs.

Fish from Jack's line, eggs, rolls, the rest of the potted meat, and a tin of peaches made a fine breakfast, washed down with hot tea. The fire died down and the sunshine came in at the cave entrance. Everyone went outside to see what sort of a day it was.

The lake sparkled blue below. The bare trees swung gently in the breeze. Nora told her mother all about the wild raspberries and strawberries and nuts, and Peggy chattered about the seeds they had planted, and the baskets they could make.

And then Captain Arnold said, "Well, I think it's about time we were going."

The children looked up at him. "Going! What do you mean, Daddy? Leave our island?"

"My dears," said Captain Arnold, "you can't live here always—besides, there is no need for you to, now. You are not runaways any more. You are our own children that we love, and we must have you with us."

"Yes," said Mrs. Arnold. "We must all go back to a proper home, and you must go to school, my dears. You have been very brave and very clever—and very happy, too—and now you can have a lovely home with us, and we will all be happy together."

"But what about Jack?" asked Nora, at once.

"Jack is ours, too," said Mrs. Arnold. "I am sure his grandfather will be glad for us to have him for always. He shall have me for his mother, and your father shall be his, too! We will all be one big family!"

Jack wanted to say such a lot but he couldn't say a single word. It was very strange. His face just went red with joy, and he held Nora's hand so tightly that he hurt her without meaning to. He was just about the happiest boy in the world at that moment.

"Mummy, I shall so hate leaving our dear, dear island," said Nora. "And Willow House, too—and our cosy cave and the bubbling spring—and everything."

"I think I might be able to buy the island for you," said Daddy. "Then, in the holidays you can always come here and run wild and live by yourselves if you want to. It shall be your very own."

"Oh, Daddy!" shouted the children, in delight. "We shan't mind going to school and being proper and living in a house if we've got the island to go back to in the holidays! Oh, what fun it will be!"

"But I think you must leave it now and come back home

for Christmas," said Mrs. Arnold. "We have our own old home to go back to—you remember it, don't you? Don't you think it would be nice to have Christmas there—and a Christmas pudding—and crackers—and stockings full of presents?"

"Yes, yes, yes!" shouted all the children.

"It's just what I longed for!" said Nora.

"I was going to buy you some red crackers yesterday, Nora," said Jack, "but I heard the great news before I had bought anything!"

"You shall all have red crackers!" said Captain Arnold, with a laugh. "Now, what about getting off in the boat?"

"Just give us time to say good-bye to everything," said Peggy. "Mummy, come down and see Willow House. We made it ourselves and it's so pretty in the summer, because you see, it's a *live* house, and grows leaves all the time!"

In an hour's time everyone was ready to leave. The hens were bundled once more into a sack and were most annoyed about it. Daisy was left, and Captain Arnold said he would send a fisherman over for her. It was too cold for her to swim behind the boat. Most of the children's stores were left, too. They would be able to use them when they next went to the island.

Peggy took the rabbit-rug she had made. That was too precious to leave. They brought the books too, because they had got fond of those. They had stored everything carefully in the inner cave, and thrown sacks over them in case of damp. They couldn't help feeling a bit sad to leave, although they knew they were going to their own happy home again.

At last everyone was in the boat. Captain Arnold pushed off and the sound of oars came to Daisy's ears as she stood pulling at the thin winter grass. She stood watching the boat as it bobbed away on the waves.

"Good-bye, dear secret island," said Nora.

"Good-bye, good-bye!" said the others. "We'll come back again! Good-bye, Daisy, good-bye, everything!"

"And now let's talk about all we're going to do at Christmas," said Mrs. Arnold, cheerfully, for she saw that the children were sad at leaving their beloved little island.

It was not long before the four children and their father and mother (for Jack counted them as his parents too, now) were settled happily in their own home. There was such a lot of excitement at first, for the children had to have new dresses, new suits, new underclothes, new socks, new shoes! Mrs. Arnold said that although Peggy had really done her best to keep them tidy, they were quite dropping to pieces!

So off they went shopping, and came back feeling as grand as kings and queens, all dressed up in their new things! Peggy looked fine in a blue coat and skirt with a little blue hat. Nora wore red, and the two boys had suits and overcoats of dark blue.

Jack felt queer in his. It was the first time in his life he had ever had anything new of his own to wear, for he had always gone about in somebody's old things before! He felt very grand indeed.

The children looked at one another and burst out laughing.

"How different we look now!" said Mike. "Think of our dirty old rags on the island! But it's good to be really properly dressed again—and the girls *do* look nice!"

It was strange at first to sleep in a proper bed again. The girls slept in a pretty room and had a little white bed each. The boys slept in the next room, and had two brown beds. At first they all wondered where they were when they awoke in the morning, but after a few days they got used to it.

Christmas drew near. They all went out to buy presents

for one another. It was most exciting. They went to London and marvelled at the great shops there. They watched all kinds of ships and boats sailing along in a big tank. They saw model trains tearing round and round a little countryside, going through tunnels, stopping at stations, just like a real train. It was all very exciting after living such a peaceful life on the island.

Christmas was lovely. They hung up their socks at the end of their beds—and in the morning what fun they had finding the things packed tightly in the long stockings! Tiny dolls in the girls', oranges, sweets, nuts, needle-books and balls—and in the boys' were all kinds of things, too. Bigger presents were at the foot of the bed, and *how* excited all the children were unpacking them!

"This is better than Christmas in the cave!" said Nora, unpacking a great big smiling doll with curly golden hair. "Oh, Jack! Did you really buy this for me? Oh, how lovely, lovely, lovely!"

Soon the bedrooms were full of dolls, books, trains, balls, aeroplanes and motor-cars! It was the loveliest Christmas morning the children had ever had—and certainly Jack had never in his life known one like it! He just simply couldn't believe his luck.

"You deserve it all, Jack," said Nora. "You were a good friend to us when we were unhappy—and now you can share with us when we are happy."

There was a Christmas-tree after tea, with more pre-sents—and as for the crackers, you should have seen them! Red ones and yellow ones, blue ones and green ones! Soon everyone was wearing a paper hat, and how the children laughed when Captain Arnold pulled a cracker and got a tiny aeroplane out of it!

"Well, you can't fly away in *that*, Daddy," cried Peggy.

"You won't ever fly away again, Daddy, will you?" said Nora, suddenly frightened in case her father and mother should fly off again and be lost, so that the four children would be alone once more.

"No, never again," said her father. "Mummy and I have made such a lot of money out of our flying now, that we can afford to stay at home and look after you. We shall never leave you again!"

It was four happy children who went to bed that night. The boys left the door open between their room and the girls', so that they might all talk to one another till they fell asleep. They could not get out of this habit, for they had always been able to talk to one another in bed on the island.

"It's been a lovely day," said Peggy sleepily. "But I do just wish something now."

"What?" asked Mike.

"I do just wish we could all be back in our cosy cave on our secret island for five minutes," said Peggy.

"So do I," said everyone, and they lay silent, thinking of the happy days and nights on the island.

"I shall never, never forget our island," said Nora. "It's the loveliest place in the world, I think. I hope it isn't feeling lonely without us! Good-night, secret island! Wait for us till we come again!"

"Good-night, secret island!" said the others. And then they slept, and dreamt of their island—of the summer days when they would go there once more, and live merrily and happily alone, in the hot sunshine—of winter days in the cosy cave—of cooking over a camp fire—and sleeping soundly on heathery beds. Dear secret island, only wait, and you shall have the children with you once again!

THE END

Everyone stared in amazement at the Secret Mountain

The Secret Mountain

Enid Blyton

The Secret
Mountain

The Beginning Of The Adventures

One bright sunny morning, very early, four children stood on the rough grass of a big airfield, watching two men busily checking the engines of a gleaming white aeroplane.

The children looked rather forlorn, for they had come to say good-bye to their father and mother, who were to fly themselves to Africa.

"It's fun having a famous father and mother who do all kinds of marvellous flying feats," said Mike. "But it's not such fun when they go away to far-off countries!"

"Well, they'll soon be back," said Nora, Mike's twin sister. "It will only be a week till we see them again."

"I somehow feel it will be longer than that," said Mike gloomily.

"Oh, don't say things like that!" said Peggy. "Make him stop, Jack!"

Jack laughed and slapped Mike on the shoulder. "Cheer up!" he said. "A week from today you'll be here again to welcome them back, and there will be cameramen and newspaper men crowding round to take your picture – son of the most famous air-pilots in the world!"

The children's father and mother came up, dressed in flying suits. They kissed and hugged the children.

"Now, don't worry about us," said their mother. "We shall soon be back. You will be able to follow our flight by reading what the newspapers say every day. We will have a fine party when we come home, and you shall all stay up till eleven o'clock!"

"Gracious!" said Jack. "We shall have to start going to bed early every night to get ready for such a late party!"

5

It was rather a feeble joke, but everyone was glad to laugh at it. One more hug all round and the two flyers climbed into the cockpit of their tiny aeroplane, whose engines were now roaring in a most business-like way.

Captain Arnold was to pilot the aeroplane for the first part of the flight. He waved to the children. They waved back. The aeroplane engines took on a deeper, stronger note, and the machine began to move gently over the grass, bumping a little as it went.

Then, like a bird rising, the wheels left the ground and the tiny white plane rose into the air. It circled round twice, rose high, and then sped off south with a drone of powerful engines. The great flight had begun!

"Well, I suppose the White Swallow will break another record," said Mike, watching the aeroplane become a tiny speck in the blue sky. "Come on, you others. Let's go and have some lemonade and buns."

Off they went and were soon sitting round a little table in the airfield's restaurant. They were so hungry that they ordered twelve buns.

"It's a bit of luck getting off from school for a couple of days like this," said Mike. "It's a pity we've got to go back today. It would have been fun to go to a cinema or something."

"Our train goes from London in two hours' time," said Peggy. "When does yours go?"

"In three hours," said Jack, munching his bun. "We shall have to go soon. It will take us over an hour to get to London from here, and you girls don't want to miss your train."

"We'll all look in the newspapers each day and see where Mummy and Daddy have got to," said Peggy. "And we'll look forward to meeting you boys here again in about a week's time, to welcome the plane back! Golly, that *will* be exciting!"

"I still feel rather gloomy," said Mike. "I really have got

a nasty feeling that we shan't see Dad and Mummy again for a long time."

"You and your nasty feelings!" said Nora laughing. "By the way, how's Prince Paul?"

Prince Paul was a boy at Mike's school. He and the children had had some strange adventures together the year before, when the Prince had been captured and taken from his land of Baronia to be kept prisoner in an old house that had once belonged to smugglers. The children had rescued him – and now Paul had been sent to the same school as his friends, Mike and Jack.

"Oh, Paul's all right," said Mike. "He was furious because the headmaster wouldn't allow him to come with Jack and me to see Dad and Mummy off."

"Well, give him our love and tell him we'll look forward to seeing him in the holidays," said Peggy, who was very fond of the little Prince.

"Come on – we really must go," said Mike. "Where's the taxi? Oh, there it is. Get in, you girls, and we'll be off. Jack and I will have time to come and see you safely into your train."

Before evening came all four children were safely back at their two schools. Prince Paul was watching for his friends, and he rushed to meet Jack and Mike.

"Did you see them off?" he cried. "Did you see the evening papers? There's a picture of Captain and Mrs Arnold in it."

Sure enough the evening papers were full of the big flight that the famous pilots were making. The children read them proudly. It was fun to have such a famous father and mother.

"I'd rather have a famous pilot for a father than a king," said Prince Paul enviously. "Kings aren't much fun, really – but airmen are always doing marvellous things!"

For the next two days the papers were full of the plane's magnificent flight – and then a horrid thing happened.

7

Mike ran to get the evening paper, and the first thing that met his eye was a great headline that said:

"NO NEWS OF THE ARNOLDS. STRANGE SILENCE. WHAT HAS HAPPENED TO THE WHITE SWALLOW?"

The White Swallow was the name given to the beautiful aeroplane flown by Captain and Mrs Arnold. Mike went pale as he read his headlines. He handed the paper to Jack without a word.

Jack glanced at it in dismay. "What can have happened?" he said. "I say – the girls will be jolly upset."

"Didn't I tell you I felt gloomy when I saw Dad and Mummy off?" said Mike. "I *knew* something was going to happen!"

The girls were just as upset as the boys. Nora cried and Peggy tried to comfort her.

"It's no good telling me they will be all right," wept Nora. "They must have come down in the middle of Africa somewhere, and goodness knows what might happen. They might be eaten by wild animals, or get lost in the forest or—"

"Nora, they've got food and guns," said Peggy. "And if the plane has had an accident, well, heaps of people will be looking and searching day and night. Let's not look on the dark side of things till we know a bit more."

"I wish we could see the boys," said Nora, drying her eyes. "I'd like to know what they say."

"Well, it's half-term holiday the week-end after next," said Peggy. "We shall see them then."

To the children's great disappointment, there was no news of their parents the next day – nor the next day either. Then, as the days slipped by, and the papers forgot about the lost flyers, and printed other fresher news, the children became more and more worried.

Half-term came, and the four of them went to London, where they were to stay for three days at their parents' flat. Miss Dimmy, an old friend of theirs, was to look after

8

them for that short time. Prince Paul was to join them that evening. He had to go and see his own people first, in another part of London.

"What's being done about Dad and Mummy?" asked Mike, feeling glad to see Dimmy, whom they all loved.

"My dear, you mustn't worry – everything is being done that can possibly *be* done," said Dimmy. "Search parties have been sent out all over the district where it is thought that Captain and Mrs Arnold may have come down. They will soon be found."

Dimmy took them all to a cinema, and for a while the children forgot their worries. Prince Paul joined them after tea, looking tremendously excited.

"I say, what do you think?" he cried. "My father has sent me the most wonderful birthday present you can think of – guess what it is!"

"A pink elephant," said Mike at once.

"A blue bed-jacket!" said Nora.

"A clockwork mouse!" said Peggy.

"A nice new rattle!" cried Jack.

"Don't be silly," grinned Paul, who was now quite used to the English children's teasing ways. "You're all wrong – he's given me an aeroplane of my very own!"

The four children stared at Paul in the greatest surprise. They knew that Paul's father was a rich king – but even so, an aeroplane seemed a very extravagant present to give to a small boy.

"An *aeroplane!*" said Mike. "Golly – if you aren't lucky, Paul! But you are too young to fly it. It won't be any use to you."

"Yes, it will," said Paul. "My father has sent me his finest pilot with it. I can fly all over your little country of England and get to know it very well."

A voice came up from the London street below. "Paper! Evening paper! Lost aeroplane found! White Swallow found!"

With a yell the four children rushed down the stairs to buy a paper. But what a dreadful disappointment for them! It was true that the White Swallow had been found – but Captain and Mrs Arnold were not with it. They had completely disappeared!

The children read the news in silence. The aeroplane had been seen by one of the searching planes, which had landed nearby. Something had gone wrong with the White Swallow and Captain Arnold had plainly been putting it right – then something had happened to stop him.

"And now they've both disappeared, and, although all the natives round have been questioned about them, nobody knows anything – or they say they don't, which comes to the same thing," said Peggy, almost in tears.

"I wish to goodness *we* could go out to Africa and look for them," said Mike, who hadn't really much idea of how enormous a place Africa was.

Prince Paul slipped a hand through Mike's arm. His eyes shone.

"We *will* go!" he said. "What about my new aeroplane! We can go in that – and Pilescu, my pilot, can take us! He is always ready for an adventure! Don't let's go back to school, Mike – let's go off in my aeroplane!"

The others stared at the little Prince in astonishment. What an idea!

"We couldn't possibly," said Mike.

"Why not?" said Paul. "Are you afraid? Well, I will go by myself then."

"Indeed, you won't!" cried Jack. "Mike – it's an idea! We've had marvellous adventures together – this will be another. Let's go – oh, do let's go!"

In The Middle Of The Night

Not one of the five children thought of the great risk and danger of the adventure they were so light-heartedly planning.

"Shall we tell Dimmy?" said Nora.

"Of course not," said Jack scornfully. "You know what grown-ups are – why, Dimmy would at once telephone Paul's pilot and forbid him to take us anywhere."

"Well, it seems horrid to leave her and not tell her anything," said Nora, who was very fond of Miss Dimmy.

"We'll leave a note for her that she can read when we are well away," said Mike. "But we really mustn't do anything to warn her or anyone else. My word – what a mercy that Paul had that aeroplane for his birthday!"

"When shall we go?" said Paul, his big dark eyes shining brightly. "Now – this very minute?"

"Don't be an idiot, Paul," said Jack. "We've got to get a few things together. We ought to have guns, I think, for one thing."

"I don't like guns," said Nora. "They might go off by themselves."

"Guns don't," said Jack. "You girls don't need to have guns. But where can we get these things – I'm sure I don't know."

"Pilescu, my pilot, can get everything we want," said Prince Paul. "Don't worry."

"But how will he know what to get?" asked Mike. "I hardly know myself what we ought to take."

"I will tell him he must find out," said Paul. "Show me where your telephone is Mike, and I will tell him everything."

11

Soon Paul was holding a most extraordinary talk with his puzzled pilot. In the end Pilescu said he must come round to the flat and talk to his small master. He could not believe that he was really to do what Paul commanded.

"I say – suppose your pilot refuses to do what you tell him?" said Jack. "I'm sure he will just laugh and tell us to go back to school and learn our tables or something!"

"Pilescu is my man," said the little Prince, putting his small chin into the air, and looking very royal all of a sudden. "He has sworn an oath to me to obey me all my life. He has to do what I say."

"Suppose he tells your father?" said Mike.

"Then I will no longer have him as my man," said Paul fiercely. "And that will break his heart, for he loves me and honours me. I am his prince, and one day I will be his king."

"You talk like a history book," said Peggy with a laugh. "All right, Paul – you try to get Pilescu to do what we have planned. He'll soon be here."

In twenty minutes Pilescu arrived. He was a strange-looking person, very tall, very strong, with fierce black eyes and a flaming red beard that seemed on fire when it caught the sun.

He bowed to all the children in turn, for his manners were marvellous. Then he spoke to Paul in a curiously gentle voice.

"Little Prince, I cannot believe that you wish me to do what you said on the telephone. It is not possible. I cannot do it."

Prince Paul flew into a rage, and stamped on the floor, his face bright red, and his dark eyes flashing in anger.

"Pilescu! How dare you talk to me like this? My father, the king, told me that you must do my smallest wish. I will not have you for my man. I will send you back to Baronia to my father and ask him for a better man."

"Little Prince, I held you in my arms when you were

12

born, and I promised then that you should be my lord," said Pilescu, in a troubled voice. "I shall never leave you, now that your father has sent me to be with you. But do not ask me to do what I think may bring danger to you."

"Pilescu! Shall I, the king's son, think of danger!" cried the little Prince. "These are my friends you see here. They are in trouble and I have promised to help them. Do you not remember how they saved me when I was kidnapped from my country of Baronia? Now it is my turn to help them. You will do what I say."

The other four children watched in astonishment. They had not seen Paul acting the prince before. Before ten minutes had gone by the big Baronian had promised to do all that his haughty little master demanded. He bowed himself out and was gone from the flat before Dimmy came to find out who the visitor was.

"Good, Paul!" said Mike. "Now all we've got to do is to wait till Pilescu lets us know how he got on."

Before the night was gone Pilescu telephoned to Prince Paul. The boy came running to the others, his face eager and shining.

"Pilescu has found out everything for us. He has bought all we need, but he says we must pack two bags with all we ourselves would like to have. So we must do that. We must leave the house at midnight, get into the car that will be waiting for us at the corner – and go to the airfield!"

"Golly! How exciting!" said Mike. The girls rubbed their hands, thrilled to think of the adventure starting so soon. Only Jack looked a little doubtful. He was the eldest, and he wondered for the first time if they were wise to go on this new and strange adventure.

But the others would not even let him speak of his doubts. No – they had made up their minds, and everything was ready except for the packing of their two bags. They were going; they were going!

The bags were packed. The five children were so

excited that they really did not know what to pack, and when the bags were full, not one child could possibly have said what was in them! With trembling hands they did up the leather straps, and then Mike wrote out a note for Dimmy.

He stuck the note into the mirror on the girls' dressing-table. It was quite a short note.

> "Dimmy Dear,
> "Don't worry about us. We've gone to look for Daddy and Mummy. We'll be back safe and sound before long.
>
> > "Love from all of us."

Dimmy had been out to see a friend and did not come back until nine o'clock. The children had decided to get into bed fully dressed, so that Dimmy would not have any chance of asking awkward questions.

Dimmy was rather surprised to find all the children so quiet and good in bed. They did not even sit up to talk to her when she came into the bedrooms to kiss them all goodnight. She did not guess that it was because they were not in their night clothes!

"Dear me, you must all be tired out!" she said in surprise. "Well, goodnight, my dears, sleep well. You still have another day's holiday, so we will make the most of it tomorrow."

All the children lay perfectly still until they heard Dimmy go into her bedroom and shut the door. They listened to her movements, and then they heard the click of her bedroom light being turned off.

"Don't get out of bed yet," whispered Jack to Mike. "Give Dimmy time to get to sleep."

So for another half-hour or so the children lay quiet – and Nora fell asleep! Peggy had to wake her up, and the little girl was most astonished to find that she had to get up

14

in the dark, and that she had on her day clothes! But she soon remembered what a big adventure was beginning, and she rubbed her eyes, and went to get a wet sponge to make her wider awake.

"What's the time?" whispered Mike. He flashed his torch on to the bedroom clock – half-past eleven. Nearly time to leave the house.

"Let's go to the dining-room and hunt round for a few biscuits first," said Jack. "I feel hungry. Now for goodness sake be quiet, everyone. Paul, don't trip over anything – and, Nora, take those squeaky shoes off! You sound like a dozen mice when you creep across the bedroom!"

So Nora took off her squeaky shoes and carried them. Jack and Mike took the bags, and the five children made their way quietly down the passage to the dining-room. They found the biscuit tin and began to munch. The noise of the biscuits being crunched in their teeth sounded very loud in the silence of the night.

"Do you think Dimmy will hear us munching?" said Nora anxiously. She swallowed her piece of biscuit too soon and a crumb caught in her throat. She went purple in the face, and tried hard not to cough. Then an enormous cough came, and the others rushed at her.

"Nora! Do be quiet!" whispered Jack fiercely. He caught the cloth off the table and wrapped it round poor Nora's head. Her coughs were smothered in it, but the little girl was very angry with Jack.

She tore off the cloth and glared at the grinning boy. "Jack! You nearly smothered me! You're a horrid mean thing."

"Sh!" said Mike. "This isn't the time to quarrel. Hark – the clock is striking twelve."

Dimmy was peacefully asleep in her bedroom when the five children crept to the front door of the flat. They opened it and closed it very quietly. Then down the stone stairway they went to the street entrance, where another big door had to be quietly opened.

"This door makes an awful noise when it is closed," said Mike anxiously. "You have to bang it. It will wake everyone!"

"Well, don't shut it then, silly," said Jack. "Leave it open. No one will bother about it."

So they left the big door open and went down the street, hoping that they would not meet any policemen. They felt sure that a policeman would think it very queer for five children to be out at that time of night!

Luckily they met no one at all. They went down to the end of the street, and Mike caught Jack's arm.

"Look – there's a car over there – do you suppose it is waiting for us?"

"Yes – that's our car," said Jack. "Isn't it, Paul?"

Paul nodded, and they crossed the road to where a big blue and silver car stood waiting, its engine turned off. The children could see the blue and silver in the light of a street lamp. Paul's aeroplane was blue and silver too, as were all the royal aeroplanes of Baronia.

A man slipped out of the car and opened the door silently for the children. His uniform was of blue and silver too, and, like most Baronians, he was enormous. He bowed low to Paul.

Soon the great car was speeding through the night. It went very fast, eating up the miles easily. The children were all tremendously excited. For one thing it was a great thrill to be going off in an aeroplane – and who knew what exciting adventures lay in store for them!

They came to the airfield. It was in darkness, except for lights in the middle of the field, where the beautiful aeroplane belonging to Prince Paul stood ready to start.

"I am to take you right up to the aeroplane in the car," said the driver to Prince Paul, who sat in front with him.

"Good," said Paul. "Then we can all slip into it, and we shall be off before anyone really knows we are here!"

An Exciting Journey

The big blue and silver car drove silently over the bumpy field until it came to the aeroplane. Pilescu was there, his red beard shining in the light of a lamp. With him was another man just as big.

"Hallo, Ranni!" said Prince Paul joyfully. "Are you coming too? I'm so glad to see you!"

Ranni lifted the small Prince off the ground and swung him into the air. His broad face shone with delight.

"My little lord!" he said. "Yes – I come with you and Pilescu. I think it is not right that you should do this – but the lords of Baronia were always mad!"

Paul laughed. It was easy to see that he loved big Ranni, and was glad that the Baronian was coming too.

"Will my aeroplane take seven?" he asked, looking at it.

"Easily," said Pilescu. "But now, come quickly before the mechanics come to see what is happening."

They all climbed up the little ladder to the cockpit. The aeroplane inside was like a big and comfortable room. It was marvellous. Mike and the others cried out in amazement.

"This is a wonderful aeroplane," said Mike. "It's much better than even the White Swallow."

"Baronia has the most marvellous planes in the world," said Pilescu proudly. "It is only a small country, but our inventors are the best."

The children settled down into comfortable armchair seats. Paul, who was tremendously excited, showed everyone how the seats unfolded, when a spring was touched, and became small beds, cosy and soft.

17

"Golly!" said Jack, making his seat turn into a bed at once, and then changing it back to an armchair, and then into a bed again. "This is like magic. I could do this all night!"

"You must settle down into your seats quickly," ordered Pilescu, climbing into the pilot's seat, with big Ranni just beside him. "We must be off. We have many hundreds of miles to fly before the sun is high."

The children settled down again, Paul chattering nineteen to the dozen! Nobody felt sleepy. It was far too exciting a night to think of sleep.

Pilescu made sure the children had all fastened their seat belts, and started the engines, which made a loud and comfortable noise. Then, with a slight jerk, the aeroplane began to run over the dark field.

It bumped a little – and then, like a big bird, it rose into the air and skimmed over the long line of trees that stood at the far end of the big field. The children hardly knew that it had left the ground.

"Are we still running over the field? asked Mike, trying to see out of the window near him.

"No, of course not," said Ranni laughing. "We are miles away from the airfield already!"

"Goodness!" said Peggy, half-startled to think of the enormous speed at which the plane was flying. The children had to raise their voices when they spoke, because the engine of the plane, although specially silent, made a great noise.

That flight through the dark night was very strange to the children. As soon as the plane left the ground its wheels rose into its body and disappeared. They would descend again when the aeroplane landed. It flew through the darkness as straight as an arrow, with Pilescu piloting it, his eyes on all the various things that told him everything he needed to know about the plane.

"Why did Ranni come?" Prince Paul shouted to Pilescu.

18

"Because Ranni can take a turn at piloting the plane," answered Pilescu. "Also there must be someone to look after such a crowd of children!"

"We don't need looking after!" cried Mike indignantly. "We can easily look after ourselves! Why, once when we ran away to a secret island, we looked after ourselves for months and months!"

"Yes – I heard that wonderful story," said Pilescu. "But I must have another man with me, and Ranni was the one I could most trust. We may be very glad of his help."

No one knew then how glad they were going to be that big Ranni had come with them – but even so, Ranni was very comforting even in the plane, for he brought the children hot cocoa when they felt cold, and produced cups of hot tomato soup which they thought tasted better than any soup they had ever had before!

"Isn't it exciting to be drinking soup high up in an aeroplane in the middle of the night?" said Peggy. "And I do like these biscuits. Ranni, I'm very glad you came with us!"

Big Ranni grinned. He was like a great bear, yet as gentle as could be. He adored little Paul, and gave him far too much to eat and drink. They all had bars of nut chocolate after the soup, and Pilescu munched as well.

The plane had been flying very steadily indeed – in fact, the children hardly noticed the movement at all – but suddenly there came a curious jerk, and the plane dropped a little. It happened two or three times, and Paul didn't like it.

"What's it doing?" he cried.

Mike laughed. He had been up in aeroplanes before, and he knew what was happening at that moment.

"We are only bumping into air-pockets," he shouted to Paul. "When we get into one we drop a bit – so it feels as if the plane is bumping along. Wait till we get into a big air-pocket – you'll feel funny, young Paul!"

19

Sure enough, the plane slipped into a very big air-pocket, and down it dropped sharply. Paul nearly fell off his big armchair, and he turned quite green.

"I feel sick," he said. Ranni promptly presented him with a strong paper bag.

"What's this for?" asked Paul, in a weak voice, looking greener than ever. "There's nothing in the bag."

The other four children shouted with laughter. They felt sorry for Paul, but he really did look comical, peering into the paper bag to see if there was anything there.

"It's for you to be sick in, if you want to be," shouted Jack. "Didn't you know that?"

But the paper bag wasn't needed after all, because the plane climbed high, away from the bumpy air-pockets, and Paul felt better. "I shan't eat so much chocolate another time," he said cheerfully.

"I bet you will!" said Jack, who knew that Paul could eat more chocolate than any other boy he had ever met. "I say – isn't this a gorgeous adventure? I hope we see the sun rise!"

But they didn't, because they were all fast asleep! Nora and Peggy began to yawn at two o'clock in the morning, and Ranni saw them.

"You will all go to sleep now," he said. He got up and helped the two girls to turn their big armchairs into comfortable, soft beds. He gave them each a pillow and a very cosy warm rug.

"We don't want to go to sleep," said Nora in dismay. "I shan't close my eyes. I know I shan't."

"Don't then," said Ranni with a grin. He pulled the rugs closely over the children and went back to his seat beside Pilescu.

Nora and Peggy and Paul found that their eyes closed themselves – they simply wouldn't keep open. In three seconds they were all sound asleep. The other two boys did not take much longer, excited though they were.

Ranni nudged the pilot and Pilescu's dark eyes twinkled as he looked round at the quiet children.

He and Ranni talked in their own language, as the plane roared through the night. They had travelled hundreds of miles before daylight came. It was marvellous to see the sun rising when dawn came.

The sky became full of a soft light that seemed alive. The light grew and changed colour. Both pilots watched in silence. It was a sight they had often seen and were never tired of.

Golden light filled the aeroplane when the sun showed a golden rim over the far horizon. Ranni switched off the electric lights at once. The world lay below, very beautiful in the dawn.

"Blue and gold," said Ranni to Pilescu, in his own language. "It is a pity the children are not awake to see it."

"Don't wake them, Ranni," said Pilescu. "We may have a harder time in front of us than they know. I am hoping that we shall turn and go back, once the children realise that we cannot possibly find their parents. We shall not stay in Africa very long!"

The children slept on. When they awoke it was about eight o'clock. The sun was high, and below the plane was a billowing mass of snowy whiteness, intensely blue in the shadows.

"Golly! Is it snow?" said Paul, rubbing his eyes in amazement. "Pilescu, I asked you to fly to Africa, not to the North Pole!"

"It's fields and fields of clouds," said Nora, looking with delight on the magnificent sight below them. "We are right above the clouds. Peggy, look – they seem almost solid enough to walk on!"

"Better not try it!" said Mike. "Ranni, you might have waked us up when dawn came. Now we've missed it. I say, I *am* hungry!"

21

Ranni became very busy at the back of the plane, where there was a proper little kitchen. Soon the smell of frying bacon and eggs, toast and coffee stole into the cabin. The children sniffed eagerly, looking down at the fields of cloud all the time, marvelling at their amazing beauty.

Then there came a break in the clouds and the five children gave shouts of joy.

"Look! We are over a desert or something. Isn't it queer?"

The smooth-looking desert gave way to mountains, and then to plains again. It was most exciting to watch.

"Where are we?" asked Mike.

"Over Africa," said Ranni, serving bacon and eggs to everyone, and putting hot coffee into the cups. "Now eat well, for it is a long time to lunch-time!"

It was a gorgeous meal, and most exciting. To think that they had their supper in London – and were having their breakfast over Africa! Marvellous!

"Do you know whereabouts our parents came down, Pilescu?" asked Mike.

"Ranni will show you on the map," said the pilot. "Soon we must go down to get more fuel. We are running short. You children are to stay hidden in the plane when we land on the airfield, for I do not want to be arrested for flying away with you!"

"We'll hide all right!" said Paul, excited. "Where is that map, Ranni? Let us see it. Oh, how I wish I had done better at geography. I don't seem to know anything about Africa at all."

Ranni unfolded a big map, and showed the children where Captain and Mrs Arnold's plane had been found. He showed them exactly where their own plane was too.

"Golly! It doesn't look very far from here to where the White Swallow was found!" cried Paul, running his finger over the map.

Ranni laughed. "Further than you think," he said.

"Now look – we are nearing an airfield and must get fuel. Go to the back of the plane and hide under the pile of rugs there."

So, whilst the plane circled lower to land, the five children snuggled under the rugs and luggage. They did hope they wouldn't be found. It would be too dreadful to be sent back to London after coming so far.

In A Very Strange Country

A number of men came running to meet the plane as it landed beautifully on the runway. Pilescu climbed out of the cockpit and left Ranni on guard inside. The children were all as quiet as mice.

The blue and silver plane was so magnificent that all the groundsmen ran round it, exclaiming. They had never seen such a beauty before. Two of them wanted to climb inside and examine it, but Ranni stood solidly at the entrance, his big body blocking the way. Pilescu spoke to the mechanics and soon the plane was taking in an enormous amount of fuel.

"Pooh! Doesn't it smell horrid?" whispered Paul. "I think I'm going to choke."

"Don't you dare even to sneeze," ordered Jack at once, his voice very low but very fierce.

So Paul swallowed his choking fit and went purple in the face. The girls couldn't bear the smell either, but they buried their faces deeper in the rug and said nothing.

A man's voice floated up to the cockpit, speaking in broken English.

"You have how many passengers, please?" he asked.

"You see me and my companion here," answered Pilescu shortly.

23

The man seemed satisfied, and walked round the plane admiring it. Pilescu took no notice of him, but began to look carefully into the engines of the plane. He noticed something was wrong and shouted to Ranni.

"Come down here a minute and give me a hand." Ranni stepped down the ladder and went to stand beside Pilescu. As quick as lightning one of the airfield men skipped up the ladder to the cockpit and peered inside the plane.

It so happened that Mike was peeping out to see if all was clear at that moment. He saw the man before the man saw him, and covered his face again, nudging the others to keep perfectly still.

Ranni saw that the man had gone up to the cockpit and he shouted to him. "Come down! No one is allowed inside our plane without permission."

"Then you must give me permission," said the man, whose quick eye had seen the enormous pile of rugs at the back, and who wished to examine it. "We have had news that five children are missing from London, and there is a big reward offered from the King of Baronia if they are found."

Pilescu muttered something under his breath and ran to where the mechanics had just finished refuelling the plane. He pushed them away and made sure nobody was still nearby. Ranni went up the steps in a trice, and tipped the inquisitive man down them. Pilescu leapt into the plane and slipped into the pilot's seat like a fish sliding into water.

There was a good deal of shouting and calling, but Pilescu ignored it. He started the plane and it ran swiftly over the ground. With a crowd of angry men rushing after it, the plane taxied to the end of the field and then rose gently into the air. Pilescu gave a short laugh.

"Now it will be known everywhere that we have the children on board. Get them out, Ranni. They were very good and they must be half smothered under those rugs."

The five children were already crawling out, excited to think of their narrow escape.

"Would we have been sent back to London?" cried Paul.

"I peeped out but the man didn't see me!" shouted Mike.

"Are we safe?" said Peggy, sitting down in her comfortable armchair seat again. "They won't send up planes to chase us, will they?"

"It wouldn't be any use," said Ranni, with a grin. "This is the fastest plane on the airfield. No – don't worry. You are all right now. But we must try to find the place where the White Swallow came down, for we do not want to land on any more airfields at the moment."

The day went on, and the children found it very thrilling to look out of the windows and see the mountains, rivers, valleys and plains slipping away below them. They longed to go down and explore them. It was wonderful to be over a strange land, and see it spread out below like a great map.

Towards the late afternoon, as the children were eating sweet biscuits and chocolate, and drinking lemonade, which by some miracle Ranni had iced, Pilescu gave a shout.

Ranni and he put their heads together over the map, and the two men spoke excitedly in their own language. Paul listened, his eyes gleaming.

"What are they saying?" cried Mike impatiently. "Tell us, Paul."

"They say that we are getting near the place where the White Swallow came down," said Paul. "Ranni says he had been in this part of the country before. He was sent to get animals for our Baronian Zoo, and he knows the people. He says they live in tiny villages, far from any towns and they keep to themselves so that few others know them."

25

The plane flew more slowly and went down lower. Ranni searched the ground below them carefully as the plane flew round in big circles.

But it was Mike who first saw what they were all eagerly looking for! He gave such a shout that the girls nearly fell off their seats, and Ranni turned round with a jump, half-expecting to see one of the children falling out of the plane!

"Ranni! Look – there's the White Swallow! Oh, look – oh, we've passed it! Pilescu, Pilesseu go back! I tell you I saw the White Swallow!"

The boy was so excited that he shook big Ranni hard by the shoulder, and would have done the same to the pilot except that he had been warned not to touch Pilescu when he was flying the machine. Ranni looked back, and gave directions to Pilescu.

In a trice the plane circled back and was soon over the exact place where the gleaming white plane stood still and silent. The children gazed at it. To think that they were looking at the very same plane they had waved good-bye to some weeks before – but this time the two famous pilots were not there to wave back.

"I can't land very near to it," said Pilescu. "I don't know how Captain Arnold managed to land there without crashing. He must be a very clever pilot."

"He is," said Peggy proudly. "He is one of the best in the world."

"I shall land on that smooth-looking bit of ground over there," said Pilescu, flying the plane lower. "We may bump a bit, children, because there are rocks there. Get ready for a jolt!"

The plane flew even lower. Then Pilescu found that he could not land with safety, and he rose into the air again. He circled round once more and then went down. This time he let down the wheels of the plane and they touched the ground. One ran over a rock and the plane tilted

26

sideways. For one moment everyone thought that it was going over, and Pilescu turned pale. He did not want to crash in the middle of an unknown country!

But the plane was marvellously built and balanced and it righted itself. All the children had been thrown roughly about in their seats, and everything in the cabin had slid to one side.

But the five children soon sorted themselves out, too excited even to look for bruises. They rushed to the door of the cockpit, each eager to be out first. Ranni shouted to them.

"Stay where you are. I must go out first to see what there is to be seen."

Pilescu stopped the engines, and the big throbbing noise died away. It seemed strange to the children when it stopped. Everything was so quiet, and their voices seemed suddenly loud. It took them a little time to stop shouting at one another, for they always had to raise their voices when they were flying.

Ranni got out of the cockpit, his gun handy. No one appeared to be in sight. They had landed on rough ground, strewn with boulders, and it was really a miracle that they had landed so well. To the left, about two miles away, a range of mountains rose. To the right was a plain, dotted with trees that the children did not know. Small hills lay in the other directions.

"Everything looks very strange, doesn't it?" said Mike. "Look at those funny red-brown daisies over there. And even the grass is different!"

"So are the birds," said Peggy, watching a brilliant red and yellow bird chasing a large fly. A green and orange bird flew round the plane, and a flock of bright blue birds passed overhead. They were not a bit like any of the birds that the children knew so well at home.

"Can we get out, Ranni?" called Mike, who was simply longing to explore. Ranni nodded. He could see no one

27

about at all. All the five children rushed out of the plane and jumped to the ground. It was lovely to feel it beneath their feet again.

"I feel as if the ground ought to bump and sway like the plane," said Nora, with a giggle. "You know – like when we get out of a boat."

"Well, I jolly well hope it doesn't," said Jack. "I don't want an earthquake just at present."

The sun was very hot. Pilescu got out some marvellous sun-hats for the five children and for himself and Ranni too. They had a sort of veil hanging down from the back to protect their spines from the sun. None of them were wearing very many clothes, but even so they felt very hot.

"I'm jolly thirsty," said Mike, mopping his head. "Let's have a drink, Ranni."

They all drank lemonade, sitting in the shade of the plane. The sun was now getting low, and Pilescu looked at the time.

"There's nothing more we can do today," he said. "Tomorrow we will find some local people and see what we can get out of them by questioning them. Ranni thinks he can make them understand, for he picked up some of their language when he was here hunting animals for the Baronian Zoo."

"Well, surely we haven't got to go to bed already?" asked Nora in dismay. "Aren't we going to explore a bit?"

"There won't be time – the sun is setting already," said Ranni. As he spoke the sun disappeared over the horizon, and darkness fell around almost at once. The children were surprised.

"Day went into night, and there was no evening," said Nora, looking round. "The stars are out, look! Oh, Mike – Jack – aren't they enormous?"

So they were. They seemed far bigger and brighter than at home. The children sat and looked at them, feeling almost afraid of their strange beauty.

Ranni kept guard overnight

Then Nora yawned. It was such an enormous yawn that it set everyone else yawning too, even big Ranni! Pilescu laughed.

"You had little sleep last night," he said. "You must have plenty tonight. In this country we must get up very early whilst it is still cool, for we shall have to rest in the shade when the sun climbs high. So you had better go to sleep very soon after Ranni has given you supper."

"Need we sleep inside the plane?" said Jack. "It's so hot there. Can we sleep out here in the cool?"

"Yes," said Ranni. "We will bring out rugs to lie on. Pilescu and I will take it in turns to keep watch."

"What will you watch for?" asked Peggy, in surprise. "Not enemies, surely?"

"Well, Captain and Mrs Arnold disappeared just here, didn't they?" said Pilescu solemnly. "I don't want to wake up in the morning and find that we have disappeared too. I should just hate to go and look for myself!"

Everyone laughed – but the children felt a little queer too. Yes – this wasn't nice, safe old England. This was a strange, unknown country, where queer, unexpected things might happen. They moved a little closer to red-bearded Pilescu. He suddenly seemed very safe and protective as he sat there in the starlight, as firm and solid as one of the big dark rocks around!

Waiting For News

Ranni provided a good meal, and Pilescu built a camp-fire, whose red glow was very comforting. "Wild animals will keep at a safe distance if we keep the fire going well," said Pilescu, putting a pile of brushwood nearby. "Ranni or I will be keeping guard tonight, and we will have a fine fire going."

Rugs were spread around the fire, whose crackling made a very cheerful sound. The five children lay down, happy and excited. They had come to the right place – and now they were going to look for Captain and Mrs Arnold. Adventures lay behind them, and even more exciting ones lay in front.

"I shall never go to sleep," said Nora, sitting up. "Never! What is that funny sound I hear, Ranni?"

"Baboons in the hills," said Ranni. "Never mind them. They won't come near us."

"And now what's *that* noise?" asked Peggy.

"Only a night-bird calling," said Ranni. "It will go on all night long, so you will have to get used to it. Lie down, Nora. If you are not asleep in two minutes I shall put you into the plane to sleep there by yourself."

This was such a terrible threat that Nora lay down at once. It was a marvellous night. The little girl lay on her back looking up at the enormous, brilliant stars that hung like bright lamps in the velvet sky. All around her she heard strange bird and animal sounds. She was warm and comfortable and the fire at her feet crackled most comfortingly. She took a last look at big Ranni, who sat with his back to the plane, gun in hand, and then shut her eyes.

"The children are all asleep," said big Ranni to Pilescu in his own language. "I think we should not have brought them on this adventure, Pilescu. We do not know what will happen. And how shall we find Captain and Mrs Arnold in this strange country? It is like seeking for a nut on an apple tree!"

Pilescu grunted. He was very tired, for he had flown the plane all the way, without letting Ranni help. Ranni was to watch three-quarters of the night, and Pilescu was to sleep – then he would take the rest of the watch.

"We will see what tomorrow brings," he said, his big

red beard spreading over his chest as his head fell forward in sleep. And then another noise was added to the other night-sounds – for Pilescu snored.

He had a wonderful snore that rose and fell with his breathing. Ranni was afraid that he would wake up the children and he nudged him.

But Pilescu did not wake. He was too tired to stir. Jack awoke when he heard the new sound and sat up in alarm. He listened in amazement.

"Ranni! Ranni! Some animal is snorting round our camp!" he called. "Are you awake? Can't you hear him?"

Ranni smothered an enormous laugh. "Lie down, Jack," he said. "It is only our good friend Pilescu. Maybe he snores like that to keep wild animals away. Even a lion might run from that noise!"

Jack grinned and lay down again. Good gracious, Pilescu made a noise as loud as the aeroplane! Well – almost, thought Jack, floating away into sleep again.

Ranni kept watch most of the night. He saw shadowy shapes not far off, and knew them to be some kind of night-hunting animals. He watched the stars move down the sky. He smelt the fragrance of the wood burning on the fire, and sometimes he reached out his hand and threw some more into the heart of the leaping flames.

A little before dawn Ranni awoke Pilescu. The big Baronian yawned loudly and opened his eyes. At once he knew where he was. He spoke to Ranni, and then went for a short walk round the camp to stretch his legs and get wide awake.

Then Ranni slept in his turn, his hand still on his gun. Pilescu watched the dawn come, and saw the whole country turn into silver and gold. When daylight was fully there he awoke everyone, for in such a hot country they must be astir early whilst the air was still cool.

The children were wild with excitement when they awoke and saw their strange surroundings. They ran round the camp, yelling and shouting, whilst Ranni cooked a delicious-smelling meal over the camp fire.

"Hie, look! Here's a kind of little lake!" shouted Jack. "Let's wash in it. Ranni, Pilescu! Could we bathe in this lake, do you think?"

"Not unless you want to be eaten by crocodiles," said Ranni.

Nora gave a scream and tore back to the camp at top speed. Ranni grinned. He went to look at the lake. It was not much more than a pond, really.

"This is all right," he said. "There are no crocodiles here. All the same, you mustn't bathe in it, for there may be slug-like things called leeches, which will fasten on to your legs and hurt you. Please remember to be very careful indeed in this strange country. Animals that you only see at the Zoo in England run wild here all over the place."

This was rather an alarming idea to the two girls. They did a very hasty wash indeed, but the three boys splashed vigorously. The air was cool and delicious, and every one of the children felt as if they could run for miles. But they only ran to the camp beside the plane, for they were so hungry, and breakfast smelt so good. The hot coffee sent its smell out, and the frying bacon sizzled and crackled in the pan.

"What's the plan for today, Pilescu?" asked Jack. "Do we find someone and ask if they know anything of the White Swallow and its pilots?"

"We are in such a remote part of Africa, that the people round here might never have seen a plane before. But Ranni is going to the nearest village to try and get news," said Pilescu, ladling out hot bacon on to the plates.

"But how does he know where the next village is?" asked Mike in wonder, looking round. "I can't see a thing."

"You haven't used your eyes," said Ranni, with a smile. "Look over there."

The children looked in the direction to which he was

pointing, where low hills lay. And they all saw at once what Ranni meant.

"A spire of smoke!" said Mike. "Yes – that means a fire – and fire means people. So that's where you are going, Ranni? Be careful, won't you?"

"My gun and I will look after one another," said big Ranni with a grin, and he tapped his pocket. "I shall not be back till nightfall, so be good whilst I am gone!"

Ranni set off soon after breakfast, carrying food with him. He wore his sun-hat, for the sun was now getting hot. The children watched him go.

"I do wish we could have gone with him," said Jack longingly. "I hope he will have some news when he comes back."

"Come, you children can wash these dishes in water from the pool," called Pilescu. "Soon it will be too hot to do anything. Before it is, we must also find some firewood ready for tonight."

Pilescu kept the children busy until the sun rose higher. Then when its rays beat down like fire, he made them get into the shade of the plane. Paul did not want to, for he enjoyed the heat, but Pilescu ordered him to go with the others.

"Pilescu, it is not for you to order me," said the little Prince, sticking his chin into the air.

"Little Paul, I am in command now," said the big Baronian, gently but sternly. "You are my lord, but I am your captain in this adventure. Do as I say."

"Paul, don't be an idiot, or I'll come and get you into the shade by the scruff of your neck," called Mike. "If you get sunstroke, you'll be ill and will have to be flown back to London at once."

Paul trotted into the shade like a lamb. He lay down by the others. Soon they were so thirsty that Pilescu found himself continually getting in and out of the plane with supplies of cool lemonade from the little refrigerator there.

34

The children slept in the midday heat. Pilescu was sleepy too, but he kept guard on the little company, wondering how big Ranni was getting on. When the sun began to slip down the coppery sky, he mopped his brow and awoke the children.

"There is some tinned fruit in the plane," he told Nora. "Get it, and open the tins. It will be delicious to eat whilst we wait for the day to cool."

Ranni did not come back until the sun had set with the same suddenness as the day before. The children watched and waited impatiently for him, and lighted the bonfire early to guide him.

Pilescu was not worried, for he knew that, although the spire of smoke had looked fairly near, it was really far away – and he knew also that Ranni would not be able to walk far when the midday heat fell on the land like flames from a furnace.

The little company sat round the fire, and above them hung the big bright stars. They all watched for Ranni to return.

"I do wonder if he will have any news," said Nora impatiently. "Oh, Ranni, do hurry! I simply can't wait!"

But she had to wait and so did everyone else. It was late before they heard the big Baronian shouting loudly to them. They all leapt up and trained their eyes to see him.

"There he is!" shouted Jack, who had eyes like a cat's in the dark. "Look – see that moving shadow among those rocks?"

The shadow gave a shout and everyone yelled back in delight.

"Ranni! Hurrah! He's back!"

"What news, Ranni?"

"Hurry, Ranni, do hurry!"

The big Baronian came up to the fire. He was tired and hot. He dropped down to the rugs and wiped his hot forehead. Pilescu gave him a jug of lemonade and he drank it all in one gulp.

"Have you news, Ranni?" asked Pilescu.

35

"Yes – I have. And strange news it is too," said Ranni. "Give me some more sandwiches or biscuits, Pilescu, and I will tell my tale. Are you all safe and well?"

"Perfectly," said Pilescu. "Now speak, Ranni. What is this strange news you bring?"

Big Ranni Tells A Queer Tale

Ranni lighted his pipe and puffed at it. Everyone waited for him to begin, wondering what he had to tell them.

"I found a small camp," said Ranni. "Not more than four or five men were there. They had been out hunting. When they saw me coming they all hid behind the rocks in terror."

"But why were they so afraid?" asked Nora in wonder.

"Well, I soon found out," said Ranni. "I can speak their language a little, because I have hunted round about this country before, as you know. It seems that they thought I was one of the strange folk from the Secret Mountain."

"From the Secret Mountain!" cried Mike. "What do you mean? What secret mountain?"

"Be patient and listen," said Pilescu, who was listening closely. "Go on, Ranni."

"Somewhere not far from here is a strange mountain," said Ranni. "It is called the Secret Mountain because for years a secret and strange tribe of people have made their home in the centre of it. They are not like the people round about at all."

"What are they like, then?" asked Jack.

"As far as I can make out their skins are a queer creamy-yellow, and their beards and hair are red, like Pilescu's and mine. They are thin and tall, and their eyes

36

are green. No one belonging to any other tribe is allowed to mix with them, and no one has ever found out the entrance into the Secret Mountain."

"Ranni! This is a most wonderful story!" cried Prince Paul, his eyes shining with excitement. "Is it really true? Oh, do let's go and find the secret mountain at once, this very minute!"

"Don't be an idiot, Paul," said Mike, giving him a push. The little Prince was very excitable, and Mike and Jack often had to stop him when he wanted to rush off at once and do something. "Be quiet and listen to Ranni."

"All the people that live anywhere near are afraid of the Folk of the Secret Mountain," said Ranni. "They think that they are very fierce, and they do not come this way if they can possibly help it. When they saw me, with my red hair, they really thought I was a man from the Secret Mountain, and they were too terrified even to run away."

"Did you ask them if they knew anything about Daddy and Mummy?" asked Peggy eagerly.

"Of course," said Ranni. "They knew nothing – but tomorrow a man is coming to our camp here, who saw the White Swallow come down, and who may be able to tell us something. But I think, children, that there is no doubt that Captain and Mrs Arnold were captured by the Folk of the Secret Mountain. We don't know why – but I am sure they are there."

"We cannot search for them, then," said Pilescu. "We must fly to the nearest town and bring a proper search party back here."

"No, no, Pilescu," cried everyone in dismay.

"*We* are going to look for our parents," said Mike proudly. "Pilescu, this is the third great adventure we children have had, and I tell you we are all plucky and daring. We will *not* fly away and leave others to follow this adventure."

All the children vowed and declared that they would

not go with Ranni and Pilescu, and the two men looked at one another over the camp fire.

"They are like a litter of tiger-cubs," said Ranni in his own language to Pilescu.

Prince Paul laughed excitedly. He knew that Ranni wanted to follow the adventure himself, and that this meant that Paul too would be with him, for he would not leave his little master now. Paul turned to the other children.

"It's all right," he said. "We shan't go! Ranni means to help us."

For a long time that night the little camp talked over Ranni's strange tale. Where was the Secret Mountain? Who were the strange red-haired people who lived there? Why had they captured Captain and Mrs Arnold? How in the world were the searchers to find the way into the mountain if not even the people round about know it? For a long time all these questions were discussed again and again.

Then Pilescu looked at his watch. "It is very late!" he exclaimed. "Children, you must sleep. Ranni, I will keep watch tonight, for you must be very tired."

"Very well," said Ranni. "You shall take the first half of the night and I will take the other. We can do nothing but wait until tomorrow, when the man who saw the White Swallow will come to talk to us."

Very soon all the camp was asleep, except Pilescu, who sat with his gun in hand, watching the moving animal-shapes that prowled some distance away, afraid to come nearer because of the fire. Pilescu loved an adventure as much as anyone, and he thought deeply about the Folk of the Secret Mountain, with their creamy-yellow skins, red hair and curious green eyes.

The big Baronian was brave and fierce, as were all the men from the far-off land of Baronia, where Paul's father was king. He was afraid of nothing. The only thing he did

38

not like was taking the five children into danger – but, as Ranni had said, they were like tiger-cubs, fierce and daring, and had already been through some astonishing adventures by themselves.

Morning came, and with it came the native who had seen the White Swallow come down. He was very tall, but with a sly and rather cruel face. Carrying three spears for him came a small, thin boy, with a sharp face and such a merry twinkle in his eyes that all the children liked him at once.

"Who is that boy?" asked Jack, curiously. Ranni asked the man, and he replied, making a scornful face.

"It's his nephew," said Ranni. "He is the naughty boy of the family, and is always running away, exploring the country by himself. Children of this tribe are not allowed to do this – they have to go with the hunters and be properly trained. This little chap is disobedient and wild, so his uncle has taken him in hand, as you see."

"I like the look of the boy," said Jack. "But I don't like the uncle at all. Ask him about the White Swallow, Ranni. See if he knows anything about Captain and Mrs Arnold."

Ranni did not speak the man's language very well, but he could understand it better. The man spoke a lot, waving his arms about, and almost acting the whole thing so that the children could nearly understand his story without understanding his words.

"He says he was hunting not far from here, keeping a good look-out for any of the Secret Mountain Folk, when he heard the sky making a strange noise," said Ranni. "He looked up, and saw a great white bird that said 'r-r-r-r-r-r-r-r,' as loudly as a thunderstorm."

The children shouted with laughter at this funny description of an aeroplane. Ranni could not help grinning, even though he knew the man had probably never seen a plane before, and went on with his translation.

"He says the big white bird flew lower, and came down

over there. He stayed behind his tree without moving. He thought the big white bird would see him and eat him."

Again everyone laughed. The tribesman grinned too, showing two rows of flashing white teeth. The little boy behind joined in the laughter, but stopped very suddenly when his uncle turned round and hit him hard on the side of the head.

"Oh my goodness!" shouted Jack in surprise. "Why shouldn't he laugh too?"

"Children of this tribe must not laugh if their elders are present," said Ranni. "This man's nephew must often get into serious trouble, I should think! He looks as if he is on the point of giggling every minute!"

The man went on with his story. He told how he had seen two people climb out of the big white bird, which amazed him very much. Then he saw something that frightened him even more than seeing the aeroplane and the pilots. He saw some of the Folk of the Secret Mountain, with their flaming red hair and pale skins!

He had been so interested in the aeroplane that he had stayed watching behind his tree – but the sight of the Secret Mountain Folk had given him such a scare that his legs had come to life and he had run back towards his village.

"So you didn't see what happened to the White Bird people?" asked Ranni, deeply disappointed. The man shook his head. The small boy watching, imitated him so perfectly that all the children laughed, disappointed though they were.

The man looked behind to see what everyone was smiling at and caught his nephew making faces. He strode over to him and knocked him down flat on the ground. The boy gave a yell, sat up and rubbed his head.

"What a horrid fellow this man is," said Pilescu in disgust. "Ranni, ask him if he can tell us the way to the Secret Mountain."

Ranni asked him. The man showed signs of fear as he answered.

"He says yes, he knows the way to the mountain, but he does not know the way inside," said Ranni.

"Ask him if he will take us there," said Pilescu. "Tell him we will pay him well if he does."

At first the man shook his head firmly when Ranni asked him. But when Pilescu took a mirror from the cabin of the plane, and showed the man himself in it, making signs to him that he would give it to him as well, the man was tempted.

"He thinks the mirror is wonderful. He is in the mirror as well as outside it," translated Ranni with a grin. "He says it would be a good thing to have it, because then if he is hurt or wounded, it will not matter – the man inside the mirror, which is himself too, will be all right, and he will be him instead."

Everyone smiled to hear this. The man had never seen a mirror before, he had only caught sight of himself in pools. It seemed as if another himself was in the strange gleaming thing that the red-haired man was offering him. He stood in front of the mirror, making awful faces, and laughing.

Ranni asked him again if he would show them the way to the Secret Mountain if he gave him the mirror. The man nodded. The mirror was too much for him. Why, he had never seen anything like it before.

"Tell him we will start tomorrow at dawn," said Pilescu. "I want to make sure that we have everything we need before we set off. Also I want to look at the engines of the White Swallow and our own plane to see that they are all ready to take off, should we find Captain and Mrs Arnold, and want to leave in a hurry!"

The children were in a great state of excitement. They hardly knew how to keep still that day, even when the great heat came down, and they had to lie in the shade,

41

panting and thirsty. It was so exciting to think that they really were to set off the next morning to the strange Secret Mountain.

"I'm jolly glad Ranni and Pilescu are coming with us," said Nora. "I do love adventures – but I can't help feeling a little bit funny in the middle of me when I think of those strange folk that live in the middle of a forgotten mountain.

The Coming Of Mafumu

Pilescu and Ranni tinkered about with the White Swallow, which stood not very far off, and with their own plane most of the day. The children, of course, had thoroughly examined the White Swallow, feeling very sad to think that Captain and Mrs Arnold had had to leave it so mysteriously.

Mike had thought that there might have been a note left to tell what had happened, but the children had found nothing at all.

"That's not to be wondered at," said Pilescu. "If they had had time to write a note, they would have had time also to fly off in the plane! As far as I can see there is nothing wrong with the White Swallow at all – though I can see where some small thing has been cleverly mended. It seems to me that Captain and Mrs Arnold were taken by surprise and had not time to do anything at all."

"Both planes are fit to fly off at a moment's notice," said Ranni, appearing beside Pilescu, very oily and black, his red hair hanging wet and lank over his forehead.

"Ought we to leave anyone on guard?" asked Mike. "Suppose we come back and find that the planes have been damaged?"

Ranni frowned. "We will lock them of course, but I don't

42

think anyone would damage them. I just hope a herd of elephants doesn't come and trample through them! We must just leave the planes and hope for the best."

Pilescu had got ready big packages of food and a few warm clothes and rugs. Paul laughed when he saw the woollen jerseys.

"Good gracious, Pilescu, what are we taking those things for? I'd like to go about in a little pair of shorts and nothing else, like that small boy wears!"

"If we go into the mountains it will be much cooler," said Pilescu. "You may be glad of jerseys then."

The day passed slowly by. The children thought it would never end.

"Why is it that time always goes so slowly when you are looking forward to something lovely in the future?" grumbled Mike. "Honestly, this day seems like a week."

But it passed at last, and the sudden night-time came. Monkeys chattered somewhere around, and big frogs in the washing-pool set up their usual tremendous croaking.

Next day, at dawn, their guide arrived, and behind him, as usual, came the little boy, his nephew, wearing his scanty shorts. The boy wore no hat at all, and the five children wondered why in the world he didn't get sunstroke.

"I suppose he's coming too," said Jack, pleased. "I wonder what his name is. Ask him, Ranni."

The boy grinned and showed all his white teeth when Ranni shouted to him. He answered in a shrill voice:

"Mafumu, Mafumu!"

"His name is Mafumu," said Ranni. "All right, Mafumu, don't shout your name at us any more!"

Mafumu was so overjoyed at being spoken to by the big Ranni that he kept shouting and wouldn't stop.

"Mafumu, Mafumu, Mafumu!"

He was stopped in the usual way by his uncle, who slapped him hard on the head. Mafumu fell over, made a face at his uncle's back, and got up again. The children were very glad he was coming with them. They really couldn't help liking the cheeky little boy, with his twinkling black eyes and his flashing smile.

Ranni closed and locked the entrance door of the cockpit. Then, with a few backward glances at the two gleaming planes, the little company set off on their new adventure. They were silent as they left the camp, for all of them were wondering what might happen in the near future.

Then Mafumu broke the silence by lifting up his shrill voice and singing a strange slow song.

"Sounds a bit like one of the hymns we have in church," said Mike. "Oh no – his uncle is going for him again. Golly, how I wish he'd stop – he is always hitting poor Mafumu."

Mafumu was slapped into silence. He came behind the whole company, sulking, carrying a simply enormous load. His uncle also carried a great many packages, balanced most marvellously on his head. Ranni explained that the natives were used to carrying goods this way and thought nothing of taking heavy loads for many, many miles.

Soon the open space where the planes had landed was left behind. The little company came towards what looked like a wood, but which was really a small forest that reached almost to the foot of the nearest mountain.

It was very dark in the forest after the glare of the sunlight. The trees were so thick, and heavy rope-like creepers hung down from them everywhere. The children could see no path at all to follow, but the tribesman led them steadily on, never once upsetting any of the many packages piled up on his head.

The chattering of monkeys was everywhere. The children saw the little brown creatures peering down at them, and laughed with delight to see a mother monkey holding a tiny baby in her arms. Other wild creatures scuttled away, and once their guide gave a loud shout and flung his spear at a large snake that slid silently away.

"Oooh," said Nora, startled. "I forgot there might be snakes here. I hope I don't tread on one. I say, isn't this an exciting forest? It's like one in a fairy-tale. I feel as if witches and fairies might come out at any moment."

"Well, just make sure you don't wander off looking for fairy castles," said Pilescu. There are probably lots of snakes and insects in the undergrowth, and you can be sure our guide is taking us by the safest path."

Mafumu was enjoying himself. He was a long way behind his uncle, for the guide led the way, and Mafumu came at the tail of the company. Next to him was Jack, and Mafumu was doing his best to make friends with him.

He picked a brilliant scarlet blossom from one of the trees and tried to stick it behind Jack's ear. Jack was most annoyed, and the others laughed till they cried at the sight of Jack with a red flower behind his ear. Mafumu thought that Jack didn't like the colour of the flower, so he picked a bright blue one and tried that.

Jack found himself decorated with this flower, and he took it from his ear crossly, whilst the others giggled again.

"Shut up, Mafumu," he said.

Mafumu was very quick at picking up what he heard the children say, even though he did not understand the words. "Shutup, shutup, shutup," he repeated in delight. He called to Ranni. "Shutup, shutup, shutup!"

Nobody could help laughing at Mafumu. He was so silly, so cheerful, so quick, and even when his uncle was unkind to him he was smiling a moment later.

He still badly wanted to make friends with Jack, and the next present he made to the boy was a large and juicy-looking fruit of some sort. He pressed it into Jack's hand, flashing his white teeth, and saying some thing that sounded like "Ammakeepa-lotti-loo."

45

Jack looked at the fruit. He smelt it. It had a most delicious scent, and smelt as sweet as honey. "Is it safe to eat this, Ranni?" he called.

Ranni looked round and nodded. "Yes – that is a rare fruit, only found in forests like these. Did Mafumu find it for you?"

"Yes," said Jack. "He keeps on giving me things. I wish he wouldn't."

"Well, tell him to give them to me instead," cried Peggy. "I'd love to have those beautiful flowers and that delicious-looking yellow fruit. It looks like a mixture of an extra-large pear and a giant grape!"

Jack tasted it. It was the loveliest fruit he had ever had, so sweet that it seemed to be made of honey. The boy gave a taste to the two girls. They made faces of delight, and Nora called to Mafumu.

"Find some more please, Mafumu; find some more!"

"Shutup, shutup, shutup," replied Mafumu cheerfully, quite understanding what Nora meant, and thinking that his answer was correct. He disappeared into the forest and was gone such a long time that the children began to be alarmed.

"Ranni! Do you think Mafumu is all right?" shouted Jack from the back of the line. "He's been gone for ages. He won't get lost, will he?"

Ranni spoke to the guide in front. The man laughed and made some sort of quick answer.

"He says that Mafumu knows his forest as an ant knows its own anthill," translated Ranni. "He says, too, that he would not care at all if Mafumu were eaten by a crocodile or caught by a leopard. He doesn't seem at all fond of his small nephew, does he?"

"I think he's a horrid man," said Peggy. "My goodness – are there leopards about?"

"Well, you needn't worry even if there are," said Ranni. "Pilescu and I have guns, and our leader has plenty of spears ready."

It was cool and dark in the forest and the little company were able to go for a long way without resting, twisting and turning through the trees. Frogs croaked somewhere, and birds called harshly. Jack spotted some brightly coloured parrots, and there were some rather queer squirrel-like creatures that hopped from branch to branch. The monkeys were most interested in the children, and a little crowd of them swung through the trees, following the company for quite a long way.

At last the forest came to an end. The trees became fewer, and the sun shone between, making golden freckles on the ground that danced and moved as the trees waved their branches.

"Well, that couldn't have been a very big forest if it only took us such a short time to go through," said Mike.

"It is really a very big one," said Pilescu. "But we have only gone through a corner of it. If we went deeper into it we should not be able to get along. We should have to take axes and knives to cut our way through."

The children were still worried about Mafumu, but he suddenly appeared again, bent nearly double under his old load and carrying a new load of the juicy-looking yellow fruit. He gave some to each child, grinning cheerfully.

"Oh, thanks awfully," said Mike. "Golly, this is just what I wanted – I *was* thirsty! This fruit melts in my mouth. Thanks awfully, Mafumu."

"Thanksawfully, shutup," said the little boy in delight.

"I think we'll all have a rest here," said Pilescu. "The sun is still high in the sky and we can't walk any further for it will be too hot once we are out of the forest. We will go on again when the sun is lower."

Nobody felt very hungry, for they were all so hot. Mafumu found some other kind of fruit for everybody, not nearly so nice, but still, very juicy and sweet. His uncle ate no fruit, but took something from a pouch and chewed that.

All the children fell asleep in the noonday sun except

47

Mafumu. He squatted down beside Jack and watched the boy closely. Jack grinned at him and even when he slept Mafumu stayed by his side.

The grown-ups sat talking quietly together. Ranni looked round at the sleeping company. "The children have done well today," he said to Pilescu. "They must have a good night's rest tonight as well, for tomorrow we must climb high."

"I wish that this adventure was over, and not just beginning," said Pilescu uneasily, fanning Paul's hot face with a spray of leaves. The boy was so sound asleep that he felt nothing.

But not one of the children wished that the adventure was over. No – to be in the middle of one was the most exciting thing in the world!

A Very Long March

For two whole days the company marched valiantly onwards. The children were all good walkers except Paul, and as Ranni carried him on his shoulders when he was very tired, that helped a good deal.

They had now come to the mountains and the guide was leading them steadily upwards. It was tiring to climb always, but the children soon got used to it. Mafumu did not seem to mind anything. He skipped along, and went just as fast uphill as down. He had picked up some more words now, and used them often, much to the children's amusement.

"Goodgracious, shutup, hallo, thanksawfully," he would chant as he skipped along, his load of packages balanced marvellously and never falling. "Hurryup, hurryup, hallo!"

"Isn't he an idiot?" said Jack. But although the children

laughed at his antics, they all liked the cheerful boy enormously. He brought them curious things to eat – toadstools that were marvellous when cooked – strange leaves that tasted of peppermint and were good to chew – fruit of all kinds, some sweet, some bitter, some too queer-tasting to eat, though Mafumu ate everything, and smacked his lips and rubbed his round tummy in delight.

On the second day, when the children were all climbing steadily, Mafumu saw a clump of bushes high up some way in front of them. They were hung with brilliant blue berries, which Mafumu knew were sweet and juicy. He took a short cut away from the path, and climbed to the bushes.

He stripped them of the blue berries and began to jump back to join the company. But on the way his foot caught against a loose stone that rattled down the hillside and fell against his uncle's leg.

In a fury the guide sprang at his nephew and caught hold of him. He beat him hard with his spear, and the little boy cried out in pain, trying his best to wriggle away.

"Oh, stop him, stop him!" yelled Jack, who hated un- kindness of any sort. "Mafumu was only getting berries for us. Stop, stop!"

But the guide did not stop, and Jack ran up to him. He wrenched the spear out of the man's hand and threw it down the hillside in anger, his face red with rage.

The spear went clattering down and was lost. The guide turned on Jack, but Ranni was beside him, talking sternly. The man listened, his eyes flashing. He said nothing, but turned to lead the way up the mountain-side once more.

"What did you say to him, Ranni?" asked Mike.

"I told him he would not get paid if he hit anyone again," said Ranni shortly. "He was just about to strike Jack. Don't interfere again, Jack. I'll do the interfering."

"Sorry," said Jack, though he was still boiling with rage. Mafumu had got up from the ground, his face and arms

49

covered with bruises. He ran to Jack and hugged him, speaking excitedly in his own language.

"Stop it, for goodness sake, Mafumu," said Jack uncomfortably. "Oh golly, I wish you wouldn't. Do let go, Mafumu!"

"He says he will be your friend for ever," said Ranni with a grin. "He says he will leave his uncle and his tribe and come and be with the wonderful boy all his life. He says you are a king of boys!"

"King Jack, the king of boys!" shouted Mike, clapping Jack on the shoulder.

"Shut up," growled Jack.

"Shutup, shutup, shutup," echoed Mafumu happily, letting go of Jack and walking as close to his hero as he possibly could.

After that, of course, Mafumu adored Jack even more than before, and Jack got used to seeing the little boy always at his heels, like a shadow. He could not get rid of him, so he put up with it, secretly rather proud that Mafumu should have picked him out to be his friend.

It got steadily cooler as they all climbed higher. The mountains seemed never-ending.

"We shall never, never get to the top," said poor Peggy, who had started a blister on one heel.

"We're not going to the top," said Mike. "All we are doing is climbing to a place where we can pass between two mountains. Ranni says we shall strike off to the east there, by that enormous rock, and make our way to a place where this mountain and the next one meet. There is a pass between them – and from there we can see the Secret Mountain!"

"Golly!" said Paul. "Are we as near as all that?"

"Well – not awfully near," said Mike. "But we'll get there sooner or later. Have you rubbed that stuff that Ranni gave you, all over your heel, Peggy?"

"Yes," said Peggy. "And I've put a wad of cotton-wool over the blister too. I shall be all right."

"Good girl," said Mike. "I don't think things like blisters ought to creep into adventures like ours!"

Everyone laughed. They had put on woollen jerseys now and were glad of them, especially when clouds rolled down the mountain-side and covered them in mist. They were glad of hot drinks, too, heated over a fire of sticks.

Mafumu always knew where water was, and he brought it to the fire in the saucepan that Ranni gave him. It was easy to make hot cocoa with plenty of sugar in it from one of the packages, and how good it tasted!

They slept in a cave that night, stretched out on the rugs. The girls cuddled together for it was very cold. Mafumu slept on nothing at all, and did not seem to feel the cold in the least. He really was a most tough little boy.

Ranni and Pilescu did not both sleep at the same time, but took turns at keeping watch – not only for any mountain leopard that might come into the cave, but also for any of the Folk from the Secret Mountain! They did not know what such strange people might do.

Mafumu was curled up on the rocky ground by Jack. Jack had offered him a share of the rug, but the boy would not take any of Jack's coverings. He even tried to cover Jack up, much to the amusement of everyone else.

"He wants to be your nurse," chuckled Mike.

"Oh, do stop making jokes like that," grumbled poor Jack. "I can't help Mafumu behaving like this, can I? He will keep on doing it."

"Tomorrow we shall see the Secret Mountain," said Nora sleepily. "I'm just longing to get my first glimpse of it. I wonder what it will be like."

"I wonder if Mafumu's unpleasant uncle can possibly tell us any way to get into it," said Mike. "It's not going to be much good gazing at a secret mountain, if we don't know the secret of getting into the middle of it!"

"Do you suppose there are halls and rooms and passages in it?" said Peggy, cuddling closer to Nora to try and get warm. "How I do love secret things!"

Mafumu took hold of Jack's rug and pulled it more closely over the elder boy and for once in a way Jack did not stop him. The boy was almost asleep. He lay there in the cave, his eyes closing.

"Goodnight, Mafumu," said Jack sleepily.

"Hallo, goodnight," answered Mafumu, happy to be with his new friends.

"Tomorrow we shall see the – the – Secret – Mountain," murmured Jack, and then fell fast asleep.

Tomorrow – yes, tomorrow!

The Secret Mountain

The next day dawned very misty. White clouds rolled round about the mountain pass, and it was difficult to see very far ahead. The children were most disappointed.

But as they walked steadily upwards towards the rocky pass between the two mountains, the sun began to shine more strongly through the mists, and soon the last fragments disappeared.

"Isn't everything glorious!" cried Mike, looking round. Below them lay the great hillside they had climbed, and in the distance, stretching for miles, they could see the rolling country of Africa. Above them towered the mountains and overhead was the blazing sky.

"All the colours look so much brighter here," said Peggy, picking a brilliant orange flower and sticking it into her hat. "Oh, Mafumu, for goodness sake!"

Mafumu had darted forward when he saw Peggy picking

52

the flower, and had plucked a great armful of the orange flowers, which he now presented to her. The little girl laughed and took them. She didn't know what to do with them, but in the end she and Nora stuck them all round their hats.

"I feel like a walking garden now," said Nora. "I wish Mafumu wouldn't be so generous!"

"Soon we shall arrive at the place from which we get our first glimpse of the Secret Mountain," said Ranni.

That made everyone walk forward even more eagerly. For three hours they climbed towards the rocky pass, the guide leading the way, finding a path even when it seemed almost impossible to get by. Sometimes there was hard climbing to be done, and Ranni and Pilescu had to pull and push the children to get them up the hillside or over big rocks. Sometimes they passed through thick little copses of strange trees, where brilliant birds called to one another. It was all unknown country and most exciting.

At last they reached the top of the pass. From here they could see the other side of the range of mountains. Truly it was a marvellous place to stand! From this mountain peep-hole the little company could see both east and west – rolling country behind them for miles, disappearing into purple hills – and in front another range of mountains towering high into the sky, with a narrow valley in between the mountains they were on, and the range opposite.

Everyone stood silent, even the guide. It was surely the most wonderful sight in the world, the children thought. Then Paul spoke eagerly.

"Which is the Secret Mountain? Where is it? Quick, tell us!"

Ranni spoke to the guide, and he raised his spear and pointed with it. He spoke shortly to Ranni.

Ranni turned to the listening children. "Do you see that mountain over there, with clouds rolling round it? Wait till they clear a little, and you will see that the mountain has a curiously flat top. You will also see that it has a yellowish look, because, so this fellow says, a rare yellow bush grows there, which at some season of the year turns a fiery red."

This all sounded rather weird. The children gazed across to the opposite mountains – and each saw the one that had clouds covering it. As they watched, the clouds uncurled themselves, and became thinner and thinner, at last disappearing altogether. And then everyone could see the curious Secret Mountain!

It stood out boldy from the other because of its yellow appearance, and also because of its strange summit. This was almost flat, like a table-top. The guide raised his spear again, and pointed, muttering something to Ranni.

"He says that he has heard that the Folk of the Mountain sometimes appear on the top of it, and that they worship the sun from there," said Ranni. "Though how anyone could see people so far away I can't imagine. However, it is quite possible that there is a way up inside the mountain to the top."

"Isn't it strange to think of a tribe of people taking such a queer home, and living there apart from everyone else?" said Jack in wonder.

"Oh, that has often happened," said Pilescu. "Sometimes there are tribes living apart from others in the middle of dense forests – sometimes on islands – sometimes even in deserts. But a mountain certainly seems one of the strangest places to choose."

"I suppose they come out to hunt, and that is how the other people know about them," said Mike.

"I think you are right," said Ranni. "Well – there's the wonderful Secret Mountain – and here we are. The mountain won't come to us, so we must go to the mountain. Shall we set off again, Pilescu?"

The guide spoke rapidly to Ranni, making faces and waving his arms about.

"He says he doesn't want to come any further," said Ranni. "Is it any good his coming?" He swears he doesn't know any way into the mountain."

"He's going to come with us all the way," said Pilescu firmly. "He may find that he knows the way in after all, once we get there! Anyway, he won't get paid if he doesn't come."

"Where *is* the money?" asked Nora. "It's not being carried along with us, is it?"

"Of course not," said Ranni with a laugh.

"Well, did you put it back into the cabin of the plane?" said Jack. "You locked that."

"No. I wrapped up the money carefully and hid it under the low brances of that big tree by the washing-pool before we left," said Ranni. "I shall tell our guide where it is when he has done his job – but not before!"

"That's a clever idea," said Peggy. Ranni turned to the man and spoke to him again. He shook his head violently. Ranni shrugged his shoulders, and bade the little company set off.

They made their way along a rocky path, leaving the guide and Mafumu behind. But they had not gone very far before loud shouts came from the tribesman, and the children saw him leaping along to catch them up. Mafumu trotted behind, his face was one big smile.

His uncle spoke with Ranni, but Ranni shook his head. The children could quite well guess what was happening – the man was asking to be paid, and Ranni was being determined. In the end the guide agreed to go with them once more, and Ranni promised to tell him where the money was as soon as they reached the Secret Mountain.

It was a good thing that their guide went with them, for the way he led them was one which they would never have found for themselves. It was a hidden way, so that the little company would not be seen by any watchers on the Secret Mountain.

Ranni and Pilescu had had no idea that there was this hidden path to the mountain. They would have tried to lead the party across the valley, over marshy ground, or through such thickly growing bushes that it would have been almost impossible to make their way through.

As it was, the tribesman avoided these, and took them to a narrow river, not much more than a large stream, that flowed along swiftly towards the mountain. This stream was almost completely covered in by bushes and trees that met above the water, making a kind of green tunnel, below which the river gurgled and bubbled.

"Golly! What an exciting river!" cried Jack, thrilled to see the dim green tunnel. "How are we going to get along? Is it shallow enough to wade down the stream?"

"In parts it would be, but I don't fancy doing that," said Pilescu. "What is the fellow doing – and Mafumu too? I believe they are making rough rafts for us!"

"What fun!" cried Paul, and he ran to watch the two workers.

Mafumu was busy bringing armfuls of stuff that looked rather like purple cork to his uncle. He had got it from a marshy piece of ground. It smelt horrible.

"Is it cork?" said Paul.

"No – it looks more like some sort of fungus, or enormous toadstool," said Pilescu. "Look at his uncle binding it together with creeper-ropes!"

In two hours' time four small rafts of the horrible-smelling cork were made. They looked rather queer and they smelt even queerer, but they floated marvellously, bobbing about on the water like strange ducks. The children were delighted. It was going to be splendid fun to float down the hidden river, under a green archway of trees, right up to the Secret Mountain!

"Our guide says that his tribe always use these queer rafts to get quickly down this valley, which they fear because of the Mountain Folk," said Ranni. "The stream goes right round the foot of the Secret Mountain, and joins a river round there. Then it goes into the next valley, which is a fine hunting-ground used by Mafumu's tribe. He says that the rafts don't last long – they gradually fall to bits – but last just long enough to take a man into the next valley with safety!"

Pilescu and Paul got on to one raft. It wobbled dangerously, but sank hardly at all into the water. There was only just room for the two of them to squat. They held on to the creeper-ropes that bound the raft together. Then down the stream they went, bobbing like corks.

Ranni and Nora went next. Mike and Peggy went together, and last of all came the guide, Jack, and, of course, Mafumu, who was determined not to leave Jack for even a minute!

It was a strange journey, a little frightening. The trees met overhead and were so thick that no sunlight pierced through to the swift stream. The only light there was glowed a dim green.

"Your face looks green!" cried Peggy to Mike, as they set off together down the strange river-tunnel.

"So does yours!" said Mike. "Everything looks green. I feel as if we must be under water! It's because we can't see any daylight at all – only the green of the trees and of the stream below."

The stream became swifter as it ran down the valley. In no place did the trees break – the tunnel was complete the whole way. The rafts were really splendid, but towards the end of the journey they began to break up a little. The outside edges fell off, and the rafts began to loosen from the creeper-ropes.

"Hie! We shall soon be in the water!" yelled Ranni. "Where do we land?"

The guide shouted something back. "Well, that's a good thing!" cried Ranni. "We're nearly there, children."

The bobbing rafts spun slowly round and round as they

57

Paul's raft spun into a pool

went along. It really was a most peculiar journey, but the children loved every minute. They were sad to see their rafts gradually coming to pieces, getting smaller and smaller!

Suddenly the stream ran into a large still pool. It ran out again the other end of the pool, but when the guide gave a loud shout, everyone knew that their journey's end had come. The pool was their stopping place. If they went any further they would go right round the mountain and into the next valley.

Ranni's raft spun into the quiet pool, and by pulling at the branches of a nearby tree he dragged himself and Paul to the bank, on which grew thick bushes. All the others followed, though Mike and Peggy nearly sailed right on, for their raft was right in the very middle of the current! However, they managed to swing it round and joined the others.

"If I don't get off my raft it will disappear from under me," said big Ranni, whose weight had made his raft break up more than those of the others. Everyone jumped off their rafts and stood on the banks of the pool. They had to stand on rotting branches and roots, for the trees and bushes grew so thickly there that the bare ground could not be seen.

"Well – we've arrived," said Pilescu. "And now – where's the mountain? We should be at the foot."

The guide, with a frown on his face, took them through the thick bushes, squeezing his way with difficulty, and came to a tall tree. He climbed it, beckoning the others behind him.

Ranni climbed up, and one by one everyone followed. They all wanted to see what the man had to show them. Monkeys fled chattering from the branches as the little company climbed upwards, helping themselves by using the long creepers which hung down like strong ropes.

Their guide took them almost to the top of the tree. It towered over the bush below, and from its top could be seen, quite close at hand, the Secret Mountain!

Everyone stared in amazement at the Secret Mountain

A Pleasant Surprise

The Secret Mountain towered up steeply. It was covered by the curious yellow bushes, which gave it its strange appearance from a distance. The bushes had yellow leaves and waxy-white flowers over which hovered brilliant butterflies and insects of every kind.

But it was the mountain itself that held the children's eyes. It was so steep. It looked quite impossible to climb. It rose up before their eyes, enormous, seeming to touch the sky. They were very near to it, and Nora was quite frightened by its bigness.

The tribesman frowned as he looked at it and muttered strings of queer-sounding words to himself. He was plainly going no further. Only the money he had been promised had made him come so far. He slid down the tree and spoke rapidly to Ranni.

Ranni told him where he would find his reward, and the man nodded, showing all his white teeth. He called to Mafumu, and the two of them disappeared into the bushes.

"Hie, Mafumu – say good-bye!" yelled Jack, very sorry indeed to see the merry little fellow going. But his uncle had Mafumu firmly by one ear and the boy could do nothing.

"Well, he might at least have said good-bye," said Peggy. "I did like him. I wish he was going with us."

"Did Mafumu's uncle give you any idea at all as to how we might get into the mountain?" Mike asked Ranni. Ranni shook his head.

"All he would say was that we should have to walk through the rock!" he said. "I don't think he really knew what he meant. It was just something he had heard."

"Walk through the rock!" said Jack. "That sounds a bit like Ali Baba and the Forty Thieves. Do you remember – the robbers made their home in a cave inside a hill – and when the robber chief said 'Open Sesame!' a rock slid aside – and they all went in!"

Pilescu and Ranni did not know the tale, and they listened with interest.

"Well, the way in *may* be by means of a moving rock," said Ranni. "But, good gracious, we can't go all round this enormous mountain looking for a moving rock! And if we did find it, I'm sure we should not know the secret of moving it!"

They were all sitting down at the foot of the tree, eating a meal, for they were hungry and tired. It was hot in the valley, even in the shade of the trees. The calls of the birds, the hum of insects and the chattering of monkeys sounded all the time. The sun was sinking low, and Pilescu made up his mind that they must all camp where they were for the night. He glanced up at the enormous branches of the tree they were under, and wondered if, by spreading out the rugs in a big fork halfway up, the children could sleep there safely.

"I don't like letting the children sleep on the ground tonight," he said to Ranni. "I daren't light a fire to keep wild creatures away, because if we do we shall attract the attention of the Mountain Folk – and we don't want to be surrounded and captured in the night. Do you think that tree would hold them all?"

Ranni glanced upwards. "The tree would hold them all right," he said. "But supposing they fall out in their sleep!"

"Oh, we can easily prevent that," said Pilescu. "We can tie them on with those creeper-ropes."

The two men had been talking to one another in their own language, and only Paul understood. He listened with delight.

"We're going to sleep up in a tree!" he told the others, who listened in astonishment. "We daren't light a fire tonight, you see."

"Goly! How exciting!" said Mike. "I really don't think anyone could have had such a lot of thrills in a short time as we've had this week!"

Pilescu made the children climb the tree whilst it was still daylight. Halfway up the branches forked widely, spreading out almost straight, and there was a kind of rough platform. Pilescu stuffed the spaces between the branches with creepers, twigs and some enormous leaves that he pulled from another tree. Then he spread out half the rugs, and told the children to settle down.

They spread themselves on the rugs, joyful to think they were to spend a whole night in a tree. Some monkeys, who had been watching from the next tree, set up a great chattering when they saw the children settling down.

"They think you are their cousins from a far-off land," said Pilescu with a broad grin. "They're not far wrong, either. Now lie still whilst I cover you with these other rugs, and then I'm going to tie you firmly to the branches."

"Oh, Pilescu – we're too hot to be covered!" cried Paul, pushing away the rug.

"It will be very chilly in the early morning," said Pilescu. "Very well – leave the rug half off now, and pull it on again later."

Pilescu and Ranni made a very good job of tying the children to the tree. Now they were safe! The two men slid down the big tree to the ground. The monkeys fled away. The children talked drowsily for a while, and Peggy tried her hardest to keep awake and enjoy the strangeness of a night up a tree.

But her eyes were very heavy, and although she listened for a while to the enormously loud voices of some giant frogs in the nearby marsh, and the curious call of a bird that seemed to say, "Do do it, do do it," over and over again, she was soon as fast asleep as the others.

As usual, Ranni and Pilescu took turn and turn about to watch. They both sat at the foot of the great tree, one at one side, the other at the other. Ranni took first turn, and then Pilescu.

Pilescu was very wide awake. He sat with his gun in his hand watching for any movement or sound nearby that might mean an enemy of some kind. He, too, heard the frogs, and the bird crying "Do do it, do do it." He heard the trumpeting of far-off elephants, the roar of some big forest cat, maybe a leopard, and the stir of the wind in the branches of the trees.

And then, towards dawn, he heard something and saw something that was not bird or animal. Something or someone was creeping between the bushes, very slowly, very carefully. Pilescu stiffened, and took hold of his gun firmly. Could it be any of the Folk of the Secret Mountain?

The Something came nearer, and Pilescu put out a hand and shook Ranni carefully. Ranni awoke at once.

"There's something strange over there," whispered Pilescu. "I can only see a shadow moving. Do you suppose it's a scout sent out by the Mountain Folk?"

Ranni peered between the bushes in the dim light of half-dawn. He, too, could see something moving.

"I'll slip behind that bush and pounce on whatever it is," whispered Ranni. "I can move away from this side of the tree without being seen."

So big Ranni slid away as silently as a cat, and crawled behind the nearest bush. From there he made his way to another bush and waited for the Something to come by.

He pounced on it – and there came a terrified yell, and a shrill voice that cried out something that sounded like "Yakka, longa, yakka, longa!"

Ranni picked up what he had caught and carried it to

Pilescu. It was something very small – something that both men knew very well. They cried out in amazement.

"Mafumu!"

Yes – it *was* Mafumu. Poor Mafumu, crawling painfully along the bushes, searching for the friends he had left the day before.

"Mafumu! What has happened?" asked Ranni. The boy told him his story.

"I went back a long way with my uncle, but he was unkind to me, and he told me he would give me to the first crocodile he saw in a river. So I ran away from him to come back to my new friends. And a big thorn went into my foot – see – so I could not walk, I could only crawl."

The poor little boy was so tired, and in such pain that tears fell out of his eyes. As dawn came stealing over the countryside, big Ranni took the poor little fellow into his arms, whilst Pilescu pulled out the great thorn from his foot. He bathed the hurt and bound it up with lint and gauze. He gave the boy something to eat and drink and then told him to sleep.

But comfortable though he was in Ranni's arms, Mafumu would not stay there. He must go to his new friends, and especially Jack!

So up the tree he climbed, and was soon snuggled down beside Jack, who did not even wake when the boy lay almost on top of him.

"Mafumu may be helpful to us," said Pilescu to Ranni. "He knows the language of the tribes around here, he knows where to find fruit and drinking water, and he can guide as well."

In the morning, what loud cries of amazement came from the tree above, when the children awoke and found Mafumu with them!

"Mafumu!"

"How *did* you get here, Mafumu?"

"Mafumu, get off me, I can't move!"

65

"Mafumu, what have you done to your foot?"

Mafumu sat up on Jack's legs and grinned round happily.

"Me back," he said, proud that he could say some English words with the right meaning. "Me back." Then he went off into his usual gibberish.

"Hallo, goodnight, shutup, what's the matter!"

Everyone laughed. Jack punched him on the back in a friendly manner. "You're an idiot, but an awfully nice idiot," he said. "We're jolly glad to see you again. I shouldn't be surprised if you help us quite a lot!"

And Jack was right, as we shall soon see!

The Wonderful Waterfall

As the little company sat eating their breakfast they talked about what would be the best thing to do. How were they to find a way into the Secret Mountain?

"You know, I believe that Mafumu's uncle knew something," said Ranni. "I rather think there is some sort of secret way in, if only we could find it."

"Ranni! I know how we could find it!" said Mike excitedly. "Couldn't we hide until we see some of the Secret Mountain Folk – and then track them to see how they get inside?"

"Yes – if we could only see some of the folk, without them seeing us!" said Ranni. "We should have to scout round a bit – it is perfectly plain that no one could possibly get into the mountain from *this* side – it's so steep. I don't believe even a goat could get up it!"

"Well – let's explore round the other side," said Mike. "Hurry up and finish your breakfast, girls. I can hardly wait."

"Of course, you realize that we shall all have to be very careful," said Pilescu. "It is quite possible that the folk in the Secret Mountain already know we are here, and are waiting to capture us."

"Oooh," said Nora, not liking the sound of that at all. "I shall keep very near to you and Ranni, Pilescu!"

"I hope you will," said Pilescu, taking the little girl's hand in his. "I would not have come on this mad adventure if I had known what it was to be. But now it is too late to draw back."

"I should think so!" cried Mike indignantly. "Why, Pilescu, things are going very well, I think. We have discovered where our parents are – and we may be able to rescue them at any time now. We've got guns!"

"Yes – but first we have to find where your parents *are!*" said Pilescu. "And how to get to them."

"Well, let's make a start," said Mike. "Come on. It will be too hot soon to explore anywhere! All my clothes are sticking to me already."

The party packed up their things. Ranni and Pilescu carried most of them, but the children had to take some too. Mafumu as usual carried his share balanced on his head. They all set off cautiously, keeping as near to the foot of the queer steep mountain as they could, and yet taking cover as they went, so as not to be seen.

It was difficult going. Mafumu was a great help, for he seemed to know the best paths at once. He went in front, with Ranni and Jack just behind him. Pilescu was at the back, his hand on his gun. He was taking no risks!

As they went round the mountain a strange noise came to their ears.

"What's that?" said Nora, alarmed. They all stood and listened. Mafumu beckoned them on, not knowing why they had stopped.

"Big noise, Mafumu, big noise," said Jack, holding up his hand for Mafumu to listen. The boy laughed.

"Big water," he said. "Big water." He was very proud of himself for being able to answer Jack in his own language. He was as sharp as a needle, and in half an hour was quite able to pick up twenty or more new words.

"Big water" said Jack puzzled. "Does he mean the sea?"

"No – I know what it is – it's a waterfall!" said Mike. "Hark! It sounds like thunder, but it's really water tumbling down the mountain-side not far off. Come on – I bet I'm right."

The little company pressed on, following their new guide. The noise grew louder. It really did sound like thunder, but was more musical. The echoes went rolling round the valley, and now and again the noise seemed to get inside the children's heads in a queer manner. They shook their heads to get it out! It was funny.

And then they suddenly saw the waterfall! It was simply magnificent. It fell almost straight down the steep mountain-side with a tremendous noise. Spray rose high into the air, and hung like a mist over the fall. The children could feel its wetness on their faces now and again from where they stood, awed and silent at the sight of such a wonderful fall of water.

"My goodness!" said Peggy, full of astonishment and delight. "No wonder it makes such a noise! It's a *marvellous* waterfall. It's coming from the inside of the mountain!"

"Yes – it is," said Mike, shading his eyes and looking upwards. "There must be an underground river that wanders through the mountain and comes out at that steep place. Golly! How are we going to get by?"

It was very difficult. They had to go a good way out of their path. The waterfall made a surging, violent river at its foot, that shouted and tumbled its way down the valley, and joined the hidden river down which they had come not long before.

Mafumu was not to be beaten by a waterfall! He made his way alongside the surging water until he came to a shallow part, where big boulders stuck up all the way across.

"Hurryup, hurryup," he said, pointing to the stones. "We go there, hurryup."

"I believe we *could* get across there," said Ranni. "The stones are almost like stepping-stones. I will carry Nora across, and then Peggy – and you take Paul, Pilescu. The boys can manage themselves."

"*I* can manage by *myself*," said the little Prince indignantly. "I'm a boy too, are'nt I?"

"You are not so big as the others," said Pilescu with a grin, and he caught up the angry boy and put him firmly on his shoulder. Paul was red with rage, but he did not dare to struggle in case he sent Pilescu into the water. As it was, Pilescu lost his footing once, and almost fell. He just managed to swing himself back in time, and sat with a bump on a big rock. Paul was almost jerked off his shoulder.

The girls were taken safely across. As Ranni had said, the stones were almost like stepping-stones, although one or two were rather far apart – but fortunately the water there was only waist-deep, so a little wading solved the difficulty. The other three boys got across easily. Mafumu jumped like a goat from one stone to another.

And now they were the other side of the waterfall. The noise of its falling still sounded thunderous, but they liked it.

"The foam is like soap-suds," said Nora, watching some swirling down the river.

The sun was now too high for any of them to go further. Even Mafumu was hot and wanted to rest. Also his foot pained him a little now, in spite of the careful bandaging. Everyone curled up in the cool shade of an enormous tree, where they could occasionally feel the delicious coldness of the misty spray from the waterfall.

"I suppose we ought to have a meal," said Ranni, too lazy to do anything about it.

"I'm so hot and tired I couldn't eat even an ant's egg!" said Jack.

"You haven't been offered one," said Peggy. "The only thing *I'd* like would be something sweet to drink."

Mafumu disappeared for a moment. He came back laden with some strange-looking fruit, that looked like half nut, half pomegranate. He slit a hole in the top-end and showed Peggy how to drink from it.

"I suppose it's safe to drink the juice of this funny fruit," said Peggy doubtfully.

Ranni nodded. "Mafumu knows what is good or not," he said. "Taste it and see what it's like. If it's nice I'll have some too!"

Peggy tipped up the queer green fruit. It was full of some thick, fleshy juice that trickled out rather like treacle. At first the taste was bitter, like lemon – but as the little girl sucked hard, a delicious coolness spread over her mouth and down her throat.

"Golly!" said Peggy. "It makes me feel as if I've got ice-cream going down me, but not at all sweet. Do have some, you others!"

Soon everyone was sucking the strange fruit. Nobody liked the bitter taste at first, but they all loved the glorious coolness that came afterwards.

"Mafumu, you are very, very clever," said Jack sleepily to the little boy, who was, as usual, curled up as near to his hero as he could manage. Mafumu grinned in delight. A word of praise from Jack made him very happy.

Soon everyone was sleeping soundly – except Ranni, who was on guard, though he found it very difficult to keep awake in such heat. The heat danced round, and everything shimmered and quivered. If it had not been for the coolness that blew over from the nearby waterfall it would have been quite unbearable.

Even the monkeys were quiet – but when they began to move in the tree and to chatter again Ranni awoke everyone. The great heat of the day was gone. If they were going to do any more exploring they must set off at once.

And soon they had a great surprise – for when they rounded a rocky corner of the yellow mountain they heard voices! They all stopped still at once, hardly daring to breathe. *Voices!* Could they be natives – or folk from the Mountain.

The voices were deep and harsh – like the voices of rooks, Jack thought. Ranni waved Mafumu forward, for he knew that the boy could move as silently as a shadow. Mafumu slid down on to his tummy and wriggled forward like a snake. It was marvellous to watch. The other children could not imagine how he could get along as quickly as he did.

Everyone else sank down quietly behind the bushes and stayed as still as mice. Mafumu wriggled forward into a thick bush. It was prickly, but the boy did not seem to feel the scratches. He parted the bush-twigs carefully and looked through.

Then he looked back towards Ranni, his face full of excitement, and beckoned him forward with a wave of his hand. The children had the amusement of watching big Ranni do his best to wriggle forward on his front, just as Mafumu had done. The enormous Baronian did very well, however, and was soon beside the boy, peering through the prickly bush.

The two of them stayed there for some time. The others waited impatiently, hearing the harsh voices of the strangers, and wondering what Ranni and Mafumu could see.

Suddenly there came a grating sound, a rolling, groaning noise – and the voices stopped. The queer noise came again, such a grating sound that it set everyone's teeth on edge! With the rolling sound of rumbling thunder the noise echoed around – and then stopped. Now only the sharp calls of the birds, the ceaseless hum of thousands

of insects and the silly chatter of monkeys could be heard
– and behind it all the roaring of the waterfall in the
distance.

Ranni and Mafumu crawled back, their faces shining
with excitement. They took hold of the other children and
hurried them to a safe distance. And in the shade of a
great rock Ranni told them what he and Mafumu had
seen.

The Way Into The Secret Mountain

"Quick, Ranni, tell us everything!" said Jack.

"We saw some of the Folk of the Secret Mountain!"
said Ranni. "They certainly do look queer. It is just as
Mafumu's uncle said – they have flaming red hair and
beards and their skins are a funny yellow. I couldn't see if
their eyes were green. They were dressed in flowing robes
of all colours, and they wore turbans that showed their red
hair."

"Golly!" said Mike, his eyes wide with excitement. "Go
on – what happened?"

"The queerest thing happened," said Ranni. "I hardly
know if I believe it or not. Well – let me tell you. As we
lay there, watching these people talking together in their
funny harsh voices, we noticed that they were near a very
curious kind of rock."

"What sort of rock?" asked Pilescu.

"It was an enormous rock," said Ranni. "It was strange
because it was much smaller at the bottom than at the top,
so that it looked almost as if it must fall over. Well, as we
watched, one of the Mountain Folk went up to the rock
and pushed hard against it."

"Why, he couldn't surely move an enormous rock!" cried Mike.

"That's what *I* thought," said Ranni. "But that rock must be one of these curious balancing rocks that can be pivoted, or swung round, at a touch, no matter how big they are. There are just a few known in the world, and this is another."

"What happened when the rock swung round?" asked Pilescu.

"It not only swung round, it slid to one side," said Ranni. "Just like the rock in the story of Ali Baba that you told me! And behind it was a great door in the mountain-side studded with shining knobs that glittered in the sun!"

Everyone stared at Ranni in silence, too excited to speak. So that was the way into the mountain! They had stumbled on it quite by accident.

"Go on," whispered Peggy at last.

"I couldn't see how the great doorway was opened," said Ranni. "It seemed to slide to one side, very quietly – but whether it was opened from the outside or the inside I really don't know. Then the rock rolled back into place again, and swung back into position with that terrific roaring, groaning sound you heard."

"And did the people go into the mountain?" asked Mike.

"They did," answered Ranni. "We saw no more of them."

Everyone sat silent for a while, thinking of the queer entrance to the Secret Mountain. So that was what Mafumu's uncle had meant when he said that to get into the mountain one had to walk through rock!

"Well – what are we going to do?" said Jack. "We know the way in – but I wonder how that great studded door is opened! Oh, Ranni – can we try to get in tonight?"

"We'd better," said Ranni. "I will try by myself and see

73

what happens. You can all find good hiding-places nearby and watch. I'll take my gun, you may be sure!"

The children could hardly wait for the sudden nightfall to come. They found themselves good hiding-places – though Jack and Mafumu found the best. Theirs was up a big tree not far from the mountain entrance. Mafumu found it, of course, and helped Jack up there. The others were behind or in the middle of thick bushes.

When the stars hung brightly, and a crescent moon shone in the sky, Ranni crept forward to the strange rock, whose black shadow was enormous in the night. Everyone watched, hardly daring to breathe in case anything happened to Ranni.

Big Ranni stepped quietly up to the rock. He thought he knew exactly where to heave, for he had seen one of the Mountain Folk move the rock and had noted the exact place. But it was difficult to find it at night.

Ranni shoved and pushed. He pressed against the rock and heaved with all his might. Nothing happened. He stopped and mopped his hot forehead, wondering which was the right place to press against.

He tried again and again – and just as he was giving up something happened. He pushed at the right place quite by accident! With a groaning roar the enormous rock swung slowly round and then slid back. The noise it made was terrific. Ranni sprang back into the shadows, afraid that a hundred Mountain Folk might come rushing out at him.

The studded door shone in the moonlight. It did not open. It stood there, big and solid, strange and silent, barring the way. Nobody came. Nobody shouted to see who had swung back the rock. Only the night-sounds came on the air, and the sound of the distant waterfall.

Everyone waited, trembling with excitement. Jack nearly fell out of his tree, he shivered so much with wonder and expectation. But absolutely nothing happened. The rock remained where it was, the door shone behind.

"Ranni! Maybe the Mountain Folk haven't heard the noise!" whispered Pilescu. "Go and try the door."

Ranni crept forward again, keeping to the deep-black shadows. Once or twice the moonlight glinted on the gun he held in his hand. Ranni was taking no chances!

The others watched him from their hiding-places. He went right up to the door. He felt over it with his hand. He pushed gently against it. He tried to slide it to one side. He tried all the studs and knobs to see if by chance any of them opened the great door. But no matter what he did, the door remained shut.

"Let us come and see," whispered Mike to Pilescu. The boy felt that he could not keep still any longer. Pilescu was also longing to go to the mountain door, so he Mike, Paul, and the two girls crept forward in the shadows.

Jack wanted to come too – and began to climb carefully down the tree, getting caught in a great creeper as he did so. Mafumu tried to untangle him, but the more he tried, the more mixed-up poor Jack got.

And then, just as Jack was almost untangled, there came a grinding, grating roar once more – and the enormous rock slid along in front of the great door and swung round slowly into its place.

Behind it, caught between the rock and the door, was everyone except Mafumu and Jack! The girls, Mike, Paul, Ranni and Pilescu were in the narrow passage between.

Ranni tried to stop the rock from sliding back into place, but once started on its way nothing would stop the enormously heavy rock. No one could escape, either, for there was no time to slip out of the trap.

Jack and Mafumu stared towards the rock in the greatest dismay. Jack leapt down from the tree, almost breaking his ankle, and ran towards the mountain.

"Are you safe, are you safe!" he shouted.

But there was no answer. The swinging rock shut the sound of voices away. Jack beat on the rock, he tried to heave it as he had seen Ranni do, and Mafumu did the same. But neither boy could find the secret balance of the rock, and it stayed where it was, colossal in the moonlight, towering above them as they shouted and hammered on it.

And then, behind the rock, the great door slid back! Jack and Mafumu heard it, and fell silent, listening. What was happening?

What indeed? When the door slid back, the little company in front of it stared with wide eyes into a great hall-like cave. It was lighted by glowing lamps, and a wide flight of steps led downwards for a little way. Up these steps came the Folk of the Secret Mountain, dressed in their flowing robes, and carrying strange yellow wands which glittered from top to bottom.

The leader was a very tall man with a bright red beard and gleaming eyes. He spoke to Ranni in language rather like that used by Mafumu. Ranni understood some of it.

"He wants us to follow him," Ranni said to Pilescu. "Got your gun, Pilescu?"

"Yes," said the big Baronian. "But it's no use using it, Ranni. There are too many of them. Put your gun away for the moment, and we'll see what happens. We are in a nice mess now. Only Jack and Mafumu are safe!"

That was a strange journey into the heart of the mountain. Big carved lamps glowed all the way, lighting up enormous flights of steps, great walls, and high rocky ceilings.

"The mountain is full of hollows which these people have made into halls and rooms," said Ranni in a low voice to Pilescu. "Isn't it amazing? Look at those great pictures drawn in colour on the walls! They are strange but very beautiful."

The children gazed in wonder at the great coloured

pictures on the rocky walls of the mountain-caves. Lamps were set cleverly to light up the pictures so that the men and animals in them seemed almost alive. The Secret Mountain was indeed a marvellous place!

At last the long journey through the heart of the mountain came to an end. The little party found themselves in a queer room, whose rocky ceiling rose too high for them to make out by the light of their lamp. Shining stones were set into the walls, and these glittered like stars in the lamplight.

A rough platform was at one end of the room. On it were piled heaps of wonderful rugs, beautifully woven, and marvellously patterned in all the brightest colours imaginable. The children sat down on them, tired out.

Pitchers of ice-cold water stood on a stone table. Everyone drank deep. Flat cakes lay on a shallow dish beside the pitchers. Mike tasted one. It was sweet and dry, quite pleasant to eat. Everyone made a meal, wondering what was going to happen.

The door to their strange room was made of strong wood and had been fastened on the outside. There was nothing to do but wait. The Mountain Folk had left them quite alone in the heart of their queer home.

"We'd better get some rest," said Ranni, and he covered up the three children with the rugs. "I don't know what to wish about Jack. I'm glad he's not caught – and yet I wish we were all here together."

"Perhaps Jack and Mafumu will find some way of rescuing us," said Peggy hopefully.

Ranni laughed shortly. "It's no good hoping that, Peggy! If he tries to get through the rock entrance, and through that big studded door, he will just find himself a prisoner!"

"Do you suppose we'll see Mummy and Daddy?" asked Nora suddenly. "They must be somewhere in this mountain too."

"Yes – that's quite likely," said Pilescu thoughtfully. "Ranni, I'll keep guard for the first half of the night. You go to sleep with the others now."

In spite of all the tremendous excitement of the day the three children were soon asleep on the soft rugs. Ranni did not sleep at first, but at last he dozed off, sitting half upright in case Pilescu needed him quickly.

But the night passed away silently and no one came to disturb them in their cell-like room. The lamp burned steadily, giving a soft light to the curious, high-roofed room. It burned until the day – and even then it still lit the room, for no daylight, no sunlight ever entered the heart of the Secret Mountain.

Mafumu Makes A Discovery

Jack was almost beside himself with alarm and despair. Mafumu kept close beside him, saying nothing at all, looking at Jack out of his big dark eyes. Both boys beat again and again on the great rock that hid the entrance to the Secret Mountain. They heard the door behind slid back into place once more – and then all was silent.

"Come," said Mafumu at last, and he took Jack's arm. He led him to where everyone had left their packs, and the two sat down together.

"What are we to do?" said Jack at last, burying his head in his hands. "I can't bear to think of everyone captured, and we can't get at them."

Mafumu did not understand. He sat there looking at Jack, muttering something in his own language. Then he made a kind of bed of the packs, and pushed Jack down on them.

"We sleep now. I find way soon," said the younger boy flashing his white teeth in the moonlight. They must wait until the morning.

Jack fell asleep at last. As soon as Mafumu saw that his eyes were closed, and heard his regular breathing he crept away from Jack. He stood upright in the brilliant moonlight and looked at the great mountain. How was he going to find a way inside?

Mafumu was not yet ten years old, but he was the sharpest boy in his tribe. He was mischievous, disobedient and wilful, but he had brains. He had lain thinking and thinking of how he might get into the Secret Mountain without going through the entrance of the sliding rock.

And into his mind had come a picture of the great waterfall. He saw it springing from the mountain-side, a great gushing fall of silvery water. He was going to see if it came from the heart of the Secret Mountain!

The boys slipped away in the moonlight. He ran until he came to the great waterfall. It was magnificent in the light of the moon, and the spray shone like purest silver. The noise was twice as loud at night, and he was half-afraid.

He glanced fearfully all round him. He was not afraid of animals or snakes – but he was afraid of being caught by the Folk of the Mountain. If he should be captured, Jack would be left helpless, for he did not know the countryside as Mafumu did.

Mafumu made his way up the mountain, keeping as close to the waterfall as he could. Several times he was drenched, but he liked that. It was cool! The night was hot, and Mafumu was bathed in perspiration as he climbed upwards. The mountain was very steep indeed. It was only by working his way from rocky ledge to ledge that he could get up at all.

At last he came to where the waterfall began. Mafumu worked his way above the fall, and found that, as he had thought, the water gushed straight out of the mountain

Mafumu crawled along the ledge

itself. There must be an underground river running through the mountain. The great hill towered above him, reaching to the clouds. Just below him the waterfall sprang from the mountain, and the fine spray clung to his skin.

He worked his way down again, almost defeated by the noise of the fall. He came to where the water shot out of the mountain in a great arch. He wriggled his way towards it, and found a rocky ledge, wide and damp, just by the fall itself.

Mafumu stood and shivered with fright, for the noise was tremendous. It flowed all around him like rumbling thunder. He edged his way behind the great arch of water, for the rocky ledge stretched all the way behind.

And there, hidden in the misty spray that hung always around and about the waterfall, Mafumu thought that he had discovered another way into the Secret Mountain! For surely, where the water was able to come out of the mountain, he and Jack would be able to go in!

The moon was now almost gone, and darkness crept across the country. Mafumu shivered. He had a curious charm round his neck, made of crocodile's teeth, and he took it into his hand to bring him good luck. He slid quickly down the mountain-side, grazing himself as he went, and bruising his ankle-bones as he knocked them against rocks and stones. But he did not even feel the hurt, so anxious was he to get back to Jack, and tell him what he had found.

He reached Jack as the dawn was breaking. Jack was awake, and very puzzled because Mafumu was gone. The boy looked white and worried. He simply had no idea at all what would be the best thing to do. He had almost made up his mind that he must try to move the rock somehow and get into the mountain so as to be with the others.

But Mafumu had other plans. In funny, broken English he tried to explain to Jack what his idea was.

81

"Big, big water," he said, and made a noise like the splashing of the waterfall. "Jack come with Mafumu see big, big water. We go into big water. Come."

Jack thought Mafumu was quite mad, but the other boy was so much in earnest that he nodded his head and said Yes, he would come.

Leaving their packs where they were, covered by boulders and stones, the two boys made their way back to the great waterfall. The noise was so deafening that they had to shout to one another to make themselves heard.

Mafumu remembered the way he had taken in the moonlight. He never forgot any path he had once travelled. He even remembered the bushes and rocks he had passed. So now he found it easy to help Jack up the rocky ledges to where the water gushed out of the mountain-side.

Jack was wet through and almost deaf by the time he reached the place where the water appeared from the mountain. He kept shaking his head to get the noise of the fall out of it – but it was impossible! It went on all the time.

Mafumu was excited. He led Jack behind the great curve of the fall, and showed him how the water thundered out just above their heads. It was a queer feeling to stand immediately under a great waterfall, and see it pouring down overhead and in front, a great blue-green mass of water, powerful enough to sweep the boys off and away if it could have reached them!

"How queer to stand behind a waterfall like this," said Jack. "Mafumu – what's the sense of bringing me here? How do you suppose we're going to crawl through water that's coming out of the mountain at about sixty miles an hour. You must be mad."

But Mafumu was not mad. He took Jack right to the other side of the ledge, and pointed to a narrow rocky path that led into the mountain, where the water ran only

82

two or three inches deep. Nearby, the river had worn a deep channel for itself – but this ledge was just above the level of the river, and had water on it only because of the continual splashing and spray that came from the fall.

"We go in here," grinned Mafumu. "We go in here, yes?"

"Golly, Mafumu – I believe you are right!" said Jack, excited. "I believe we can go in here! Though goodness knows how far we'll get, or where it will take us."

"We go now," said Mafumu. "Hurryup, hurryup."

The boys squeezed themselves on to the rocky ledge. If they had slipped into the great torrent of water that poured out, that would have been the end of them. But they were careful to hold on to bits of jutting-out rock, so as not to fall. The ledge was damp and slippery. The air was full of fine spray. It was queer to be squeezing by a great river that became a waterfall two or three feet away from them!

The rocky ledge ran right into the mountain, keeping a foot or two above the level of the deep hidden river. The boys made their way along it. Soon they had left behind the thunder of the waterfall, and the mountain seemed strangely silent. Just below them, to their left, ran the underground river, silent and swift.

"It's dark, Mafumu," said Jack, shivering. It was not only dark, but cold. No sunshine ever came up the secret river! But soon a queer light showed from the roof and walls of the river tunnel.

It shone green and blue. Mafumu thought it was very odd, but Jack knew that it was only the strange light called phosphorescence. He was glad of its pale gleam, for now they could see more or less where they were going.

We shan't fall down into the river now and be swept out into the waterfall," he thought. "My goodness, Mafumu was clever to think there might be a way into the mountain, where the river came out and made a fall! I should never have thought of that in a hundred years! Wouldn't it be marvellous if we could rescue everyone!"

After a long crawl along the ledge the tunnel opened out into a series of caves, some large, some small. The boys marvelled at some of them, for the walls were agleam with queer bright stones. Mafumu did not like them.

"The walls have eyes that look at Mafumu," he whispered to Jack. Jack laughed – but he soon stopped, for his laugh echoed round and round the caves, and rumbled into the heart of the mountain and came back to him like a hundred giant-laughs, very queer and horrible.

On through the river-caves went the two boys, silent and rather frightened now. Then they came to what seemed a complete stop

"Mafumu! The river is in a tunnel here, and the roof almost touches the top of the water!" said Jack in dismay, "We can't get any further."

Mafumu waded into the river. It was not running very swiftly just there, for it was almost on the level. It was deep, however, and the boy had to swim. He began to make his way up the tunnel to see how far he could go with his head above the water. His head knocked against the roof as he swam – and presently he found that the water touched the roof! So he had to swim under the water, and hoped that before he choked the roof would rise a little and give him air to breathe!

Mafumu was a good swimmer, and was able to hold his breath well – but his lungs were almost bursting by the time that he was able to find a place to stick up his head above the water and breathe again. Even so, the roof fell low again almost at once, and the water bobbed against it. How far would it be before it rose again and Mafumu could breathe?

He had to try. There was nothing else to do, unless he and Jack were to go right back. So he took an enormous breath, dived down and swam vigorously below the water, trying the roof with his hand every now and again to see if he could come above the water and breathe.

He was rewarded. The roof suddenly rose up and the tunnel became a large cave! Mafumu waded out of the water gasping and panting, delighted that he had not given up too soon!

He sat down for a few minutes to get all the breath he could. He had to go back and bring Jack through now! He did not know if the other boy could swim under water as well as he, Mafumu, could!

Back went Mafumu, knowing exactly where to rise and breathe, and where to dive under and swim back to where Jack was anxiously awaiting him, wondering what in the wide world had happened!

Mafumu tried to explain to Jack what he was to do. Jack understood only too well!

"Lead on, Mafumu," said the boy, taking a deep breath. "I'm a good swimmer – but I don't know if I'm as good as you are! Go on!"

So into the river went both boys, swimming below the water where it touched the roof, and coming up, almost bursting, in the place where the roof lifted a little so that they might breathe.

Then into the water they went again, shivering, for it was icy-cold, and once more swam as fast as they could up the low tunnel, their heads bumping the roof till they came thankfully to where the tunnel opened out into the large cave! They crawled out of the water, panting, and sat down to get their breath. Their hearts beat like great pumps, and it was some time before both boys could go on.

"Now which way?" wondered Jack, looking all round at the gleaming cave. "There are three or four archways leading out of this cave, Mafumu, with the river winding silently through the middle. Which way do we go?"

Inside The Mountain

Mafumu was running all round, peering first through one rocky archway and then through another. He stopped at last and beckoned to Jack. Jack went over to him, wondering what the other boy could see, for he was plainly excited.

No wonder Mafumu was excited! Peering through the little archway he had seen an enormous flight of steps leading upwards through the mountain! The steps were cut out of the solid rock, and were polished and shining. At the foot hung a great lamp, very finely made, which gave a curious green light.

The boys stood at the bottom of the rocky stairway, staring upwards. Where could it lead to?

"Shall we go up?" whispered Jack, his whisper starting a rustling echo all around him. Mafumu nodded. In silence the two boys began to climb the great stairway. It went up for a great way, wide and easy to climb. Then it curved sharply to the right and became a curious spiral staircase, still cut into the rock.

"I believe it leads up to the top of the mountain!" said Jack, quite out of breath. "Let's sit down and have a rest. My legs are really tired with all this climbing."

They did not notice that a wooden door opened on to the stairway just behind them. They sat there in silence, resting themselves. And then suddenly they heard the harsh voices of the Folk of the Mountain! The boys looked round quickly and by the light of one of the green lamps hanging at a curve of the stairway they saw the door. It was just opening!

The boys did not know whether the folk would go up

the stairway or down, and they hadn't time to choose! They simply tumbled themselves down the steps, came to a curve and waited there, their hearts thumping, and their legs trembling.

"If they come down the stairway we shall be seen!" thought Jack desperately. "They will touch us as they pass, because the stairway is so narrow."

But the Folk of the Mountain went *up* the stairway, not down! The boys heard their footsteps and their voices disappearing into the distance. They crept back up the stairway to the door – and it was open!

"Golly! What a bit of luck!" Jack whispered to Mafumu, who, although he did not understand the words, knew what Jack meant all right. The boys slipped in through the open door and found themselves in an enormous gallery that ran round the most colossal hall they had ever seen.

"This must be a kind of meeting-hall," thought Jack, gazing down from the rocky gallery to the great floor below. "I bet it's right in the very middle of the mountain! Golly! What a strange place it is!"

Steps led up from the great hall in many directions. They led to fine wooden doors, studded and starred with gleaming metals. The Folk of the Mountain had a strange and mighty home! There was no one at all to be seen and the deep silence seemed very queer. Enormous lamps hung down from the roof, swinging slightly as they burned. Deep shadows moved over the floor as the lamps swung, and Mafumu stared, for he had never seen such a place in all his life.

"Mafumu! Those people will be coming back soon, I expect," said Jack in his ear. "Come on. We must get down into this hall and go up a stairway to see if we can find where the others are. Hurry!"

The boys slipped down into the great hall. They stood there in the shadows, wondering which flight of steps to take. They chose the nearest one, a wide, shallow stretch that led to an open doorway.

Up they went, and through the doorway. A long, dark passage lay before them, with rocky walls and ceiling. They went down it, and turned into another one. They heard the noise of voices and stopped.

No one had heard them, so they crept on again, and came out through a big archway that led into a fine cave. Its walls were hung with the skins of animals and with curtains of shining material. The floor was covered with rich rugs. On them sat the Folk of the Secret Mountain.

How queer they looked in the light of the swinging lamps! The men all had flaming red beards and hair, and their faces looked a sickly yellow. The women were wrapped up to their noses, and showed neither hair nor chins! The boys knew they were the women because they spoke in high-pitched, shrill voices.

All of them were working at something. Some were making rugs. Others were weaving with bright-coloured strands that looked like raffia. Some were hammering at things that the boys could not see.

"We'd better go back," whispered Jack, pushing Mafumu. "Come on. If we're seen here we'd be taken prisoner."

The boys crept back. Mafumu was frightened, for the Folk of the Mountain had looked so strange! The two boys went back until they came to another door. It was shut. They pushed against it and it opened.

The room inside was very odd. It held nothing at all but a rope ladder that went up and up and up into the darkness of the roof!

"There must be a narrow hole that goes up for a long way," whispered Jack. "I wonder where the rope ladder leads to. Sh! Mafumu – there's someone coming!"

Sure enough, voices and footsteps could be heard once more. Mafumu gave a groan of fright, caught hold of the rope ladder, and was up it in a trice, disappearing into the darkness of the high roof at once. Jack thought it was a good idea and he followed as well.

Just in time! Three men came into the little room, shut the door and began to talk in their harsh voices. Jack and Mafumu stayed still on the ladder, for they knew that if they climbed higher the ladder would shake and the men would guess someone was up there.

The men talked for ten minutes, and then went out. The two boys climbed up the ladder at once. They thought they would be safer at the top than at the bottom!

The ladder was fastened to a ledge, and opposite the ledge was another door, strong and heavy. It was bolted on the outside with great heavy bolts that looked impossible to move!

"Somebody's bolted in there," whispered Jack. "Do you suppose it's Peggy and Nora and Mike and the rest of them?"

Mafumu nodded. Yes – he felt sure they had stumbled on the prison of the rest of their little party! He began to pull at the bolts.

Although they were heavy, they were well oiled and ran fairly easily when both boys pulled at them. One by one they slid the back. There was a kind of latch on the door, and Jack slid it up. The door opened.

Not a sound came from the room inside. The boys hardly dared to peep round the door. What would they see? Surely if their friends were in their they would have made some sound, said something or shouted something!

Jack pushed the door wide open and went boldly inside, far more boldly than he felt! And what a surprise he got!

The rest of their party were not there – but Captain and Mrs Arnold were! They lay on piles of rugs in the corner of the dimly lit cave, looking pale and ill. They watched the opening of the door, thinking that someone was bringing them food.

When they saw Jack they sprang to their feet in the greatest amazement! They stared as if they could not believe their eyes. They felt they must be dreaming.

"Jack! Jack! Is it really you?" asked Mrs Arnold at last. "Where are the others – Mike, Peggy and Nora?"

Mike, Peggy and Nora were Mrs Arnold's own children, though she counted Jack as hers too, because he had once helped the others when they were in great trouble. Jack stared at Captain and Mrs Arnold in joy. He flung his arms round Mrs Arnold, for he was very fond of her.

"There isn't time to talk," said Captain Arnold quickly. "Jack has opened our prison door. We'd better get out whilst we have the chance! Follow me. I know where we can go and talk in safety."

He led the way out of the room, taking with him some flat cakes and a pitcher of water. He stopped to fasten the bolts behind him, so that anyone coming that way would not notice anything unusual. Then, instead of going down the rope ladder, Captain Arnold took a little dark passage to the right that led steeply upwards. Before very long, much to the two boy's amazement, they came into a vivid patch of sunlight!

"There are sun-windows cut into the steep sides of this mountain here and there," said Captain Arnold. "The Folk of the Mountain use them for sun-bathing. It is impossible to escape through them because the mountain falls away below them, and anyone squeezing out of a sun-window would roll to the bottom at once! We are safe here. Sometimes my wife and I have been taken here to get a bit of sun, and no one ever comes by."

"Tell us everything, Jack," begged Mrs Arnold. "Quick – what about the others?"

Jack and Mafumu were very glad indeed to curl up in the warm sunshine and feel the light and warmth of the sun once more. They munched the cakes and drank the water whilst Jack quickly told his whole story. Captain and Mrs Arnold listened in the greatest astonishment.

"Well, you have had amazing adventures before – but, really, this is the most extraordinary one you children have yet had!" said Captain Arnold. "And now, let me tell you *our* adventures!"

He told them how he had been forced down to mend something that had gone wrong with the White Swallow. Whilst he was mending it, the Folk of the Mountain had come silently up and captured them. They had been taken off to the secret mountain, and had been kept prisoners ever since.

"We don't exactly know why," said Captain Arnold. "But I'm afraid that the Folk of the Mountain don't mean us any good! They are worshippers of the sun, and I believe they have a great temple-yard up on the top of this mountain where they make sacrifices to the sun. I only hope they don't mean to throw us over the mountain-top to please the sun-god, or something like that!"

"Good gracious!" said Jack, going pale. He had read in history books of ancient tribes who had worshipped strange gods and made sacrifices to them. He had never dreamed it could happen today. "What about the others? Will the Mountain Folk do that sort of thing to them too?"

"Well, we must see that they don't," said Captain Arnold. "The others are in the mountain somewhere – and we must find them! Have you finished your cakes, Jack? Well, we will leave this warm sun-trap now and explore a little. I don't expect anyone will find out that we are gone until the morning, as our guards had already brought us our food for the day. We have a good many hours to hunt for the others!"

At first Mafumu was very shy of the two strange people, but when he saw how Jack chattered to them he soon began grinning and showing his white teeth.

"Me Mafumu," he said. "Me Mafumu. Me Jack's friend!"

"Well, come on, Mafumu. You must keep with us," said Captain Arnold. "Follow me along this passage, and we'll see where it leads us to!"

On The Top Of The Mountain

Meanwhile, what had happened to the others? They had slept restlessly in their underground room, with the lamp burning beside them. They only knew when morning came because their watches told them that it was six o'clock.

"I'm hungry," said Mike, yawning. "I hope they give their prisoners plenty to eat in this Secret Mountain!"

No sooner had he spoken than the door was unbolted and two red-haired men came in, the folds of their brightly coloured robes swishing all around them. They carried fresh water and some more of the flat cakes in a big dish. They also brought fruit of all kinds, which the children were delighted to see.

"I do wonder what has happened to Jack and Mafumu," said Mike. "What will they do, do you think, Ranni?"

"I can't imagine," said Ranni, taking some of the fruit. He and Pilescu were far more worried than they would tell the children. They hated the sight of the queer red-haired folk – though both Ranni and Pilescu looked curiously like them sometimes, with their bright red hair and beards. But their eyes were not green, nor was their skin yellow.

Towards the end of the long and boring day, the door was flung open, and one of their guards beckoned the little company out. They followed their guide down long, winding passages, cut out of the mountain rock itself, and at last came to a great door that shone green and blue in the light of the swinging lamps above.

The door slid to one side as they came near it, and behind it the children saw a great flight of steps going up and up. The steps shone with a strange golden colour, and shimmered from orange to yellow as the little company began to climb them.

At every two-hundredth step the stairway, still wide and golden, curved round, and ascended again. The children were soon tired of the endless climb. They sat down to rest.

Behind them came a company of the Folk of the Mountain, chanting a strange and doleful song. Nobody liked it at all. It was horrid.

Many times the company sat down to rest. Ranni and Pilescu felt sure that the stairway led to the summit of the mountain. It was a marvellous piece of work, that stairway, beautiful all the way. Here and there, set at the sides, were glittering lamps in the shape of a rayed sun. These were so bright that the children could hardly bear to look at them.

"I think we must be going to the very top of the mountain," said Ranni. "It's soon sunset – and sunworshippers usually pray to the sun at sunrise or sunset. We shall probably see them at their worship!"

Ranni was right – but he did not guess what an extraordinary place the summit of the mountain was!

Panting and tired, the little party climbed the last of the flight of steps. They came out through a great golden door into a vast corridor, with tall yellow pillars built in two rows.

"Goodness!" said Mike, stopping in amazement. "What a view!"

That was the first thing that struck everyone. The view from the top of the Secret Mountain was simply magnificent. All around rose other mountains, some high, some lower, and in and beyond stretched the green valleys, some with a blue river winding along. It took the children's breath away, and made them feel very small indeed to look on those great mountains.

After they had feasted their eyes on the glorious scenery all around them, they turned to see what the summit of the Secret Mountain was like. It was very strange. For one thing, it had been levelled till it was completely flat. There was an enormous wide space in the centre, floored with some kind of yellow stone that shone yellow and orange like the flight of steps up which they had come. Around this wide space, on three sides, were long pillared corridors – and on the fourth side was a great temple-like building, overlooking the steepness of the eastern side of the mountain.

The children, with Ranni and Pilescu, were taken to the great temple. The wind was very rough and cold on the top of the mountain and everyone shivered. A red-haired man came up and flung shimmering cloaks around their shoulders. These were lined with some kind of wool, and were very warm indeed.

Everyone was taken to the top of the temple, where a tall, rounded tower jutted. From this tower they could see the setting sun, falling over the rim of the western sky. As the sun disappeared, the Folk of the Secret Mountain fell on to their knees and chanted a weird song.

"A sort of prayer to the sun, I suppose," said Ranni grimly. He spoke to Pilescu in his own language. "I don't much like this, do you, Pilescu?"

Prince Paul pricked up his ears. "Why don't you like it, Ranni?" he asked. Ranni would not tell him. All of them watched the sun. It disappeared suddenly over the edge of the world. At once the countryside was plunged into darkness, the valley and mountains disappeared from sight, and only the shimmering of the golden floor lighted the summit of the queer mountain.

A tall, red-haired man went into the centre of the shining courtyard, and spoke loudly and violently. Ranni listened and tried to understand as much as he could.

"What is he saying?" asked Mike.

94

"As far as I can make out he is asking the sun to stay away and let the rain come," said Ranni. "It seems that the rain is very much overdue, and these people are praying to the sun to dress himself in the thick clouds that will bring the rain they want. I expect they have crops somewhere on the mountain-side and are in danger of losing them if the rains don't come!"

That night the little party slept on rugs in the cold, wind-swept temple. They were all alone on the mountain-top, for their guards disappeared behind the yellow sliding door, slid it back into place again and fastened it with great long bolts. Ranni and Pilescu explored the temple, the courtyards and the corridor by the light of a torch – but there was no other door down into the mountain save the big shining one. It was as impossible to leave the top of the mountain as it had been to leave their underground room the night before.

How everyone wondered where Jack and Mafumu were, and if Captain and Mrs Arnold were anywhere near! They did not know that the four were together! When they had left the sun-trap, they had taken the passage that led inwards, and walking as quietly as they could, had come across a queer collection of store-rooms. No one was there, so they had explored them thoroughly.

In one store-room, cut out of the solid rock, were dyes and paints of all kinds. Captain Arnold examined them closely. "Look," he said, "this explains the red hair of the Folk of the Mountain. This is a very strong red dye, and these people use it for their hair, to scare any strangers they meet. And see – this is the curious yellow pigment they use for their skins!"

Everyone looked at the flat pots he was holding. They were full of the yellow ointment that the Secret Mountain Folk used on their skin! No wonder the Folk looked so very queer! They dyed their hair and painted their skin yellow!

When Jack knew this he no longer felt afraid of the

curious appearance of the mountain people. Golly! If it was only paint and grease there was nothing strange to be afraid of! He took one of the flat pots of yellow grease and put it into his pocket. "It will be interesting to take home!" he said cheerfully.

"If we ever *do* get home," thought Captain Arnold to himself. They left the store-rooms and went on down a curving passage that had a very high roof. Soon they heard a noise – and they came to the banks of the underground river, which swirled along through the mountain, black and swift. It was strange to see it there, running through an enormous cave.

"We shall get lost in this mountain if we are not careful," said Captain Arnold, stopping and looking round. "I wonder if we are getting anywhere near where this river rushed out of the mountainside, Jack."

Jack asked Mafumu, and the boy shook his head. "Long, long, long way," he said mournfully. "Mafumu not know way."

The party of four went across the cave and left the swirling river behind. They were not sure that it was the same one that made the waterfall. Captain Arnold felt certain that the mountain held two or three rivers, that all joined to make one. It was no use to follow the one they had just left.

Soon they came to a curious door, quite round and studded with a strange pattern of suns. Behind it they heard voices! "What are they saying, Mafumu?" whispered Jack.

Mafumu pressed himself as close to the door as he dared. His sharp ears picked up the voices – and as he listened Mafumu grew pale under his dark skin! He crept back to the others.

"They say that the sun-god is angry," whispered Mafumu. "They say that he is burning up the mountains because he has no servant. He needs a servant before he will hide his head in the great clouds and bring rain. And it is from one of us that he asks for a servant!"

Mafumu spoke partly in his own language and partly in Jack's. The other boy understood him and told Captain and Mrs Arnold what he had said. The Captain was silent for a long time.

"It is what I feared," he said. "One of us will be thrown down the mountain-side to lessen the anger of their sun-god! We must try to reach Mike, Peggy, Nora and the others at all costs, as soon as we can. We must warn them!"

A Strange Journey – And A Surprise

As Captain Arnold was speaking the round door was flung open, and a tall, red-bearded man came out. It was dark in the passage, and he did not see the little company pressed against the wall. He was about to step out into the passage when there came the sound of running feet – and someone with flowing robes rushed up from the opposite direction.

There was a sharp talk, and then an excited shouting and calling. Mafumu pressed himself against Captain Arnold and whispered in his ear.

"We run quick, quick!"

Captain Arnold knew at once that their escape had been discovered, and that they must get away from there quickly. But where were they to go?

"Back to the river!" he whispered to Mrs Arnold, and the four of them made their way silently and swiftly down the passages to the dark river. Behind them they felt sure they heard the sound of voices and footsteps.

They went right to the bank of the river. "We could get in and go across to the other side, where that high rock is, and hope that our heads wouldn't show above the water," said Jack.

But just then Mafumu made a curious discovery. He ran to Jack, caught hold of his arm, and whispered something excitedly, pulling at Jack all the time to make him follow him. The boy went – and saw what Mafumu had so unexpectedly found. It was a small boat, of a curious shape, painted in curving stripes.

"Look! Let's get in and go down the river!" said Jack. "I can hear someone coming now, quite plainly!"

There didn't seem anything better they could do. So they all packed themselves into the funny rounded boat and pushed off down the dark river. There were paddle-like oars in the boat, but Captain Arnold did not need to use them because the current took them along strongly.

That was a very strange journey through the heart of the Secret Mountain. Sometimes the river ran through big caves, which gleamed with green phosphorescent light. Sometimes it ran through dank tunnels, and the four in the boat could feel the slimy walls as they floated through. Once the river opened out into an enormous pool, whose sides lapped the walls of a high cave.

Mafumu was terrified. He clung to Jack tightly, and muttered strings of strange-sounding words, fingering his necklace of crocodile teeth. Jack was sorry for the other boy, especially as he felt afraid too!

The river swirled along fast. Sometimes the boat knocked against rocks and nearly upset. Once Mrs Arnold almost fell overboard, and Captain Arnold only just snatched at her in time. Everyone wondered where the journey would end.

It ended in a most astonishing manner. The river suddenly became much less violent, and the current seemed to fall away to nothing. The boat almost stopped and Captain Arnold had to use the paddles to get it forward. They were in a fairly wide tunnel with a low roof, and not far ahead there seemed to be an archway, through which a bright light shone.

"We're arriving somewhere," said Captain Arnold. "Well, we can't go back, so we must go forward! I wonder what that bright light is!"

They soon found out! The boat went slowly forward, passed through the archway – and the four found, to their enormous amazement, that the river flowed through what looked like a big and most magnificent room!

The floor was of great smooth stones, polished till they shone. The walls were covered with brilliant hangings, all the colours of the rainbow, and the ceiling which was domed in glittering stones, rose up high and beautiful. From it hung the great gleaming lamp that gave the bright light the four had seen through the archway.

Stone tables stood here and there, and there were piles of soft rugs on the floor. Great vases and pitchers stood about filled with the brilliant flowers of the countryside. Three parrots screeched in a golden cage and five little monkeys huddled together in a corner.

Through the middle of this strange apartment, hidden right in the heart of the mountain, flowed one of the many underground rivers that gurgled their way towards the openings in the mountain rock through which they could fall down the hillside.

"This reminds me of a fairy-tale!" said Mrs Arnold in the greatest amazement. "What are we going to do? Get out and explore this extraordinary place? It's like a palace or something, built underground!"

No one was in the enormous, beautiful room except the parrots and the monkeys. Captain Arnold wondered whether or not to let his little party get out of the boat, which was still flowing gently along. And then he caught sight of something just ahead of him on the river.

It was a great golden gate stretched across the water! How strange! The boat would certainly be able to get no further, unless they could open the gate. Captain Arnold had a queer feeling that it would be better not to land in the strange room, but to go on, and see if by chance he could open the gate and go on his way.

So the boat went on towards the shining gate – and that was the end of their queer journey! For sitting along the banks of the river beside the gate were about a dozen of the red-haired Folk of the Mountain! As soon as they saw the boat coming they leapt to their feet in amazement and shouted and pointed!

The boat came to a stop by the gate. "It's all up now," said Captain Arnold in disgust. "We can't escape any further! They've got us!"

Sure enough, they were prisoners in about half a minute! The boat was pulled to the bank, and the Mountain Folk dragged the little company from their boat. They seemed astonished to see Jack and Mafumu.

"They don't know that Jack and Mafumu are here, of course," said Captain Arnold. "They know *we've* escaped because our cave is empty, but they didn't know anything about these two boys! Look – they are taking us back to that strange and beautiful room."

They passed through a great doorway into the big apartment they had just floated through. But now it was no longer empty! On a kind of throne at one end sat a tall, red-bearded, yellow-skinned man, whose eyes glinted strangely as he gazed down at the four people before him.

"He must be their chief or king," said Captain Arnold. "I don't like the look of him much."

Behind the chief stood a company of the Mountain Folk, all with flaming red beards. They held curious spears that glittered from end to end, and from their heads rose shining sun-rays that gleamed as they turned to one another. Mafumu was so frightened that he could hardly stand and Jack had to hold him up.

The big chief spoke in a harsh and stony voice. Only Mafumu understood a little of what he said, and what he heard made him tremble, for he knew that these sun-worshippers meant to throw one or more of them down the mountain-side as a kind of sacrifice to the sun. The red-bearded chief gave a sharp order, and at once the men with spears closed round the four and completely surrounded them.

They were marched off through the great room, with the screeching of the three parrots sounding in their ears. And they were taken to the top of the mountain, where the rest of the party were! But the way they went was quite different from the way that the others had taken!

They were marched to a small room in which stood what looked like a cage of gold, beautifully carved and worked. "Look!" said Jack, pointing upwards. "There's a hole going through the roof of this room, up and up and up!"

There was – and it was there for a curious purpose, too. It was to take the cage upwards, just as a lift-shaft holds a rising lift. The golden cage was a kind of simple lift – but the ropes that hauled it up were pulled by men and not by machinery.

The little party were crammed into the cage, with four of the Mountain Folk. The door was shut. One of the men shouted a sharp order – and immediately twenty men began to haul strongly on some massive ropes that hung down from another hole in the roof.

The cage shot upwards like a lift! Mafumu was terrified, he had never even been in a lift before! The others were amazed, but they showed no fear, and Mrs Arnold bent down to comfort the poor little boy.

Up and up they went, sometimes fast, sometimes slow, right to the very top of the mountain. They came to a stop underneath a round and gleaming trap-door, which was bolted underneath. One of the men slid back the bolts, pressed a spring and the door opened upwards, falling back silently on its hinges. The cage rose slowly once again, and when it was level with the ground it stopped.

The door of the golden cage was opened, and everyone stepped out. Captain and Mrs Arnold looked round. They had no idea where they were at first – and then they realized that they were on the very summit of the Secret Mountain! They held their breath as they looked at the magnificent view!

The cage-lift had come up through a hole right in the very middle of the vast courtyard that spread over the top of the mountain. Jack took a quick look round and wondered if any of the others were there, but he could see no one.

They *were* there, of course! They were in the temple, eating some of the fruit that had been brought to them, having wrapped themselves up well in the rugs, for the wind that blew across the mountain at that time of year was strong and cold, despite the hot sun.

It was Prince Paul who saw the strange and surprising sight of the cage-lift coming up in the middle of the courtyard! He was looking out through the open doorway of the temple, and to his very great amazement he saw what seemed to be a big trap-door slowly open and bend itself back. He swallowed his mouthful in surprise, and choked. Mike banged him on the back.

"Don't! Don't! Look! Look!" choked poor Paul, trying to point through the doorway. But everyone thought he was upset because he was choking, and Peggy took a turn at banging him between the shoulders.

Paul saw the golden cage rise up through the trap-door opening. He saw Captain and Mrs Arnold, Jack and Mafumu get out, with their four guards, and his eyes nearly fell out of his head with amazement and delight. He went quite purple in the face, and leapt to his feet.

"*Look!*" he yelled to the others. And at last they looked. When they saw the unexpected appearance of eight people in the middle of the smooth courtyard, and when Mike, Peggy and Nora saw that two of them were their own father and mother, what an excitement there was!

With shouts and shrieks the children rushed down the temple steps and ran towards the little company in the courtyard. In half a minute they were hugging their father and mother, exclaiming over them, thumping Jack on the back, shouting a hundred questions, and hugging little Mafumu, who was quite overjoyed at seeing all his lost friends so suddenly again.

"This *is* a surprise! This *is* a surprise!" everyone kept saying. And, indeed, it was!

The Escape Of Ranni And Pilescu

When everyone had calmd down a little, they lookd round to see what had become of the four guards who had come up in the cage-lift with Jack and the others. But they were gone! They had silently stepped into the golden cage once more, and had disappeared from sight into the heart of the mountain!

Captain Arnold ran to where the trap-door lay smoothly in the floor of the courtyard. He tried to get his fingers between the edges of the door and the stone of the courtyard – but they fitted so exactly that it was impossible.

"In any case it will be locked and bolted the other side," he said. "There's no way of escape there. How did *you* get here, Mike? Through this trap-door?"

103

Mike told him about the enormous flights of shining steps that led up to the golden door. He showed the newcomers the door itself, but no matter how they tried they could not slide it back.

The children were all so excited at seeing their father and mother again, and at having Jack and Mafumu once more, that they forgot their worries and chatted happily, telling one another their adventures. Only the grown-ups looked grave, and talked solemnly together, apart from the children.

"Somehow we must think of a way to escape," said Pilescu. "These Folk of the Secret Mountain are savage and ignorant. They think that the sun is angry with them, and they want to give him a servant to make their peace with him. Which of us will be chosen for that? I don't like to think."

"None of us is safe," said Captain Arnold. "Is it possible to lie in wait for the guards who come to give you food, Pilescu, overpower them, and escape down the golden stair?"

"We could try," said Ranni doubtfully. "But I fear it would be no use. Still, it seems the only thing to do."

At that moment Jack came up. He had been showing the other children the queer pot of yellow paint that he had taken from the storeroom among the caves in the mountain. He looked very peculiar because he had tried out some of the paint on his own face, and his skin was now as bright yellow as the Folk of the Mountain!

Ranni and Pilescu, who did not know about the pigment, stared at him in horror.

"Jack! What is the matter with you?" cried Pilescu. "Are you ill?"

"Very!" grinned Jack. "I think I must have got yellow fever, Pilescu! Have you got any medicine to make me better?"

The other children crowded round, giggling and

laughing, and Pilescu knew it was a joke. He looked closely at Jack.

"You have got yellow paint on your face," he said. "You look like one of the Folk of the Mountain!"

"And you, Pilescu, would look *exactly* like one if you painted *your* face," said Jack, "because you have a flaming red beard as they have. But yours is a real red beard, not a dyed one!"

No sooner had Jack said these words than the same thought flashed into Pilescu's head and Captain Arnold's at the same moment. Pilescu snatched the pot of pigment from Jack and looked at it. He dipped his finger into it and rubbed it over the back of his hand. At once his skin gleamed the same yellow as the skin of the Mountain Folk.

"I've thought the same thing as you, Pilescu," said Captain Arnold, in excitement. "If you used this paint you would pass for one of the Secret Mountain people! You and Ranni both have the bright red hair and beards of Baronian men – if you paint your skin yellow, you will look very like the Folk of the Mountain – and maybe our way of escape lies through you!"

Immediately all was excitement. Everyone talked at once. Everyone thought it was a simply marvellous idea. In the end Captain Arnold silenced the party and spoke seriously to them all.

"We must lose no further time in talk," he said. "I propose that both Ranni and Pilescu paint their faces with this yellow pigment and try to escape with the guards when they come. If only they can find their way back to where our planes are, they may be able to find some way of rescuing us all. It's the only chance that I can see."

"There are some robes in the temple with the rugs!" cried Mike. "I tried them on this morning. They would fit Ranni and Pilescu. Come and try them!"

In the greatest excitement the little company went to

The chief stood majestically on the tower

the temple. Ranni and Pilescu tried on the coloured robes and they fitted well enough. The flowing garments looked strange on the two big men, and everyone laughed.

Captain Arnold carefully rubbed the curious yellow pigment into the skin of the Baronians' faces, necks and hands. With the flowing robes, yellow skin and flaming beards they looked exactly like the Folk of the Secret Mountain! Poor Mafumu, unused to extraordinary happenings of this sort, could harldy believe that it was still Ranni and Pilescu, and he shrank away from them in fear.

"It is getting near the time when sun-worshippers come to pray to the sun at sunset," said Captain Arnold looking over the mountains to where the sun was swinging down towards the edge of the world. "Maybe many of the Mountain Folk will come, and then you can mix with them easily enough when they go!"

It was decided that Ranni and Pilescu should hide behind two great pillars near the sliding door. If they were not discovered they could mix with the Mountain Folk as they went down the stairs again, and might escape unseen in that way.

The sun swung lower – and suddenly, from behind the great golden door came the sound of chanting. It was the Mountain Folk coming to sing their prayers to the sun! The door slid to one side, and up the shining stairway came scores of the curious Folk, their beards gleaming red in the setting sun.

The leader went to the tower of the temple. All the rest spread themselves out on the flat courtyard, and flung themselves down on their faces when the man in the temple sounded a loud and echoing bell. They chanted a sad and doleful dirge for about ten minutes, whilst Captain Arnold and the rest looked on.

Behind the big pillars Ranni and Pilescu waited their chance. As soon as the sun disappeared over the edge of

107

the world and darkness fell on the mountain the people stood up and ranged themselves in lines. Then still singing, led by their tall leader, they made their way back to the stairway that led down into the dark mountain.

And, slipping to the end of the lines, went two red-bearded folk that did not belong to the mountain! Ranni and Pilescu joined the company, and tried to do exactly as the men in front did. They passed through the shining doorway and down the golden stairs. The door slid back silently into place – and Ranni and Pilescu were gone from sight!

"They've gone!" said Jack, slipping his hand through Mike's arm. "They've gone! Oh, I do wonder how they'll get on. I do hope they won't be caught!"

No one came to disturb them again that evening. The little party went into the temple and tried to find the most sheltered corner. The mountain wind blew without stopping, day and night, and it was difficult to find anywhere that was not full of draughts. The girls cuddled up to Mrs Arnold, and the boys and Captain Arnold found a bigger corner and piled rugs over themselves.

They all slept soundly that night, in spite of the cold. Captain and Mrs Arnold were glad to be with their children again, and hoped against hope that somehow Ranni and Pilescu would find a way to escape from the mountain and bring help to the prisoners.

For two days nothing happened. The Folk of the Mountain came up once at sunrise and once at sunset to chant their strange songs and prayers. Guards came to bring food and water. Curiously enough they did not miss Ranni and Pilescu at all – partly because Captain Arnold had told the party to split up, and be in various places on the summit of the mountain, instead of all together.

"Then when our guards come, they will not be able to count us up, because we shall be all over the place!" said Captain Arnold. "And unless they actually go to look for everyone they will not guess that two of our party are missing!"

But the guards did not think for one minute that anyone *could* be missing! After all, no one could escape down the trap-door for it was bolted underneath – and no one, so they thought, could escape down the golden stairway without being seen. So the little party lived peacefully for two days, with no excitements at all.

Then things began to happen. The golden cage once more came up through the trap-door in the centre of the vast courtyard! Mrs Arnold happened to be standing nearby and she had a great surprise when she saw the trap-door suddenly rise up and the golden cage appear. She ran to tell the others. They came to watch who was coming.

The chief himself walked from the golden lift! He was very tall, and very thin. His beard flamed in the sun, and his clothes swung round him like shimmering water as he walked. His yellow skin was wrinkled and drawn. He was an old, old man, but powerful and with piercing, eagle-like eyes.

He gave a sharp order. Men stepped out from the cage and came behind him. He walked solemnly to the temple, where he chanted several prayers to the sun in a strong harsh voice. Then he turned to his servants rounded up the little company of prisoners, and brought them before the chief. He ran his strange eyes over them and then looked at his servants in surprise. It was quite plain that he thought someone was missing!

He asked a sharp question. The servants hurriedly counted the prisoners and then sent two of their number to search the summit of the mountain thoroughly.

"They've gone to find Ranni and Pilescu," whispered Jack. "Well, they won't find them here!"

And they didn't, of course, though they hunted in every corner and cranny. Ranni and Pilescu had disappeared completely.

The chief was angry. His eyes flamed, and his mouth became hard and straight. He addressed his servants fiercely, and they flung themselves on their faces before him. No one but Mafumu could understand what he was saying, and even Mafumu could not understand everything!

The chief walked majestically over to the company of prisoners and looked into each one's face. No one flinched except poor Mafumu, who was in a state of real terror, partly because he was afraid of the yellow-skinned chief and partly because he knew something that the others didn't know!

The chief was choosing who was to be the servant of the sun! He glared into Jack's face. He stared closely at poor Nora and Peggy. He took Paul's chin in his hand and peered at him. Nobody liked it at all.

Mafumu was very sad. Whom would the chief choose? Somebody must be the sacrifice to the sun. And poor Mafumu would have to break the news, for no one else understood what the yellow-skinned chief was doing!

The Servant Of The Sun

The tall chief took hold of the little prince and called out some strange words to his followers. At once two men stepped forward and took the frightened boy. He did not know what they were going to do with him, but he was determined not to show that he was afraid.

So, rather white, he stood up proudly and looked the chief straight in the face. Mike and the others felt proud of him.

Paul was marched off alone He was taken to the golden

110

door, which slid back silently. Then he disappeared down the stairway, and the door once more shut like magic. Captain Arnold stepped forward angrily.

"What are you going to do to the boy?" he cried. "Bring him back!"

The chief laughed the turned on his heel. He went up to the tower of the temple and began what seemed like a long prayer to the sun.

It was left to poor trembling Mafumu to break the news to the others. In his few English words he tried to explain that little Paul was to be the servant of the sun. Everyone listened in amazement and horror. Captain and Mrs Arnold who had feared that something like this could happen ever since they had been brought to the temple on top of the mountain, looked despairingly at one another.

"I can't see how we can possibly save him," said Captain Arnold at last. They all sat down in the shade, and Peggy and Nora began to cry. If even grown-up people couldn't do anything, then things were indeed in a bad way!

Mike and Jack and Mafumu talked together. Jack would never give up hope. He was that kind of boy. But Mike was full of dismay, and as for Mafumu, he was simply shivering with worry and fright. He kept as close to Jack as he could, as if he thought that Jack would protect him from everything.

Jack was very edgy, though he didn't show it. "I wish you'd do something instead of shivering all over me," he said to Mafumu, pushing the boy away.

"Give him a pencil or a notebook to play with," said Mike. "He's only a little kid, and you can't blame him for being a bit scared."

Jack put his hand into his pocket and brought out a diary. He had been keeping the tale of their adventures there, day by day. He handed it to Mafumu.

"Here you are. Play with this over in the corner there,"

he said. Mafumu took the notebook eagerly. He turned over each page one by one, rubbing his fingers over the pages in which Jack had written. He could not understand anything, of course, because he could not write or read.

He came to where Jack had written the day before. After that the pages were blank. Mafumu was puzzled. Why was nothing written in one half of the book? He rolled himself over beside Jack and pointed to the blank pages.

Jack tried to explain to Mafumu. "Today I write, tomorrow I write, but not till the day has gone," he said.

"Jack, what's the date today?" asked Mike idly. "I've really lost count of the days, you know! I don't know if it's Sunday, Monday, Tuesday, or what – or if it's the tenth, eleventh, twenty-first, or thirtieth of the month!"

"Well, I can tell you, because I've written down our adventures every day," said Jack. "It's Wednesday – and it's the sixteenth. Look."

Mike took the diary. He glanced at the next day, and gave an exclamation.

"Oh, Jack! Look what it says for tomorrow!"

"What?" asked Jack, surprised.

"It says there will be an eclipse of the sun," said Mike. "I do wonder if we'll see it here?"

"Let's ask your father," said Jack. So the two boys went across to Captain Arnold, with the faithful Mafumu following at their heels.

"Dad! It says in Jack's diary that there is an eclipse of the sun tomorrow!" said Mike. "Do you think there is any chance at all of seeing it here?"

"What's an eclipse of the sun?" asked Peggy. "I know we've learnt about it in school, but I've quite forgotten what happens."

"It's quite simple," said Mike. "All that happens is that the moon on its way through the sky passes in front of the sun, and blocks out the sun's light for a little while. It

112

eclipses the sun's light, and for a time the world looks queer and strange because there is no sunlight in the daytime!"

Captain Arnold sprang to his feet. To Mike's enormous surprise he snatched Jack's diary from him and looked at what was printed there in the space for the next day.

"Eclipse of the sun, 11.43 a.m.," he read. "Is this this year's diary? Yes! My word! Eclipse of the sun *tomorrow!* It's unbelievable!"

He spoke in such an excited voice that everyone came round him at once.

"What's the matter? Why are you so excited?" cried Mike. Only Mrs Arnold guessed. Her eyes were bright and hopeful.

"I'll tell you. Listen carefully," said Captain Arnold. He lowered his voice, for although he did not think that any of the Mountain Folk were listening anywhere, or could understand a word he said, he was not taking any chances.

"Mike has told you what an eclipse of the sun means. It means that the moon passes exactly in front of the sun, and it only happens rarely. If we were in England the sun would not be competely hidden by the moon – but here in Africa it will, and the whole countryside will become as dark as night!"

The children listened in excitement. What a strange happening it would be!

"Now these Mountain Folk are sun-worshippers," said Captain Arnold. "It is quite plain that they have the custom of throwing unfortunate people over the mountain-side to sacrifice to the sun, when they want to please him, or ask him to grant a prayer. I am afraid that our little Paul has been chosen, and will be beyond our help tomorrow unless we do something. And now I see what we can do!"

"What?" cried everyone.

"Well, we will get Mafumu to explain to these people,

113

when they next come up here, that I will kill the sun tomorrow, unless they set Paul free!" said Captain Arnold.

"How do you mean – kill the sun?" asked Nora in wonder.

"Well, to them, when the eclipse happens, it will seem as if the sun is being killed!" said Captain Arnold, smiling. "They won't know that it is only the moon passing in front of the sun that is blocking out the light – they will really think I have done something to the sun they worship!"

"Oh, Captain Arnold – it sounds too good to be true!" cried Jack. "Won't they be amazed? I wonder if they will set us all free if we do this."

"Probably," said Captain Arnold. "We can do our best, anyway. Now, I wonder if the Mountain Folk will come up at sunset tonight, and sing their mournful prayers!"

But, to everyone's great disappointment, not a single person came. No word was heard of the little Prince. Nothing happened at all. Captain and Mrs Arnold felt uneasy about Paul, but they did not tell the others.

"Probably there is a great hunt going on in the mountain for Ranni and Pilescu!" said Captain Arnold. "I do wonder what has happened to them. If only they have managed to slip out of the rock-entrance, and find help somewhere."

The night passed. It was cold up on the mountain-top and everyone slept as usual muffled up in the soft warm rugs. The children missed Prince Paul and were sad when they thought of him. They knew he must be feeling very lonely and frightened all by himself, no matter how brave a face he put on when the Mountain Folk were there.

The dawn came, and the whole sky around was full of dancing silvery light.

"You can see such an enormous lot of sky from the top of a mountain," said Mike, gazing all round. "Look – there comes the sun!"

114

The golden sun rose slowly into the sky and the children watched it. It was so beautiful that each child was filled with awe.

"It's certainly the king of the sky!" said Mike. "I really am not surprised that these strange wild tribes worship the sun! Oh dear – I do miss Paul. I wonder where he is."

They soon saw him again. Mike spied the trap-door slowly open in the middle of the big courtyard, and he called out to the others.

"Someone's coming. Look!"

They all looked. The golden cage rose slowly through the space left by the trap-door, and in it the children could see the tall chief with his flaming red beard, two servants – and a small figure dressed in the most wonderful shimmering robes they had ever seen.

"Why – it's Paul dressed like that!" cried Mike in amazement. "And look what he's got on his head!"

Paul was certainly dressed in a very queer manner. He wore the shimmering golden garments down to his feet, and the flowing sleeves even covered his hands. On his head was a great head-dress made in the likeness of a glittering sun, with golden rays springing upwards.

The boy looked magnificent, and he walked very proudly. He had guessed that he was to be the servant of the sun, and he was afraid – but he was going to show Mike and the others that he was brave and courageous. He walked behind the chief, and sent a cheerful though rather quivery smile at his friends.

"Dear Paul. Good little Paul," said Nora.

"I do feel proud of him," said Mike, with a funny little break in his voice.

And then Captain Arnold stepped forward and shouted in such a tremendous voice that everyone jumped.

"*Stop!* I command you to *stop!*"

The tall chief stopped in his walk and glared round at Captain Arnold. He did not understand the words that the

115

captain said – but he understood their meaning. There was no mistaking that at all!

"Come here Mafumu," commanded Captain Arnold. The little boy came to him, trembling. "Tell the chief that I will kill the sun if he does anything to Paul," said the Captain. Mafumu did not understand, so Jack explained as best he could in simple words.

Mafumu nodded. He knelt down before the chief, and banged his forehead on the ground before him.

Mafumu cried out some strange words to the chief, and then banged his forehead on the ground again. The chief frowned and looked at Captain Arnold. He said something sharp to Mafumu.

"Chief say no, Captain will not kill sun," said the little boy. "He say that when the sun is high, high, high, Paul will go to the sun."

"When the sun is high," repeated Captain Arnold. "That means noon – twelve o'clock – and the eclipse is due at about a quarter to. Well – that will just about do it! Tell the chief I *will* kill the sun unless he sets us all free, Mafumu."

But the chief laughed in their faces. He set off towards the tower of the temple, Paul following behind in his shimmering robes. Everyone watched them go – and how the children hoped that the eclipse of the sun would actually happen. It seemed too strange a thing to be really true.

The Sun Disappears!

The little company of prisoners were not allowed to go into the temple that morning. The two servants stood at the door and prevented anyone from entering. Mike could see the figure of Paul up on the tower with the tall chief, who was muttering and chanting all kinds of weird words to the sun. Paul waved to Mike once, and Mike waved back.

"It's all right, Paul. You needn't be afraid," shouted Mike. "We're going to save you!"

But the wind took away his words and Paul did not hear. He stood there bravely, the wonderful head-dress he was wearing shining and glinting in the sun.

As the sun rose higher and the day gew hotter, Captain Arnold and the rest of his party found what shade they could. There was always a big wind blowing on the summit of the high mountain, but even so the rays of the sun as it rose high were flaming hot.

At about eleven o'clock the great golden door slid open, and an enormous company of Mountain Folk came singing up the shining stairway. They were dressed in shimmering robes rather like Paul's, and looked marvellous as they trooped out on to the great courtyard. Their faces were yellower than ever, and the men's beards had been freshly dyed and flamed like fire.

They ranged themselves over the courtyard and then began to dance a strange dance. Their feet stamped, their robes swung and shimmered, their voices rose and fell in a queer chant.

"A sort of sun dance," said Captain Arnold. Everyone was worried and anxious, but they could not help marvelling as they watched the curious sun-worhippers performing their extraordinary dance.

Captain Arnold glanced at his watch. It was half-past eleven. He looked anxiously up at the sun, which was almost at its highest point. No moon could be seen, of course, for the sun was so bright. But it was there all right, travelling through the sky.

An enormous gong boomed out from the temple. One of the servants of the chief was sounding it. The children had seen it there, but there had been nothing to bang it with – and now it was sounding over the mountain-top, booming its great solemn note all around. The valleys below took up the note and threw it back – and soon, from everywhere around, the echoes came back until it seemed as if the whole earth and sky were filled with the booming of the gong.

At once all the sun-worshippers fell on their knees. The chief waited until the sound of the gong had died away and then he spoke in a loud voice. He brought Prince Paul forward, and the boy stood there on the temple tower, his robes blowing and shining in the wind.

"Captain Arnold, will the eclipse start soon?" asked Jack nervously. He was terribly afraid that something would happen to Paul before they could prevent it. Captain Arnold glanced at his watch.

"It will begin in two minutes," he said. "Now, *I* am going to take a hand in this game! Watch me!"

He ran with quick, light steps to the tower. The servants at the entrance were taken by surprise, and he slipped through easily. He raced up the stone steps and in a moment or two was standing beside the chief and Paul.

And then things began to happen! Captain Arnold turned to the great sun and shook his fist at it. He shouted at it! He snatched a knife from his belt and threw it high into the air at the sun! The knife made a great curve in the air and disappeared over the mountainside!

118

The great chief knelt before Captain Arnold

119

"He kills the sun, he kills the sun!" shouted Mafumu, who suddenly understood what Captain Arnold was pretending to do. The Mountain Folk understood Mafumu's shout and rose to their feet in alarm and confusion. The servants of the chief ran to capture Captain Arnold – and then a strange thing happened.

A tiny piece seemed suddenly to be bitten out of the sun! A small black shadow appeared at one side! The moon was beginning to pass in front of it, and was hiding a very small piece.

Mafumu saw it and was astonished. He pointed at the sun, and shouted in alarm. "The sun is being eaten! See, see!"

A great silence fell on the mountain-top. Everyone was watching the sun in the sky, covering their faces with their hands, and looking through their fingers to avoid the brilliance. The servants who had come to capture Captain Arnold watched, too, trembling.

The moon passed further in front of the sun and a bigger piece became completely dark. A moan of fear came from the watching Mountain Folk. They did not understand what an eclipse of the sun was, and they really thought that their precious sun was being killed!

Not one of them guessed that it was merely the moon passing in front of the sun and blocking out its light for a while. They fell on their faces and muttered all kinds of strange prayers. And when they looked up again they saw that half of the sun was gone!

And now the world began to look queer and unearthly. The sunlight dwindled and died. A queer half-light came over the whole countryside. Birds stopped singing. The monkeys in the trees huddled together, frightened. The frogs thought that night was coming and began to croak.

The children were afraid too, although they knew quite well that it was only an eclipse they were watching. They had never seen one before, and this was a complete eclipse, with every bit of daylight and sunlight gradually going from the world they looked upon. As for poor Mafumu he had never in his life been so frightened. He crouched on the ground shivering like a jelly, and Jack did his best to comfort him.

The chief up on the tower was watching the dying sun with fear and amazement. He too was trembling. Could it be that this man was really killing their wonderful sun-god who shone so brightly in the sky each day? He could not understand it. He threw out his arms to the sun, and shouted to it, trying to comfort the failing sun, and to make it shine brightly again! Captain Arnold folded his arms, looked very stern, and it really seemed for all the world as if he were the conjurer who had worked the trick!

And now even stranger things happened! The sky became as black as night and the stars came out. They shone brilliantly, and starlight lighted the earth instead of sunlight.

"Don't be afraid," Mrs Arnold said to the scared children, who had not expected this. "The sun is gone now, lost behind the moon – so, of course, it is like night-time, and the stars shine out. You must remember that the stars are always in the sky, all through the day – but we don't see them because daylight is so bright. But now that the daylight has gone, we can see the stars shining.

It all seemed simple enough when Mrs Arnold explained it – but the terrified Mountain Folk had no idea of what was really happening, and they were quite mad with fear and terror. They shouted and moaned, and beat their foreheads and dropped to their knees.

Up on the tower it was quite dark. Captain Arnold caught hold of the astonished little prince and whispered in his ear.

"Go down the stone steps and join the others, Paul. No one will stop you now. You are safe."

Paul made his way to the steps and went down them

121

thankfully. He felt his way to the children, and clasped Mike's hand in joy. Mike put his arms round him, and the others clustered round Paul, who felt strange in his flowing garments.

"The eclipse came just at the right moment to save you, Paul, old boy," said Jack in his ear. "You're safe now. You *were* brave. We were awfully proud of you."

Paul's heart glowed. He had often been laughed at because he was rather a baby – and now he felt a hero! He kept close to the children and watched the rest of the eclipse.

As soon as Captain Arnold saw that the sun was completely gone, he began to shout, pretending that he was threatening the lost sun. The chief went down on his knees and begged for mercy, quite certain that Captain Arnold was the most powerful magician in the whole world!

Then gradually the moon passed right across the sun, and a little bit of one side began to show again. The stars slowly disappeared as the moon passed from the sun, and the strange half-light appeared once more. This was too much for the Mountain Folk. It was bad enough to have seen the sun die, as they thought – but now something else was happening, and they could not bear it.

Shouting and groaning, they rushed to the golden stairway and poured down it, slipping and falling as they went. The two servants who had been on the tower went too, deserting their chief in their fear. He was left on the tower, kneeling down before Captain Arnold.

Gradually the sun became itself again as the moon passed right across it, and the black shadow fled. The glorious daylight flooded the mountains, and the golden sun poured its rays down once more. Birds sang again. The monkeys chattered in delight. The brief and unexpected night was gone, and the world was itself again.

Captain Arnold took the frightened chief by the shoulder and led him firmly down the steps. He called to Mafumu.

"Mafumu, tell the chief he must let us all go now, or I will

122

kill his sun again," commanded the Captain. Mafumu understood. He was feeling better now that the sun had come back, and he thought that Captain Arnold must be the most powerful man in all the world. No matter how often the others explained what had really happened, Mafumu would never, never believe anything but that Captain Arnold had done something to the sun!

Mafumu, feeling important and grand, said something to the chief. The man was angry that such a small boy should speak in that way to him, and he took no notice at all. He strode away from Captain Arnold and went towards the trap-door, which was still lying open, flat on the ground. The golden cage was there awaiting him.

"Mafumu, tell him that we are going down the golden stairway, and that his servants must let us out of the rock-entrance," said Captain Arnold. Mafumu shouted at the chief. The man nodded, and entered the cage. In a trice he was gone, and the trap-door still lay flat on the ground, for he had not troubled to bolt it.

"Well, *he's* gone, and so has everyone else," said Mike, with a laugh. "My word – what an adventure! I don't mind saying that I felt very queer myself when the sun began to disappear and the stars shone out. I could do with something to eat. Let's go and get some of those flat cakes from the temple before we go down the stairs."

"Well, hurry then," said Captain Arnold. "I want to go whilst the going is good!"

The boys ran to get the cakes and some fruit. They brought it out in the flat dishes, and joined Captain and Mrs Arnold and the girls, who were walking towards the golden door.

But as they came near, the door began to slide silently shut! Captain Arnold gave a shout and ran towards it.

"Hurry! They are shutting us out!"

He got there just as the door completely closed. There it rose above him, a tall, shining door, as wide as a great gate – fast shut.

"They've tricked us!" shouted the Captain angrily, and he hammered on the door. But there was no handle, no latch, nothing to get hold of or to loosen. There was no getting through that enormous door it was plain!

Big, Big Bird That Sings R-r-r-r-r-r!

"The trap-door!" shouted Mike. "We can escape through that. The chief has left it open!"

The boys ran helter-skelter across the vast courtyard to where the opening was. They were half-afraid that the trap-door would close before they got there. But it didn't.

The four boys stood by the lift-opening and looked down. The lift-shaft ran straight down below their feet, cut out of solid rock. The golden cage was not to be seen, of course. The opening looked dark and narrow as it disappeared into the darkness of the heart of the mountain.

"I don't see how we could escape down there," said Mike. "We would need a tremendous long rope to begin with – which we haven't got – and also, just suppose the lift came up as we went down!"

"That golden cage was pulled up and down by ropes, wasn't it?" said Mrs Arnold. "Well, surely those must still be running down one side of the opening."

"Of course they must," said Captain Arnold. "We'll look for those."

But the ropes that sent the lift up and down had been cut! Captain Arnold found them easily enough, running in a cleverly cut groove at one side of the lift-opening. But when he pulled at them they came up in his hand, not more than ten feet long! Somehow they had been cut and were of no use at all!

"We may as well shut the trap-door," said Captain Arnold, in disgust and disappointment. "It is dangerous to leave it open in case one of you goes and tumbles down the hole. Well – we really are in a fix now!"

"How all the Mountain Folk must be laughing at us!" said Mike. "We are nicely caught! Can't get down, and can't get up – here we are stuck on the top of a mountain for the rest of our lives!"

Captain Arnold did not like the look of things at all. He was afraid that the Folk of the Secret Mountain would open the sliding door and spring on them during the night. But he said this only to Mrs Arnold, for he did not want to frighten the children.

"Well, we've all had a great deal of excitement today," he said. "Let's go into the cool temple, have a good meal, and a rest."

So into the temple they went, and were soon munching away at the flat cakes and the sweet juicy fruit. Then the children and Mrs Arnold settled themselves down for a rest whilst Captain Arnold kept watch. It was arranged that either the Captain, Jack or Mike should keep guard, so that at any rate the little party would not be taken unawares.

The night came as suddenly as usual. The stars flashed out brightly, and the world of mountains lay peacefully under the beautiful starlight. Captain Arnold went to examine the trap-door to make sure that no one could come upon them from there, and then he went to look at the sliding door. But it was still fast shut and there seemed to be no sound from the other side at all.

The night passed peacefully. First the Captain kept watch and then the two boys. But nothing happened. The dawn came, and the sun rose. The children awoke and stretched themselves. They were hungry – but, alas, except for a few of the flat cakes, there was no food left at all.

"I hope they are not going to starve us out," said Mike hungrily, as Captain Arnold shared out the few cakes between the party. "I shouldn't like that at all."

"This adventure is exciting, but awfully uncomfortable," said Nora.

At about ten o'clock the great golden door slid back again. Up the stairs came the Folk of the Mountain – but this time they carried shining spears! They were on the warpath, that was plain!

Captain Arnold had half-expected this. He made the children go into a corner, and he went to meet the tall chief, with Mafumu close beside him to talk for him.

But the chief was in no mood for talking. He too carried a spear, and he looked very fiercely at Captain Arnold.

"Tell him I will kill his sun again, Mafumu," said the Captain desperately.

"Chief say he kill you first," said poor Mafumu, his teeth chattering. And, indeed, it certainly looked as if this was what the chief meant to do, for he lowered his spear and pointed it threateningly at Captain Arnold.

The Captain had a revolver. He did not want to shoot the chief, but thought he might as well frighten him. He drew his revolver and fired it into the air. The noise of the shot echoed round the mountains in a most terrifying manner. The chief jumped with fright. All the Mountain Folk began to jabber and shout.

But one, cleverer than the others, aimed his spear at Captain Arnold. The shining weapon flew through the air, struck the gun in the Captain's hand, and sent it flying to ground with a clang. None of the Mountain Folk dared to pick it up, and Captain Arnold did not dare to either – for a different reason! He was not afraid of the revolver – but he *was* afraid of the spears around him!

126

The chief shouted out a harsh order, and twelve men ran up with spears. They took hold of all the little company, and before ten minutes had gone by, each grown-up and child was bound with thin, strong ropes!

"What will they do with us?" said Nora, who was very angry because her wrists had been bound too tightly.

Nobody knew. But it was plain that the little party were to be taken below into the heart of the mountain. They were not to be left on the summit.

"I expect the chief is afraid we will do something to his beloved sun if he leaves us up here," said Jack. "I wish another eclipse would happen! What a shock it would give them all!"

The chief gave orders for the captives to be taken down the shining stairway – but just as they were about to go, there came a most extraordinary noise!

At first it was far away and quiet – a little humming – but soon it grew louder and louder, and the mountain-side echoed with the sound of throbbing.

"R-r-r-r-r-r!" went the noise. "R-r-r-r-r-r! R-r-r-r-r-r!"

The Folk of the Secret Mountain stopped and listened, their eyes wide with amazement. This was a strange noise. What could it be?

The children were puzzled at first too – but almost at once Jack knew what the noise was, and he lifted up his voice in a shout.

"It's an aeroplane! An aeroplane! Can't you hear it? It's coming nearer!"

Captain Arnold was amazed. He knew that it was the noise made by the throbbing of aeroplane engines – but what aeroplane? Surely – surely – it could not be the White Swallow?

The noise came nearer – and then a black speck could be seen flying towards the mountain-side. It really *was* an aeroplane – no doubt about that at all!

The Mountain Folk saw it too. They cried out in surprise and pointed to it. "What are they saying, Mafumu?" shouted Jack.

"They say, 'Big, big bird, big, big bird that sings r-r-r-r-r-r-r!'" said Mafumu, his eyes shining and his teeth flashing. The children laughed, excited and eager. Something was going to happen – they were sure of it!

The aeroplane came nearer and nearer, growing bigger as it came. "It *is* the White Swallow!" shouted Captain Arnold. "I'd know the sound of her engines anywhere, the beauty! Ranni and Pilescu must have somehow got back to the planes, made the White Swallow ready for taking off – and flown up in her."

"Can they land here?" cried Paul.

"Of course!" said Mike. "Look at this great smooth courtyard – an ideal landing-ground if ever there was one! Oh, if only Ranni and Pilescu know this mountain when they see it, and they come here!"

The aeroplane came nearer, rising high as it flew, as if it were going to fly right over the summit of the mountain. The Mountain Folk were terrified, and crouched to the ground. The aeroplane, gleaming as white as a gull, circled overhead as if it were looking for something.

"It's going to land, it's going to land!" yelled Jack, jumping about even though his hands and legs were bound. "Golly, what a shock for the red-beards!"

The white aeroplane circled lower – and even as it made to land there came another noise echoing around the mountains.

"R-r-r-r-r-r! R-r-r-r-r-r!"

"That's *my* aeroplane; I bet it is, I bet it is!" yelled Prince Paul, his face red with excitement as he tried his hardest to get rid of the ropes that bound him, "I'd know the sound of *my* aeroplane anywhere too!"

Whilst the White Swallow made a perfect landing,

128

running gracefully on her big wheels over the enormous flat courtyard, the second aeroplane could be seen rising slowly up the mountain-side.

"It's Paul's blue and silver plane," cried Peggy. "Oh, my goodness – this is too thrilling for anything! Look who's in the White Swallow! Ranni, Ranni, Ranni!"

A Thrilling Rescue!

The chief and his servants were full of amazement and fear when they heard the noise of the aeroplanes and saw them coming. When the White Swallow zoomed immediately overhead all the Mountain Folk fell down in fear and moaned as if they were in pain.

"Look out! You'll be hurt by the plane!" yelled Mike, when the White Swallow made to land. The terrified people leapt to their feet and ran helter-skelter to the sides of the courtyard. The plane missed everyone, and it was good to see Ranni's smiling face as he jumped down from the cockpit. He glanced at the Mountain Folk but none were near, and ran across the courtyard to the prisoners. He pulled a fierce-looking knife from his belt and cut them all free.

The children crowded round him, hugging him and raining questions. "You should have seen me yesterday!" yelled Paul, who was now very proud of his narrow escape. "I wore clothes of gold and sun-rays on my head!"

Captain and Mrs Arnold were delighted too, though the Captain kept a stern eye on the Mountain Folk, who were crowded together, trembling, watching the aeroplane.

"They look as if they expect it to jump on them, or bark at them or something," grinned Jack.

"I think it would be a good thing if we took off at once," said Ranni. "You never know when these people will find their senses and start making things unpleasant for us! They've only got to damage our plane and we are done for!"

"Here comes Pilescu with *my* plane!" cried Paul in delight, as the big blue and silver aeroplane circled overhead, making a tremendous noise. The mountains around threw the echoes back, and the aeroplane sounded like a rumbling thunderstorm! Round and round it circled, and the Mountain Folk gave groans of terror and threw themselves on their faces again.

The little prince's plane made just as good a landing as the White Swallow. It let down its wheels and lightly touched the ground, running along smoothly over the enormous courtyard.

"Really, it is a perfect landing-ground!" said Captain Arnold, watching. "Smooth, big, and with plenty of wind!"

The blue and silver plane came to a stop. The door of the cockpit opened as the engines stopped. Pilescu looked out, his eyes hidden by sun-glasses. Ranni had not worn them, and the sight of Pilescu gave the Mountain Folk an even bigger fright!

Half of them rushed to the big stairway and disappeared down it, shouting. The other half, with the chief, knelt on the ground, the chief muttering something.

"He say, 'Big chief want mercy!'" grinned Mafumu, who was now enjoying himself immensely.

"Well, if he thinks I'm going to throw him down the mountain-side or take him off in the planes, he's mistaken," said Captain Arnold. "I shan't take any notice of him at all. Come along – we really ought to get off at once. It is a miraculous escape from great danger."

"The two planes will easily take us all," said Mike joyfully. "Who's going in-which ?"

"Ranni, Pilescu, Paul, Jack and the girls can go in Paul's big plane," said Captain Arnold. "I'd like Mike with us – and Mafumu had better come with me too. We can't leave him here."

They all began to climb up into the two cockpits. It didn't take long. Pilescu took the controls of his plane and looked round.

"All ready?" he asked. Then he looked again. "Where's Paul? I thought he was to come in this plane."

"He's not here," said Jack. "I expect he climbed into the White Swallow. I know he always wanted to fly in her."

"Right," said Pilescu, and pulled at a handle. But Ranni stopped him.

"We *must* see if Paul is in the other plane!" he said. "We don't want to arrive in England and find that Paul isn't in either plane!"

Ranni opened the door of the cockpit again and leaned out. He yelled to the White Swallow. "Hallo there! Have you got Paul all right?"

"What?" yelled Captain Arnold, who was just about to take off.

"Is PAUL with you?" shouted Ranni.

"No," shouted back Captain Arnold, after a quick look round his own plane. "I said he was to go with you. The White Swallow isn't big enough for more than four."

Ranni went white. He loved the little Prince better than anyone else in the world – and here they were, about to take off from the mountain-top without Paul! Whatever in the world had become of him?

Ranni leapt out of the plane. Nora called to him. "Look. Isn't that Paul over there in the temple?"

Ranni rushed towards the temple, imagining that all kinds of dreadful things were happening to the little prince. He took out his gun, quite determined to give the whole of the Mountain Folk the worst shock of their lives if they were taking little Paul a prisoner again!

Nobody but Paul was in the temple. He was in a corner struggling with something. Ranni gave a roar.

"Paul! What is it? We nearly went without you!"

Paul stood up. In his arms was the beautiful shimmering robe of golden cloth that he had worn the day before, and over his shoulder he had slung his sun-ray headress. Young Paul was determined to take those back to school with him, to show his admiring friends. How else would they believe him when he told them of his great adventure?

He had slipped away from his party when no one was looking, for he had felt certain that Captain Arnold would say no, if he asked if he might go and get the garments. The clothes had been difficult to gather up and carry, and Paul did not realise that the planes were starting off so soon!

"Hallo, Ranni! I just went to get these sun-clothes of mine," said Paul. "You haven't seen them, Ranni. Look, you must. . . ."

But to Paul's enormous astonishment Ranni gave him a resounding slap, picked up the boy, clothes and all, and ran back to the big blue and silver plane with him. The Mountain Folk, seeing Ranni run, began to jabber, and one or two picked up their spears.

A gleaming spear flew past Ranni's big head. He dodged to one side, sprang up the ladder of the cockpit and threw Paul on to a seat.

"The little idiot had gone into the temple to get his sun-clothes!" said Ranni, angry and alarmed because they had so nearly gone without Paul.

Paul was angry too. He sat up on the seat. "How dare you hit me?" he shouted to Ranni. "I'll tell the King, my father. He'll, he'll, he'll . . ."

"Shut up, Paul," said Jack. "I'll slap you myself if you say any more! You might have stopped us escaping. The Mountain Folk are looking rather nasty now."

132

Sure enough some of them were creeping towards the planes, spears in hand. Both planes started up their engines. The throbbing noise arose on the air again. The Mountain Folk shrank back in alarm.

The White Swallow took off first. Gracefully she rose into the air, circled round twice, and then made off over the mountains. Then the blue and silver plane rose up and she was off too.

Jack looked downwards. Already the Secret Mountain looked far off and small. He could just see the folk there running about like ants. How angry they must be because their prisoners had escaped in such an extraordinary way!

"Well, we're off again," said Jack to the girls. "And glad as I was to see the Secret Mountain, I am even gladder to leave it behind! Cheer up, Paul, don't look so blue! We're safe now, even though you nearly messed things up!"

Prince Paul was feeling very foolish. "Sorry," he said. "I didn't think. Anyway, thank goodness I've got the sun-clothes. Won't the boys at school think I'm lucky! I shall dress up in them and show the Head."

Eveyrone laughed. It was exciting to be in the plane again. Jack called to Ranni.

"Ranni! You haven't told us your adventures yet. How did you escape from the Secret Mountain?"

"It was unexpectedly easy," shouted back Ranni, who was sitting beside Pilescu. "No one suspected that Pilescu and I were anything but ordinary Mountain Folk when we went down the golden stairway with them. We went down and down for ages and at last came to a big cave where most of them seem to live."

"Oh yes, Mafumu and I once saw that," said Jack. "Go on, Ranni."

"We didn't like to go and sit in the cave in case somebody spoke to us and we couldn't answer in their language," said Ranni. "So we waited about in a passage until we saw a little party of the Mountain Folk going along with spears. We thought they must be going hunting so we joined them, walking behind them."

"How exciting!" said Nora. "Didn't they guess who you were?"

"Not once," said Ranni. "We followed them down all kinds of dark passages until we came into the big hall-like place whose steps lead up to the rock-entrance. They worked a lever and the big door slid open. Then they set that great rock turning and sliding, and the way was open to us!"

"You *were* lucky," said Jack. "I wish I had shared that adventure."

"It wasn't quite so good after that," said Ranni. "We had to find our way back to the planes and we got competely lost up in the mountain-pass. We found our way at last by a great stroke of luck – and arrived at the planes, very tired indeed, but safe!"

"It didn't take you long to get them going," shouted Peggy. "Did you find it difficult to spot the Secret Mountain?"

"No. Very easy," said Ranni. "It looks so yellow from the air – and besides, it's the only one with a flat top."

"I say! What's the White Swallow doing?" cried Jack suddenly. "It's going down! Is it going to land, Ranni?"

"It looks like it," said Ranni. "I wonder what's the matter! My word, I hope nothing has gone wrong. This plane is large but it won't take everyone."

The White Swallow flew lower still. Below was a fine flat stretch of grass, and the plane was making for that. It landed easily and came to a stop.

"We must land too, and see what's up," said Ranni, looking worried. So the blue and silver plane circled round too, and flew slowly towards the flat piece of grass. It let down its wheels and landed gently and smoothly, running along for a little way and then stopping.

134

Captain Arnold was already out of his plane and was helping little Mafumu down.

"What's the matter? Anything wrong?" yelled Ranni, climbing from his cockpit. "Let me come and help!"

Goodbye To Mafumu – And Home At Last!

Captain Arnold looked round and shook his head. "No – there's nothing wrong," he said. "But we can't take Mafumu to England with us! He would be miserable away from his own people. His own folk live near here – look, you can see the village over there – and I am taking him home.

"The children will want to say good-bye to him," said Ranni at once. "Little Mafumu has been a good friend to us. We couldn't have rescued you without his help. Hie, Jack – bring Paul and the girls to say good-bye to Mafumu. We're leaving him here."

Everyone climbed from the two aeroplanes. The children were sad to say good-bye to their small friend. They had grown very fond of cheeky Mafumu, and they did not want to leave him behind at all.

"Can't we possibly take Mafumu home with us?" asked Paul. "Do let's. He could live with us – and he could come to school with Mike and Jack and me!"

"Mafumu wouldn't be happy," said Ranni. "One day we will all pay a visit to him again, and see how he is getting on. I shouldn't be surprised if some day he is made chief of his tribe – he is brave and intelligent, and has all the makings of a fine leader."

"I hope that uncle of his won't hit him too much," said

Jack. "Golly, look – all the people are running out from the village. Have they seen Mafumu, do you think?"

Sure enough, from the little native village nearby came many men, women and children. They had seen Mafumu, and although they had been unsure about the aeroplanes, they felt that the "big roaring birds" as they called them could not be very dangerous if Mafumu was in one of them!

Mafumu's uncle was with the people. Jack wondered if he would take hold of the little boy and give him a shaking for having run away from him back to his friends. He glanced at Mafumu to see if he was afraid. But the boy held himself proudly. Was he not friends with these people? Had he not helped them? He felt a real king that day.

"Mafumu, take this for a parting present," said Prince Paul, and he gave Mafumu his best pocket-knife, a marvellous thing with a bright gold handle. Mafumu was overjoyed. He had often seen Paul using it, and had not even dared to ask if he might borrow it. Now it was his own! Mafumu could hardly believe his good luck.

And then, of course, everyone wanted to give little Mafumu something. Nora gave him a bead necklace, and Peggy gave him her little silver brooch with P on. Mafumu pinned it onto his shorts!

"P doesn't stand for Mafumu, but as he doesn't know his letters it doesn't matter," said Peggy. "What are you giving Mafumu, Mike?"

Mike had three fine glass marbles which he always carried about with him in his pocket. He gave them to Mafumu, whose eyes grew wider and wider as these presents were given to him! His teeth flashed white as he grinned round at everyone.

Jack gave him a pencil. It was a silver one, whose point went up or down when the bottom end was screwed round. Mafumu thought this was very clever and he was

136

overjoyed to have the wonderful pencil for his own. He threw his arms round Jack and gave him a big hug.

"Shut up, Mafumu," said Jack uncomfortably, for the others were giggling. But Mafumu hadn't finished he hugged Jack again and again, so tightly that Jack nearly fell over.

"Shut *up*, Mafumu," said Jack again. Mafumu at last let go. His eyes swimming in tears, for it nearly broke his little heart to part from Jack. He had nothing of his own to give Jack – except his very precious necklace of crocodile teeth! He took it off, muttered a few words over it, and then pressed it into Jack's hand.

"No, Mafumu," said Jack. "No. I know quite well that you think these crocodile teeth are your special good luck charm and keep you from danger. I don't want them."

But Mafumu would not take no for an answer, and in the end Jack put the crocodile necklace into his pocket, feeling a funny lump in his throat. Dear old Mafumu – it wasn't easy to part from him.

Ranni gave the boy a little mirror for himself. Pilescu gave him a notebook to scribble in with his new pencil. Captain Arnold gave him an odd pair of sunglasses, which were in a locker at the back of the White Swallow. These nearly sent Mafumu mad with joy. He at once put them on, and looked so peculiar that everyone shrieked with laughter.

And then Mrs Arnold gave the boy a photograph of all the children. It was one that she always took about with her, and was in a brown leather folding frame. Mafumu was so pleased that he did a kind of war-dance, holding all his gifts above his head, and wearing his sunglasses over his eyes. Everyone laughed till their sides ached.

The folk from the village had come nearer and nearer, full of amazement to see Mafumu receiving gifts from his friends. Mafumu took off his sunglasses and beamed round at the children.

137

"Goodbye," he said, in English. "Goodbye. Come again. Mafumu is your friend."

Everyone hugged Mafumu and then they got back into the planes. The villagers came right up to Mafumu when they saw that the others were safely in the "big roaring birds." Mafumu's uncle was jealous. He wanted the necklace that Nora had given to little Mafumu. The boy glared at his uncle. Then, with a quick movement, he put on his sunglasses and shouted in a most warlike manner.

With shrieks the whole of the villagers ran away, Mafumu's uncle running the fastest. Then Mafumu, with slow and stately steps, stalked after them, feeling himself a very chief of chiefs! That was the last sight the children had of their small friend, for the two planes took off. Mafumu turned for a moment and waved. Then, too proud to feel sad just then, he went on his way to his village, feeling quite certain that his cruel uncle would not try many more tricks on him!

"I do hate leaving Mafumu behind," sighed Peggy. "I really do hate it. He's quite one of us."

"Jack's lucky to have those crocodile teeth," said Paul.

"And you're lucky to have that glorious, shimmering robe and sun-ray head-dress," said Peggy. "I wish I had it!"

"I'll lend it to you whenever you want it," said Paul generously. "I truly will."

The aeroplanes were flying well and fast. Nora looked down to see if they were still over mountains and she gave a cry.

"We're over the Secret Mountain again! Look, everybody! We must have gone out of our way to take Mafumu back – and now we're flying the opposite way home."

Everyone looked down. Yes – there was the Secret Mountain, with its curious yellow colouring. And there was the flat top, with the vast smooth courtyard on which had happened their most exciting adventures.

"Wasn't the eclipse fun?" said Nora.

"And didn't Paul look marvellous when he came up that stairway dressed in those wonderful robes?" said Peggy.

"And wasn't it glorious when we stood on the top of the mountain and suddenly heard the roar of the White Swallow's engines?" said Jack.

"I wish we could have this adventure all over again," said Paul. "It was a bit too exciting at times, but I like exciting things."

"Well, let's hope the adventure is finished as far as excitement and danger are concerned," said Ranni. "I've had quite enough, I can tell you! All I want now is to get back to England safely, and see you all safe and sound at school again!"

"School! Fancy going back to school after all this!" cried Paul. "I don't want to. I want to go off flying in my plane again, Ranni."

"You can want all you like, but school is the best and safest place for *you*," said Ranni. "And, anyway, you have plenty to tell the boys. My word, they'll think you a hero, you may be sure!"

"Will they really?" asked the little prince, his eyes shining. "I'm not really a hero – but I wouldn't a bit mind people thinking me one."

The planes flew on steadily. At last they came to a big airport, where they landed. They took in fuel and the children had a good meal. Captain Arnold sent a message to England to say that they were all safe and sound. Then off they set again.

The children slept the night through peacefully. Adventures were lovely – but it *was* nice to feel safe again. They began to look forward to seeing England and Dimmy, and to telling their tremendous story.

And at last they were home! They landed at the big airport, and what a crowd was there to welcome them! Photographers ran up to take their picture, people crowded up to clap them on the backs and to shake hands, and Captain Arnold had to speak a few words into a microphone to say they were safely back at last!

Then they all squeezed into two cars and off they went to London and to Dimmy. They chattered and laughed, excited and proud. It was grand to be back home again, and to be welcomed in such a lovely way.

Dimmy was standing on the steps to welcome them herself. The children tumbled out of the cars and rushed to her, shouting their news.

"We've been to Africa!"

"We found a Secret Mountain!"

"Paul was nearly made a sacrifice to the sun!"

"An eclipse came, and the people thought we had killed the sun!"

"Well, you'll certainly kill *me* if you hug me like this!" said Dimmy, her eyes full of happy tears, because she was so thankful to see them again. She had been terribly worried and anxious when all the children had left her so suddenly – but now everything was all right!

That evening Captain Arnold had to go off to broadcast his story. It was to be at a quarter past nine, after the news. The children switched on the radio and listened in. It was fun to hear Captain Arnold's deep voice booming into the room as he began the tale of their adventures.

Dimmy listened in amazement. She had already heard bits and pieces from the children, but here was the tale told in full, just as it might be written in a book. It was marvellous!

For half an hour the tale went on – and then it was over. Dimmy switched off the radio.

"Well, well," she said, "we've been through some adventures together, children – but this one is the most exciting of all. Did it really happen? Could such things happen to ordinary children like you?"

"Well, they *did!*" said Jack, and he showed Dimmy his

necklace of crocodile teeth. "Look here – these are teeth from a crocodile that nearly ate Mafumu one day. His father and uncles killed it, and gave Mafumu some of the teeth. And he gave them to me."

"I wonder what Mafumu is doing now," said Mike. "Wasn't he a fine friend? We wouldn't be here now if it wasn't for old Mafumu."

"And you're not going to be *here* much longer," said Dimmy, getting up. "It's long past your bedtime!"

"*Bed*time! Is there such a thing as *bed*time?" said Peggy. "I'd forgotten all about it! We haven't been properly to bed for weeks. I don't think I shall really bother about bedtime any more."

"Well, *you* may not – but I shall!" said Dimmy. "Come along, all of you. *Bedtime!* There are biscuits and lemonade for those who come now – and none for those who dawdle!"

So biscuits and lemonade it was, and a long, long talk in the bedrooms! And then Dimmy firmly switched off the lights, tucked everybody up, said, "No more talking," in a very stern voice – and left them.

We must leave them, too, dreaming of their adventures – dreaming of the strange, far-away Secret Mountain!